ALSO BY ERIN SOMERS

Stay Up with Hugo Best

The Ten Year Affair

A NOVEL

Erin Somers

Simon & Schuster

NEW YORK   AMSTERDAM/ANTWERP   LONDON
TORONTO   SYDNEY/MELBOURNE   NEW DELHI

Simon & Schuster
1230 Avenue of the Americas
New York, NY 10020

For more than 100 years, Simon & Schuster has championed authors and the stories they create. By respecting the copyright of an author's intellectual property, you enable Simon & Schuster and the author to continue publishing exceptional books for years to come. We thank you for supporting the author's copyright by purchasing an authorized edition of this book.

No amount of this book may be reproduced or stored in any format, nor may it be uploaded to any website, database, language-learning model, or other repository, retrieval, or artificial intelligence system without express permission. All rights reserved. Inquiries may be directed to Simon & Schuster, 1230 Avenue of the Americas, New York, NY 10020 or permissions@simonandschuster.com.

This book is a work of fiction. Any references to historical events, real people, or real places are used fictitiously. Other names, characters, places, and events are products of the author's imagination, and any resemblance to actual events or places or persons, living or dead, is entirely coincidental.

Copyright © 2025 by Erin Somers

All rights reserved, including the right to reproduce this book or portions thereof in any form whatsoever. For information, address Simon & Schuster Subsidiary Rights Department, 1230 Avenue of the Americas, New York, NY 10020.

First Simon & Schuster hardcover edition October 2025

SIMON & SCHUSTER and colophon are registered trademarks of Simon & Schuster, LLC

Simon & Schuster strongly believes in freedom of expression and stands against censorship in all its forms. For more information, visit BooksBelong.com.

Book text design by Paul Dippolito

Manufactured in the United States of America

ISBN 978-1-6680-8144-0

For Josh

The Ten Year Affair

One

Cora met Sam at a twice-weekly baby group in their small town. They sat on blue plastic mats in the back room of an overpriced children's clothing store. Their infants squirmed in front of them on sheepskins. The room smelled like breast milk and baby heads and cruciferous vegetables boiled down to weakened, mealy fibers one mom had brought in Tupperware and was trying to feed her ten-month-old.

"That baby doesn't want broccoli," said Sam.

He had a toothpick stuck to his lower lip. His mouth was sexy; the toothpick was not. He offered one to Cora. She took it so she could touch his hand. It tasted like cinnamon. Of all available affections, this one was openly oral, wholly about his lips and tongue, either keeping them busy or drawing attention to them. *So, which was it?* she asked him.

"Neither," he said. Now he was using it to prod his incisors at the gum line. "Just something to do."

"To be a man and kill time chewing a wet stick," she said.

Across the room, the weeping child ingested a bite from the Tupperware and his mother called out triumphantly, "See?"

It was the two of them against Broccoli Mom. That much was clear. They exchanged numbers to seal the alliance.

Cora lived with her family on the side of town colloquially known as the mountain side. The house had views from four different rooms. There it loomed, beyond the back deck. It was brown now, bare, but when they had moved in the previous summer it had been lush and green, crawling with hikers. A gouge up its center marked the place where a funicular once ran, and Cora stared at it as she sat at the kitchen counter nursing Miles.

"I met someone sort of interesting," she said to Eliot.

He was cooking dinner, opening and closing cabinets, taking out bowls, spices, a bag of carrots, consulting a cookbook, recycling cardboard packaging and retrieving it again when he realized he hadn't read the directions. He seemed to relish making a lot of noise.

"Good!" he said. "What's her name?"

"Sam. It's a him."

"That's okay. Men and women can be friends."

"Well, yeah."

"What does he do?"

"I don't know. All I know is we hate the same lady."

Their three-year-old, Opal, came in. She had a blanket draped over her shoulders and the blanket had a baby doll caught in its fringes. The doll had been stripped of its clothing down to its peach-colored body and was being pulled along, making a scraping sound on the tile. Neither Cora nor Eliot moved to disentangle it.

"Can I watch the iPad?" said Opal.

Cora said yes at the same time Eliot said no.

Then Cora said, "Okay, whatever, no."

"You said yes before," said Opal.

"Yeah, but Dad said no."

"Dad's not boss," said Opal.

"It's a family," said Cora. "I don't think we need to apply the structure of boss and underling. Opal, why don't you color instead?"

Eliot had located a brush and was using it to glaze salmon. He wore a green pullover sweatshirt from the Museum of Natural History and the horn-rims he'd had since she met him. He'd cleaned the kitchen before he started and emptied the dishwasher. He looked good. He'd been working out. Cora thought: He's better than Sam.

"You should try hanging out with this Sam," he said. "Human contact would be good for you."

"Eh. He probably sucks," said Cora.

"Bad word," said Opal.

"Baby, go color," said Cora.

"Why do you think he sucks?" said Eliot.

"Bad word," said Opal again.

"I guess because he lives here."

"We live here," said Eliot. "We don't suck."

"Bad word."

"O," said Cora. She put a hand on Opal's head. "I will give you one hundred dollars to go color."

"Okay."

She exited the room singing. Through the kitchen doorway, they watched her sit at the small table in the dining room they kept stocked with her art supplies and pick up a red crayon. She looked like an adult sitting there, like Cora actually. She had Cora's dark blond hair, and something in her carriage was the same, some angle of her shoulders or curve of her neck.

"Does she know what a hundred dollars is?" said Eliot.

"I don't know."

"You should give this person a chance."

Had she sort of manipulated him into saying it? Eliot flipped a piece of fish and glazed some more. He was oblivious. You could picture him flipping and glazing as a comet came screaming into the atmosphere and the world ended. Would he even look up?

"You need a friend here," said Eliot. "I made a friend."

"No, you didn't. Who? Oh, Klaus? He's not your friend."

Klaus was Eliot's racquetball partner, whom he had met through a sign-up sheet at the gym. They played a couple times a week, then went out for a beer. Cora had met him once, also at the gym. She'd been incredibly sweaty from running on the treadmill. He seemed nice enough: German, stocky, divorced. "Eliot's wife," he'd said, shaking her hand. Eliot never mentioned him outside the context of racquetball.

"He is," insisted Eliot. "We see each other on a regular basis. We know each other's kids' names. Sometimes he buys the drinks and sometimes I do."

"But you're not baring your soul to him. You don't have an emotional connection to Klaus. He's an acquaintance. You're not calling Klaus up crying like, oh, Klaus. Klaus from racquetball who I met on a sign-up sheet. Help."

"How do you know I'm not doing that?"

She switched Miles to the other side. He was a good eater, which Opal hadn't been and still wasn't. "Because I know."

Eliot messed with a burner, the one in front that never wanted to light. It clicked without catching and filled the kitchen with the smell of gas. A new stove was on their list of repairs labeled Not an Emergency Yet. He searched the junk drawer for a lighter, removing take-out menus.

"We haven't been here that long," she said.

She had always made friends easily, but they had moved here without knowing anybody and then she'd had a baby. Her old friends were childless, preoccupied with their lives in the city. It was not the town's fault, but she took it out on the town. If she was lonely here, there must be something wrong with it. It must be terrain-based. It must be—should they check the census results?—that the people were dull and vain, duller and vainer than they were back in the city.

Eliot found a lighter and held it to the burner. It lit with a dramatic whoosh. Probably the stove belonged on the Emergency list, alongside the dryer that ran incessantly unless you unplugged it and the back door that hovered two inches above the doorjamb. Also, a mushroom was growing out of a crack in the bathroom tile, and when you pulled it out, it only grew back.

"You would feel better if you had someone to talk to who wasn't me," he said.

She conceded that yes, of course. Everyone needed someone to talk to. He put the lighter back in the drawer and wondered aloud how you fixed a stove if you didn't want to buy a new one. Should they hire a plumber? Was that who dealt with gas lines? Or maybe he could fix it himself if he looked on YouTube?

"Call the landlord," she said.

"Funny."

To their amazement, they owned the house. In their early

relationship, they had written off the possibility of ever being stable enough, rich enough, to buy one. Until recently, they had rented a fifth-floor walk-up in Flatbush. Opal had slept in a vestibule in lieu of a proper bedroom. The bathtub was three quarters the size of a regular tub and touched the bottom of the toilet. They could hear the neighbors arguing late into the night about whether or not they should have a baby. "You shouldn't," Cora and Eliot would whisper at the wall.

But then Cora's father had died and she'd received enough money for a down payment on a house. When the dream you dared not dream came to pass, well, that was great. A house: what joy! But also, a house: janky stove? Persistent mushroom? Door that was not, per se, a door? Their landlord used to deal with issues like these. When they'd moved in, they hadn't even owned a hammer. Still, it was *their* janky stove, *their* mushroom that could not be deterred by God or man. That meant something, didn't it?

Cora said, "You shouldn't try to do it yourself. You're gonna blow up the house."

Eliot stirred risotto. He was not done talking about her need for friendship.

"Will you do me a favor and try?" he said. "If not with this person, with someone else?"

"All right. I'll try."

"Twenty minutes until dinner. You don't have to sit with me in here. You can go be free if you want."

She stuffed her breast back in her shirt and went to go try to be free.

* * *

Broccoli Mom was at baby group the next Tuesday, talking to another woman about something called elimination communication. You could and should start potty training at birth, she explained. The method was simple. You held your child over a toilet at regular intervals all day long. You had to stay until the kid went. If the kid screamed, you let him. If he resisted, you ignored him.

"Why though?" said Sam.

He had the toothpick going again. He was no taller than Cora, but his hair was almost to his shoulders. She wondered: am I actually attracted to him or does he just have long hair?

Broccoli Mom unsnapped her baby's onesie, preparing him to eliminate.

"To make life easier for yourself down the road. On average it takes them a year to get the hang of it. So, at one your child is already potty trained."

"But you've spent a year holding him over a toilet," said Sam. "How is that easier?"

He had an older kid, he went on, Jack. Jack was three now and they'd recently potty trained him the regular way. It had taken a few weeks and there had been one disastrous accident, at the Met actually, that was a nightmare, but otherwise it had been fine.

"You changed three years of diapers," said Broccoli Mom. "Think of what you could have done in that time. You could have learned a musical instrument."

Sam replied, laughing, that he definitely would not have used the time to learn a musical instrument. Most likely he would have used it to dick around on his phone. Two minutes here, three minutes there, fifteen times a day: these were not usable chunks. Especially when it came to learning something new.

"Well, that's on you," she said. "Isn't it? Whether you use your time productively is on you."

By now other talk in the room had quieted and everyone looked at Broccoli Mom. It was interesting to be in an openly tense situation for a change. Cora studied her. She had a silver bob ending at her chin—it was fashionable these days to be ambiguously old, even if you were young—and wore a kind of kimono open over a pair of jeans and a T-shirt. Sam had picked up his baby, maybe defensively.

Cora said, "Does it work?"

"Watch," said Broccoli Mom.

She brought a Cookie Monster potty out from behind her and sat her kid on it. The kid started screaming.

"Hoby, sweetie," she said. Her voice had an edge of menace.

"What's the communication piece of this?" said Cora.

Broccoli Mom had to talk loudly to make herself heard over Hoby. "It's about reading your child's cues. Using body language and intuition to determine when he has to go. It originates in hunter-gatherer cultures in the developing world. Much more natural than diapers."

They watched as Hoby tried to thrash himself off the potty. Broccoli Mom kept him from doing this with one hand on each small shoulder. At ten months old, Hoby didn't seem close to getting the hang of it. His face scrunched in misery. Cora had to look away. She zeroed in on the picture of Cookie Monster on the front of the potty. He held a cookie in one hand. Who thought that was a good idea? Putting a picture of food on a toilet?

Broccoli Mom began making a persistent psssss sound through her teeth, a low hiss. "It helps. They start to associate the sound with—"

There was more. There was a whole philosophy of diaper-free childrearing endorsed by a naturopathic pediatrician with a French last name and a bestselling book. There was a specific sound for piss and a specific sound for shit, and you were supposed to make the sounds as you forced your kid, who could not sit, as such, to sit on the toilet.

"It's working," said Broccoli Mom. "He's going to do it. Look."

They watched Hoby attempt to pee. What choice did they have? They were in this airless room while it snowed outside. They were killing the afternoon. Cora strained for the sound, the faint patter in the bottom of the potty. Hoby had given up crying and had his head in his hands. Two wisps of dark hair were arranged across his pate like a comb-over.

Sam looked at Cora but didn't say anything. His face was slightly haggard, probably from caring for an infant all day, and he had stubble on his chin. He chewed his stick and smiled. The savagery of middle-class parents began early, almost instantly. They set you in the center of a room and made you pee on command. Later, they got mad if you didn't become a doctor.

A minute slid by on the neon wall clock. In front of her, Miles swam on his tummy, straining to lift his neck. Sam's little girl spit up and he changed her onesie and cleaned her face with a cloth.

"I'm not sure he's going to do it," said Cora, finally.

Sam said, "It's okay if he doesn't. We get the gist."

Broccoli Mom turned to them. "You two don't know what you're talking about. He will do it. Everything that's alive pees eventually."

"Plants?" whispered Cora.

Another minute passed and Hoby did not pee. They settled in to wait.

* * *

That night, Eliot got high while Cora put the kids to sleep. She could see him out on the front porch, fractured and blurred by the stained-glass panel in the front door. He did this every night. There were lots of ways to cope and this was his. Rafe supplied the pot. Cora had no clue who Rafe was. Some buddy of Eliot's from way back.

"You don't know Rafe?" Eliot said, a lot.

No, she didn't know Rafe. Who was Rafe?

"You do," said Eliot. "He lived in that apartment with eleven other guys?"

Cora remembered the apartment, but not Rafe. It was a loft in Bushwick they'd divided up into twelve plywood stalls. Each of them lived in his own stall. Before she was with Eliot, she had slept with some of the twelve. Every time, she had almost freaked out about the livestock feeling of having sex in a stall. She had not slept with Rafe, though. She could not place him. But it made sense that someone Eliot had known at twenty was now his dealer. People never went away, not really. If they did it was only to resurface years later in the dumbest way possible.

Eliot came back inside holding his bowl. She followed him to the kitchen, where he took an ice cream sandwich from the freezer and began to unwrap it.

"How was today?"

Eliot had returned to work after only a month of leave. He had done the same with Opal: it was what his job gave him. As a result, he did not understand, would never understand, what Cora's days were like. He didn't know the tedium of caring for an infant alone. He didn't grasp the physical demands, the grueling all-the-time-ness. This was not his fault, or maybe it was. In the evenings, he'd ask how things had gone that day, and she'd say, fine, good, no major casualties. Sometimes she would add "except my personhood." Haha, they would both say. Hahaha. Then they would move on to talking about his workday.

"I went to that baby group."

"That's good. I'm glad you're doing that."

"A woman tried to make her baby piss in front of us."

"I don't get it. Aren't babies pissing basically nonstop?"

"Not this one. He held his ground."

She told him about the Cookie Monster potty, the way Broccoli Mom insisted Hoby sit there.

"And this is what people are doing these days?" he said.

"It's what this one lady is doing. It's a hack she thinks she's found."

Except Hoby had not peed. Hoby had won. They'd watched in silence until the hour ended, and Broccoli Mom suddenly had somewhere to be. She had to go pick up her other kid, Hoby's sibling, Walter. Walter attended a progressive school one town over where, in warmer months, classes took place in a meadow.

"A meadow?" Cora had said. "Like a field?"

Broccoli Mom said, "Exactly. It's called the Meadow Project. You should look it up. Everything you need to know can be learned in a meadow."

The way she said the last part, fast and sort of robotically, made it sound like it had come from a brochure. Cora tried to imagine what you could learn in a meadow. Math? Well, yeah. English? Definitely. Science? If you brought the beakers and whatnot outside. Most subjects, come to think of it, could be taught anywhere. By that point, Hoby had let himself flop to the ground. Broccoli Mom snapped up his outfit and said goodbye.

"He wasn't even smiling," Cora told Eliot. "He didn't know he'd won."

She watched him laugh into his ice cream sandwich. He had his elbows on the counter. His left eyelid drooped behind his glasses, which it always did when he was stoned. It made him look sleepy and a little languid and a little young. He was two years older than she was—thirty-two to her thirty—but when he was stoned, he looked younger, like he had when they met.

"Do you want to have sex?" she said.

She had recently been cleared by her doctor. Eliot turned on the Bluetooth speaker they kept on the counter and started listening to an interview. It seemed to be with Gilbert Gottfried. They had a two-hour window before Miles woke up.

"Not tonight," said Eliot. "You've got to put in a request before—"

He indicated the front porch.

"Why are you listening to this?" she said. "What is this?"

"It's a podcast. Rafe recommended it. You wouldn't think it would be good, but it is."

Rafe again. The amount they talked about Rafe was really something.

"Can we do less Rafe in general?" said Cora.

He shushed her because Gilbert Gottfried had started talking again.

"Don't you find his voice annoying?" she said.

"It's horrible. One of the worst."

"It can't be his real voice. Does he ever not do it?"

"I'm not sure. I think he always does it."

She wanted more from him, but what she wanted couldn't be wrung from a conversation about Gilbert Gottfried. She stood another minute trying to think of some way to make him pay attention to her.

"Well, enjoy," she said, finally.

"See you up there."

On the days the group did not meet, Cora took Miles for long walks. Even in winter, the town was beautiful. The mountain disappeared into low silver clouds. Down near Main Street, the falls, which only froze in the most extreme cold, continued to churn bluish white. It had a particular smell as you walked by, organic, like moss or algae, with a note of brine, a note of metal. Then, once you'd passed, came the smell of burgers from the restaurant overlooking it.

It was a town with a waterfall five blocks from the pharmacy. A mountain half a mile from the library. There was a big modern art museum down near the railroad tracks, and residents got free admission. The train station sat right on the river and gulls swooped overhead while you waited. On weekends, crowds came up from the city, spent money at stores with words like "apothecary" in their names, and remarked that the air smelled sooo good.

These were the qualities that had sold them on living there when they had visited the previous spring. First, they hadn't wanted to live somewhere ugly; they'd done that for long enough. They'd wanted trees and train access, businesses you could walk to. Cultural life of one form or another. But mostly, it had to have a feel. It was a middle-class town—Eliot called it the last middle-class town—but it undeniably had a feel.

When it got too cold, she took Miles to the coffee shop staffed by young people with lip rings and neon Carhartt hats. She ordered a latte and sat at a table with a view of the door. When Miles fussed, she nursed him, but mostly he slept. What was she doing there? She was waiting for Sam. They did not have plans to meet, but he'd need to get out of the house with the baby, and where else would he go?

Men entered pushing strollers. None of them was Sam. Some were close to being Sam but ultimately were not. A man in a beanie rolled over her foot and apologized. His stroller was an Uppababy, the larger model with leather details that cost a grand.

"Sorry. It steers like a tank."

She peered inside. "How old?"

"Eighteen months. It's been a trip."

He smiled at her and he was not unhandsome. Then he said his baby's name was Maurice and that Maurice had to get home for his nap because Maurice got super-cranky if Maurice didn't get a full three hours and Maurice's mom would blame him if Maurice was a wreck by dinnertime because Maurice didn't eat enough when Maurice was like that and for some reason it was even hard for Maurice to fall asleep when he got too tired.

"It's like, Maurice, just go to sleep, man," he concluded. "Does that happen to your baby?"

"Oh definitely."

"Well, nice talking."

Cora said, "Good luck."

It was hard not to think: Sam would never say Maurice so many times in a row.

She left the coffee shop and steered Miles home, got him into the car, drove to Happy Tree to pick up Opal, chatted with Opal's teacher, remarked on the new artwork on the wall, agreed to bring in paper plates for an upcoming class party. They got home and she carried both kids inside, which took two trips, and their belongings, which took a third. She asked Opal what she wanted to do and Opal said, not in so many words, gorge on television. They did this, side by side on the couch until it got dark out and Eliot came home and started cooking dinner. Another day had passed. No major casualties.

One of the moms who was always at the group had white-lady dreads and wore brown hemp pants with a brown hemp shirt. She sat beside Cora the next week, where Sam usually sat, and introduced herself as Liz. Cora started to tell her the spot was saved but then felt stupid and didn't.

    She texted Sam, *Are you coming?*

    No response.

    Liz laid her baby out in front of her. It was one of those big babies you sometimes saw. Ninety-ninth percentile, legs like stacked marshmallows. Miles looked measly by comparison. The baby dragged herself toward him and put a hand in his eye. Cora gently removed it.

    Liz said, "Yeah. She grabs eyeballs. Sorry. Bonnie, knock it off."

    Bonnie spotted a wooden dog in the vicinity of Broccoli Mom and lost interest in Miles. Liz began describing a podcast she'd heard, about women who had orgasms while giving birth. It was fascinating, she said. It hadn't been studied as much as it should have because it impacted only women. If men were the ones who had babies you better believe there'd be exhaustive research by now. There'd be a pill you could take to make it easier for you to get off while giving birth.

"Here," she said.

She fished in her bag and pulled out a grubby tangle of earbuds. She straightened them out and plugged them into her phone and before it was clear what was happening, shoved one in Cora's ear. She put the other in her own ear and they sat listening to the voice of a woman describing the orgasm she'd had during labor.

I came so hard, said the voice. *I never wanted it to stop. It felt different from sex because it was . . . the pressure . . . it's hard to describe . . . it originated inside me, on the other end. The top. And as it was happening, at the height of it, there was a baby forcing its way through me. Through my gigantic cervix.*

The door opened and Sam entered and took off his shoes. He wore socks printed with fir trees and a chambray shirt. His jeans were only mildly terrible. Cora knew by then that his baby was named Penelope and she was exactly one week older than Miles.

She took the earbud out. "Okay. I mean, that's awesome, but . . ."

Sam settled in on her other side, mouthing *Sorry.*

"I had an orgasm during labor," said Liz. "Or anyway, I was close. That's why I'm interested. They say it happens with big babies." She motioned at the pale globe of Bonnie's head. "It either totally fucks you up forever or you come."

Cora caught Sam's eye and looked away to keep from laughing. Again, he offered her a toothpick and again she accepted.

"What was your labor like?" Liz asked Cora. "Did you come?"

Cora had received an epidural in her spine and a button she could press for more Percocet. She pressed it a lot, even after the nurse told her to taper off so she could feel when to push. She definitely hadn't come. Both of her births had been routine and terrifying. Primitive, in spite of the technology. So much blood plus a placenta that came flopping out of you at the end like a jellyfish.

"It was normal," said Cora. "Three days in the hospital."

"A hospital," said Broccoli Mom. "Interesting."

"Is that bad?"

"No, of course not. It's a choice every woman has to make for herself. Personally, I was too afraid of the cascading interventions to consider a hospital. If things don't move fast enough, they induce you and before you know it, they're giving you a C. Not to mention the high mortality rates for mothers of color."

Cora looked at her for a long moment. "You're white."

"Yes, but it's the principle," said Broccoli Mom. "Anyway, my doula is a genius and my birth experience was life changing. For both me and my partner."

"All birth experiences are life changing," said Sam. "They result in a baby."

He shimmied Penelope out of her tiny hoodie and placed her on her stomach. Cora's relief at his being there was immense.

In bed that night, she looked Sam up on the internet. His social media accounts were private, and she didn't want to make the first overture, but she saw his work head shot, and she saw his job description. He was something called the chief storytelling officer at a start-up that wanted to disrupt mortgages. Google revealed a couple of other photos: one of him holding a beer at a baseball game, another taken at an aquarium with a blurry shark in the background.

His wedding registry from five years ago was public. Sam Powell and Julie Morgan. They'd asked for a toaster, a KitchenAid mixer, the pasta attachment for the KitchenAid. They asked for stemless wineglasses, linen napkins, a matching tablecloth. A set of stainless-steel pots and plain white cereal bowls and cash contributions to their honeymoon fund. None of these items meant anything—it was all what everyone asked for.

Eliot came in with his eye drooping behind his glasses and began recounting something Klaus had told him that day at racquetball. Klaus's wife, Freda, had run off last year with a food photographer named Jonathan, leaving Klaus with two kids. Jonathan had abs and the most insane happy trail he'd ever seen. Freda and Jonathan liked to do psilocybin mushrooms and FaceTime him to tell him how sorry they were for ruining his life. The way Eliot knew about the abs and the happy trail was that Jonathan was shirtless on the calls and Klaus had shown him a screenshot. Wasn't that gross? Eliot wanted to know.

"What is?" said Cora. "The screenshot?"

"The running away with Jonathan."

He started stripping off his clothes.

"I tell you this to demonstrate that Klaus is my friend. We confide. What are you doing there? Don't say work emails. You told them you weren't going to answer any."

Cora was a content manager at a company that owned a group of publications about digital marketing. She'd only been there for a couple years but had become senior in her department. She held a lot of the institutional knowledge, and her colleagues had seemed panicked about her going on leave. Oddly, they needed her, or acted like they did, though the decisions she made struck her as inconsequential.

"It's not work emails," said Cora. "It's not anything."

She looked at the aquarium picture again. The focus was so soft she could barely make out Sam's face. The ground appeared damp; he had one foot in a shallow puddle. Why was it on the internet? Eliot slid in next to her and started reading a manuscript for work. He was an editor of serious-minded nonfiction at a prestigious publishing house. It paid badly and he worked constantly, read constantly, lay with his laptop or a manuscript on his chest constantly, but he cared about it a lot.

He glanced at her computer screen. "Who's that?"

"The baby group guy. Sam."

"Who?"

"I told you about him. Remember? I said he probably sucks?"

"So does he?"

"I don't know."

"Does he work at an aquarium?"

"I don't think so. I mean, I know he doesn't. He's trying to disrupt mortgages."

"Disrupt them how?"

"It's an app. I think you apply for a mortgage through the app and the app alerts you if you qualify."

"That doesn't already exist? What did we do? We used a website, didn't we? We entered some basic information? Wasn't it pretty fast?"

Cora had been shocked by how fast. She'd prepared for rejection. The two of them owning a house? It seemed like they were getting one over. They had recently—or it felt like recently—known people who slept in plywood stalls. Their lives had been that squalid, that tenuous. Cora had spent years as a waitress and then a paralegal before finally getting a job in media. Eliot had begun at the lowest level at his imprint and climbed glacially. Yet they had qualified with their real finances. They had qualified and talked it over and looked at houses in various towns. They had made a budget and chosen one and closed. Last spring, they sat with lawyers signing documents in a room lined with leather-bound volumes. Birds sang outside and the mountain was a patchwork of greens.

"I don't know how the app is different," said Cora.

Eliot returned to his manuscript. He had a pen behind his ear.

"I might have a drink with him sometime," said Cora. "Instead of the baby group."

She didn't know why she'd said it; she and Sam hadn't discussed it. She had thought about it though. They didn't need the group. They didn't need the other parents, the odd sense of competition, the trotting out of new age strategies. They didn't need to sit on the floor in a cross-legged position while some lady talked about orgasms.

"Midday drink," said Eliot. "Hmm."

"Don't you drink during the day all the time?"

"For work. And not all the time. Those days are gone. Everything hot and sexy about publishing is gone. Gone but not forgotten. Anyway, I'm only kidding. Get hammered at noon if you want. It's fine."

"I'm not going to get hammered. I'm going to have one drink."

"It doesn't bother me. Do what you want."

He returned to his manuscript. It was a book about Russia, he'd told her. Specifically, the history of bad traffic in Moscow. He was deciding now whether he wanted to acquire it. Would enough people want to read about traffic patterns in Moscow to make this project commercially viable? Were traffic patterns in Moscow sufficiently exciting to think about for the next two years?

"Do you want to have him over?" said Eliot. "You know, with his wife?"

Cora thought about her interactions with Sam so far. She felt possessive of him. She thought Eliot and Sam would get along. She could picture their pleasant, dick-swinging camaraderie. The way they'd know common people from the schools they'd attended. The way they'd bond over totems of millennial soft masculinity: craft beer and Knausgaard and basketball and socialism.

"It's too soon," said Cora. "I just met him. He might be a murderer."

"Good point. Take our baby around him a few dozen more times to make sure."

The door opened and Opal materialized in pajamas. Her hair was damp from the bath. She wanted to know what happened when you died. Eliot capped his pen and looked at Cora. There was the question of what you should tell kids, how honest you should be. Cora thought they deserved the truth, delivered gently.

She took Opal's hand. "Nothing happens. You aren't there anymore."

"But where do you go?"

"Nowhere. I know that's difficult to understand. I barely understand it myself."

"Can Grandpa see me wherever he is?"

Cora's father had died when Opal was two. He'd had a heart attack in the parking lot of a Whole Foods, where her mother had sent him for brown sugar. He had been trying to cut down on his bag usage, so he died holding the sugar in his hand. Or maybe he had dropped it. Cora didn't know. Opal hadn't come to the funeral and they thought she would forget about it.

Opal didn't forget.

"No," said Cora. "Well, the problem is, he isn't anywhere. He also can't see? Because he doesn't have eyes, or anything else . . ." She tried again. "He's in your heart. Though, not really him. His memory is there. And not literally your heart. Your mind. He's in . . . the air? Nope. Not the air."

Cora's father had been cremated, but she didn't want to broach the topic of cremains. That was objectively scary. *They put his body in an oven and burned him to ash. Sweet dreams!*

"He's nowhere, honey. I don't know how else to describe it. Can you go to sleep now? I'll walk you in there."

She closed her computer and steered her daughter back to her room. Opal had the biggest bedroom so Cora and Eliot could have the mountain view. There was a striped rug on the floor and a pastel tent in one corner. Opal got into bed and Cora situated her stuffed animals according to Opal's hierarchy: not by size, but by standing in her affection. She kissed Opal on the forehead and each cheek. Then she turned to leave.

"Is heaven real?" said Opal.

"Who told you about heaven?"

"Alasdair at school."

Cora was tired. She tried to summon an image of Alasdair from the legion of kids at Happy Tree she saw for three minutes every day and couldn't come up with anything. Alasdair was no one in particular. Another toddler with a bowl cut sounding off about heaven.

"Some people think it is and some don't. We don't know for sure."

"Do you think it is?" said Opal.

"No, honey. But it's nice. It's a beautiful idea. You can believe it if you want."

Opal considered this, staring at the glow-in-the-dark stars on the ceiling. Cora had spent an afternoon attempting to arrange them into the shapes of constellations. She hadn't been successful. They looked random, except for one of the dippers, which resembled a large, crude bucket.

"Why are you smelling your hand?" said Opal.

"I wasn't," said Cora more sharply than she meant to. "Go to sleep now, Opal. You need sleep to grow."

She had been caught by her three-year-old smelling her hand for traces of cinnamon.

But then one day he didn't show, even though he'd said he would. Cora sat next to Liz again, and this time Cora told her birth story in detail. It had taken fifteen hours. Toward the end, her OB had threatened her with an episiotomy, which had scared her sufficiently to get Miles out. She had needed three ugly black stitches anyway. Afterward, she bled for forty-one days. Surpassing the great flood, she joked.

"I bled for a month, give or take," said Liz.

"I recently passed a clot the size of a fist," said another mom, who Cora had never seen before. The baby in front of her was maybe six weeks old.

There were no men present and Cora tried to feel comforted by this all-woman space where she could be disgusting without judgment. These are my sisters in disgustingness, she thought feebly. Liz took over and started talking about orgasms again.

Apparently, she also knew a lot about something called the postpartum orgasm. What did postpartum mean in this context? Cora wondered. Any orgasm you had for the rest of your life?

At the end of the hour, she zipped Miles into his snowsuit and went home. Eliot had taken an early train back from the city and stood in the kitchen eating fistfuls of organic cheddar popcorn from the bag. Opal ate baby yogurt after baby yogurt sitting on the counter. Miles nursed as Cora sponged dried tomato sauce off the backsplash. Eliot took off his jacket so he could eat popcorn more comfortably.

"I propose a getaway," said Cora.

"Where to?" said Eliot.

"Where are they in those Gauguins? With the fruit and the women?"

"Tahiti."

"Yeah. Tahiti. Let's book a trip."

"I wish."

"It'll be great. We'll lie on the beach. Drink cocktails out of coconuts. Stay in one of those villas out over the water."

Eliot put his mouth directly under the faucet and turned it on.

"Wow," said Cora.

"There are no glasses." He wiped the back of his mouth with his hand. "They're racist, those Gauguins. I read an article about it. You know, the noble savage? He's got a mixed legacy."

"Oh," said Cora.

"Plus, the girls in the paintings were children. Definitely too young to be sexualized."

"Right, okay. No vacation then."

"We could go to the movies. You love the movies."

"I guess," said Cora. "Why?"

"For a change of scene. Isn't that what you're getting at?"

Cora shook her head. A movie wouldn't do it. It lasted two hours. At the end you were still wherever you were. Plus, the kids wouldn't do well there. Miles would cry, then nurse, then cry again. Opal couldn't be made to sit still. They'd tried it once before and she was barely heavy enough to hold the seat down. It kept folding in on her, half forcing her out through the bottom. She'd spent most of the movie on Cora's lap.

"We'll go away soon," said Eliot. "This summer."

Opal threw her empty yogurt cup on the floor and said, "Done."

She ran out of the room and went upstairs and a moment later they heard a scream.

"Mushroom!" she shouted.

The mushroom was back. Days would pass with no signs of it, sometimes weeks, and suddenly there it would be again, fully formed, white stem, slick brown cap. So repulsive was the mushroom that Cora could not stand to pull it out. She'd send Eliot and even he used a wad of paper towels, unwilling to touch it with his bare hand.

"Is there a guy we can call to get rid of the mushroom forever?" said Cora.

"A guy?" said Eliot.

"You know what I mean. A professional mushroom exterminator."

"I've never heard of that."

"What are we supposed to do then? Keep pulling it out every couple of days until we die?"

"So it seems," he said.

He grabbed a handful of paper towels and headed upstairs.

* * *

In front of their eyes, Hoby learned to use the toilet. One afternoon he sat on Cookie Monster's head and peed of his own free will. He looked resigned; he'd accepted his fate.

The whole room cheered and a few moms said, "Go, Hoby!" and "Yay!"

Broccoli Mom beamed. "Eleven months old." She repeated it slowly, looking directly at Cora. "Eleven. Months. Old."

This woman, thought Cora. She was cruel and she was righteous and Hoby had her for life. She pictured him in therapy years later: *I feel weird about the bathroom and my mother. Not to mention everything else.*

She turned to Sam and said, "Let's leave here and never come back."

"Okay," said Sam.

They bundled the kids into their outerwear. The town was small and Cora knew she would see Broccoli Mom again. They would end up on a committee together when the time came. Their kids might be classmates, friends, even a couple. But anything could happen between now and then. Broccoli Mom might move or Cora might. That comet might appear, and so on.

Outside, snow swirled down without sticking. She followed Sam to the bar on Main Street that also served ramen and hosted punk shows. Light came in through the dirty front windows in sepia bands. Sam wore Penelope in a sling. Cora had Miles in the stroller. She lifted the visor to check on him. He slept. His eyes were closed, his lashes so long and dark and individuated she could have counted them. She could not resist kissing his sweet, soft forehead.

"You don't like that woman, do you?" said Sam.

They'd gotten beers and removed their jackets. Sam's hair stood out, staticky from his hat. Now that she was facing him head-on, she found that he was better looking than she'd realized. Square-jawed and symmetrical with heavy brows. He studied her face too, which made her nervous.

"Yeah. No. She's . . . " She motioned around for how to describe Broccoli Mom. "A bad person."

Sam asked if she had other kids and she said yes, and told him about Opal.

"She's at Happy Tree, fucking shit up."

Sam said, "Jack fucks shit up at Bright Horizons."

"How is Bright Horizons anyway? It's got a nicer playground."

"It's okay. They don't seem totally into him. They want him to, I don't know, hide his light."

He seemed embarrassed he'd said this.

"You mean talk less?"

"Pretty much. Sing less, too. Laugh less. Do everything less. It's all right. We're making it work. It's where we could get in when we moved here."

They had moved two years ago from Carroll Gardens, where they'd thought they'd live forever. Then they'd had Jack and found out how expensive kids were. They'd known this going in, everyone did, but they hadn't known. Childcare was the cost of a second rent. No one had put it to them just that way. Get ready to pay two rents. In the city it was about double what you'd pay anywhere else. And so, this town, Bright Horizons and bright horizons. It didn't emasculate him to admit that moving had been scary.

"Oh no?" said Cora.

"Should it?"

"Maybe."

They drank their beers, citrusy and strong, and exchanged biographical information. She was from Connecticut, right outside the city. He was from the Boston suburbs. These upbringings were effectively identical, she said, and he protested, insisting Boston was distinct. They had both gone to college in New York, and lived there after, in the early millennium, when it was gritty and fun. They both missed it, but less and less all the time, and were glad, on the whole, that they had left.

"What do you do for work?" said Cora.

She knew already but she wanted to see if he'd say the phrase "chief storytelling officer."

"I have a stupid content job. I write things for an app. I'm partly remote. That's why I'm the one on leave. My wife is a real person, a lawyer. She's needed. Whereas I . . . no one needs an app that qualifies you for a mortgage in under two minutes."

"Maybe they do."

"I don't think so, but thanks."

He asked her what she did and she told him.

"That's interesting," said Sam.

"Guess what?" said Cora. She dropped her voice and beckoned him to lean in. "It's not."

They stayed like that for a second, a couple inches apart. His face smelled like hops and the cinnamon of his toothpicks. It seemed like they were going to kiss, but no, that couldn't be, could it? Then they did kiss, quickly, spontaneously, almost like a joke. He briefly bit her lower lip. They sat back and looked at each other. She found herself out of breath. There was a moment of mute surprise: they had not meant to do it.

THE TEN YEAR AFFAIR

Finally, Cora said, "Do you want another one?"

The light coming through the window was tinged with blue. It was two p.m. and night had begun, proto-night, the long slide into darkness.

"We have to leave," he said. "We can't have a second drink."

But there was nowhere they had to be, nothing they had to do. Except go raise their children. They ordered another round.

Cora and Sam kept the twice-a-week appointment, but ditched the group. They passed the remaining months of parental leave this way. They'd get a coffee, or sometimes a beer, at one of the places on Main Street. Afterward, they'd push their babies uphill, through the residential neighborhoods at the base of the mountain. Cora caught glimpses of him in her periphery and their shoulders brushed. When this happened, they'd look at each other for a loaded moment, until one of them found a reason to look away. She felt ridiculous, exhilarated, guilty. She was married and so was he. Eliot, she thought. My children. But then their shoulders would touch again and she'd look at him and he'd be shaking his head and half smiling.

"We should just go ahead and have sex," she said one afternoon.

He said, "Come on."

But she was serious. She wanted to fuck him. It was physical only, but had grown strong. She had no control over it, she told him. She became a slavering animal in his presence. He laughed.

"I shouldn't have said anything," said Cora.

"No, I'm glad you did. It's the way you put it."

He told her he wanted to fuck her too, but there was nothing animal about it, it was more about liking Cora as a person. Cora found it hard to believe that it was just about liking her. Liking was a mild way to feel. Did he want to fuck everything he liked? His computer? Grapefruit seltzer? A scattering of ducks on a pond where he wasn't expecting to see ducks?

He said, "You're attracted to me. I get that. But do you actually like me?"

"What's with the emphasis on liking all the time?"

"Don't you have feelings?"

She did have feelings. The feelings were she wanted to get fucked onto the astral plane and not think about her life for a second. But this clearly wasn't the right thing to say, so she reached into the feelings bag and yanked out "I'm crazy about you." Sure, why not? It was bland, liking-adjacent. It was not necessarily a declaration of love. He seemed to accept it.

"Okay," he said. "But what about our families? Your husband."

It would not be good for their families, she admitted. It was not the right thing to do by any standard you might introduce. She didn't consider herself a cheater; she hadn't done it in the past. To begin thinking of herself this way would represent a big shift.

He said, "Can't we just be friends then? It's sad to me, the idea of not knowing you."

"If I wanted a friend, I'd find a woman," she said. "No offense."

"So, if we can't be friends, what are we supposed to do. Have a ten-year affair?"

They were silent. Their generation did not take off its clothes, did not put its keys in a bowl by the front door. Sex between men and women had become taboo in their generation, where everyone was striving, not incorrectly, to be an equal. Even the word "affair" had the ring of obsolescence, like a cigarette or an adman or a chaise lounge.

"I'm kidding," he said at last.

But the affair was there now. It was between them. Somewhere in the multiverse their alternates checked into a hotel room where the afternoon light came in at a slant and hit a champagne bucket just so. It was a cliché, but wild and enjoyable because it was happening to them, this mythic thing they'd heard about, this thing in quotes: "an affair."

Two

Two vectors ran parallel through Cora's existence. One was what you might call reality, with bills and the mushroom in the bathroom and the endless depositing and retrieving of children. The other was her affair with Sam, technically fictional, its lies and illicit meetings, the racing pulse of infatuation.

Sometimes one was more present than the other. When one of her kids got sick, the affair was suspended for almost a week. She went back to work, and this took precedence for a while, until the old routines kicked in. The small talk and two p.m. granola bar, the rote cheer of email communication. Other times the affair was the more prominent of the two. In moments of boredom, in waiting rooms, on transit.

But mostly they stayed in balance.

So Cora sat in a mind-numbing meeting as she met Sam in a darkened steakhouse. She made a suggestion about SEO while they each drank an ice-cold martini. There was coffee in the meeting at least, a big bitter carafe of it, and she refilled her cup as she reached for his cock under the table. Sam brushed back her hair from her ear, whispered something, and her boss rapped his knuckles on the conference table, made a dumb joke about the moment everyone had been waiting for, and brought it around to monthly stats.

As she boiled water for pasta, she walked with Sam through a rainstorm. She tripped and he caught her coming off a street corner while she put her children to bed. During the hour-long drama that she watched with Eliot, she was blowing Sam in the backseat of his car. While she was running out to pick up milk, she was running out to pick up milk so she could meet him in the dairy aisle of ShopRite and have him furtively put his hand up her skirt for thirty seconds before heading home.

And as she tweezed her eyebrows, looked up whale facts with Opal, fed herself or other people, picked up toys, answered work emails at ten p.m., ran on a treadmill, locked herself in the bathroom for no reason she could immediately determine, she thought of him. She thought of him always in both time lines. In one it was with longing and despair and the other with longing and regret. She longed for him while she longed for him. She yearned while she yearned. She pined while she pined, and so on.

In reality, Cora took the train into the city for work three times a week. Two days she worked from home. Miles went to the baby room at Happy Tree, where a woman named Trina with a kind face and broom-yellow hair took care of him. It was devastating to leave him. On the train, at the office, she looked at pictures. Miles sleeping. Miles the day he'd first smiled. Miles rolling over, precociously, at eight weeks old. Miles in blue. Miles in yellow. Miles looking like an old man, a head of state, Churchillian in a striped onesie.

Work had gone on in her absence, with no obvious disruptions.

"What did I miss?" she asked her colleague Lily, and Lily took her to see the new snack machine. The snacks were the same, but the technology had improved. There was now a more futuristic mechanism grabbing the food. There was a touch screen instead of a keypad. Prices had gone up twenty-five cents across the board.

"That's it?" said Cora.

"Pretty much," said Lily.

It had been chaos for the first week she was out, and then it had normalized. They shouldn't have been so nervous, Lily told her. She felt silly about that. After all, it was just marketing. Not even marketing, but writing about marketing. No real emergencies were possible.

They returned to their desks, which faced each other. The plant on Cora's hadn't died, though it looked listless.

Lily said, "I watered it some. I didn't always remember."

Cora opened her email for the first time since before leave and saw she had 30,852 messages. She told Lily and Lily laughed and wondered how one would begin with 30,852 messages. Delete them all, said something inside of Cora. There was not an easy way to do it, so she spent a few hours on it. Selecting all the messages on one page, moving them to the trash.

Then it was lunchtime and she ate a Greek salad from a plastic container. Toward the bottom she found a single blueberry, and this made her retch. She had forgotten about salad place cross contamination. In the depths of maternity leave, she had looked forward to returning to work. She had thought of it as autonomy.

Her mother called as she was finishing up.

"I'm at work," said Cora.

"I know. I'm at my desk too."

She said this happily, as if it was the best place you could ever be. Cora's mom was an ob-gyn. The palette of her office was Georgia O'Keeffe. The shelf behind her desk held pottery in organic shapes. There were parameters around who was allowed to bother her and when, and a receptionist with a firm yet friendly manner answered the phone and made excuses for her. So, yes, it was probably nice to be there.

"Is there something specific?" said Cora.

"Oh no, just congratulating you on getting through it. I know it wasn't easy."

"Thanks."

"Are you feeling good?"

"I'm . . . " She looked at her browser. There were still sixteen thousand messages to delete. "Yeah. Just catching up."

"You know, your kids are going to see that you're a woman with a career and that's good for them. It was good for you and Drew."

Drew was Cora's brother, who worked as a tennis pro in La Jolla. Cora wondered if it had actually been formative for him to observe his mother's successful career in obstetrics. Had Cora internalized the message herself? She had a ho-hum desk job where she could delete thirty thousand emails without it making a difference. Still, her mother was probably correct that children should see their parents self-actualizing.

"I'm sure that's true," said Cora.

"Well, I'll let you get back to it. I know you're probably slammed."

"Thanks for calling, Mom."

Late in the day, after all the emails had been deleted, she went and spoke to her boss. He was a guy of about forty-five with the outdoorsy look of a rock climber. His name was Ryan. He wore rectangular glasses, a navy fleece, and a carabiner on his belt, connected to nothing. He asked to see a picture of Cora's baby, and Cora could tell he was being polite, like maybe he'd taken a management course where someone had instructed him to do so.

"He's so cute," he said. "Miles, right?"

Cora had sent an email out to everyone at work after Miles had been born. A picture of him in a tiny hospital-issue hat, his weight and time of birth. Ryan had taken note, or maybe he had double-checked the email before she came in. This too seemed like a pointed effort to connect.

She showed him a video of Miles laughing. He opened his mouth, revealing hard, pink gums.

Ryan said, "No teeth."

"Soon."

She put her phone away. It seemed like enough.

"Anything else I should know about?" asked Cora.

He glanced around the room as if something might jog his memory. "Oh! Have you seen the new snack machine?"

"Lily showed me."

"Cool, right?"

Cora said, "Very cool."

Sam called her after several weeks back at work, and they met up for a drink. Winter was ending; the snow had mostly melted and the sidewalks had dried. They chose a new bar on Main

Street that also served food. Too much information was posted everywhere. Scrawled by hand on the chalkboard behind the bar, crowding the menu in tiny sans serif. The bar had a philosophy, it seemed, involving ethics, sustainability, and animal by-products, and it required a lot of explaining.

"This used to be a dive," said Sam. "Before you city people showed up."

He always talked about what the town had been like when he first moved there as if he'd arrived in the 1890s to pan for gold and settle the place. He and his wife had not even been among the first wave of gentrifiers.

"Didn't you move here from Brooklyn?" she said.

"Yeah, but before."

Sam had gone back to work, too. He looked handsome and unhappy in office casual. This was his checked-shirt self, his Metro North self. This was what he wore when he interacted with people Cora would never meet. He showed her a new trick he'd learned with his toothpick. He used his tongue to flip it over the long way. He had to stretch his mouth open wide to do it. She willed him to touch her and he didn't.

Their drinks arrived and he began immediately with the intense conversation. He had not enjoyed their time apart. He thought of her often. He was suffering. Since they could not have sex, he said, he wanted a legitimate way to know her. He wanted to install her in his life. He wanted her as a permanent fixture.

"Sounds like what you really want is a new sink," she said.

"You have a great personality. You know that?"

Her whole life, people had railed on about her personality. Such a smart girl—woman! Such a smart woman. And funny. It got worse (better) as she got older. Kind, empathetic, a good parent. That was nice, right? That was what you wanted. But couldn't this one man objectify her?

"Okay," she said.

"I'm serious. I think all four of us should hang out. My wife, your husband."

"Does your wife know how we talk to each other?"

"I might tell her. It's not impossible that I'll tell her. I try to be honest with her."

"So, you want me to be friends with her. But she'll just know, it'll just be out there, that I'm a slavering animal. Self-described."

They stared at each other. He attempted to do the toothpick trick and choked and half puked it out. In the other time line they were laughing at a joke one of them had made. In the other time line, his hand was on her thigh and no one had just sort of thrown up. Her hair looked better over there, too.

"How about instead of all that I send you one nude?" said Cora.

Sam laughed. "No."

"Just one. A tasteful one. Not too porny."

"I want to have you as a friend," he said again. Have her. Have.

Someone already had her though. It was Eliot. In their kitchen the next morning, she said to him, "To what degree do you feel like you have me?"

He was eating, smearing an apple with almond butter and taking big demonstrative bites.

"Like possess you?"

"Yes."

"Zero," he said.

"No, but you do."

Long pause while he smeared and bit. "Not really."

"You do. I have obligations to you. You have access to me. I exist to you on certain terms. I'm your wife. You have me. You get to have me."

"I don't think about it like that."

"How do you think of it?"

He had finished now, tossing the core into the trash. They all had to get out of the house in the next ten minutes. Eliot first, on his bike, a straight shot downhill to the train station. And then Cora with the kids, a more complicated task.

"We're best friends. We have two kids together. I enjoy being around you. You're fun. We both elect to be here."

"You're saying you like me."

"Exactly," he said. "Yo, hand me one of those."

He meant a napkin. She gave him a look. She was nursing Miles. Opal sat on her foot playing with a Barbie doll.

"Not because you're my property, because you're right there. God, fine, I'll get it." Eliot retrieved a napkin. "I don't possess you. Don't I constantly encourage you to hang out with other people?"

He looked at his watch. "Shit, we have to go. We can talk more about this tonight."

They rushed around zipping lunch boxes, filling water bottles, slipping kids' arms into coats, jogging back upstairs for forgotten items. Cora crouched to tie Opal's shoes. She knew they would not talk about it again that night. Conversations truncated by family chaos had a way of never resuming.

She gave in. They had Sam and his wife over for dinner. The wife went by Jules and had no apparent bad traits except that she allowed the toothpicks. She even took one herself after dinner when Sam offered them around. Eliot took one too. It was unseasonably warm, balmy for early spring. They sat outside on the deck sucking their wood splinters, drinking wine, and talking about pre-K. Night crawled diagonally across the yard.

In the time line that contained their affair, Sam and Cora were alone. The leaves were a dark blue previously only seen in dreams. The strap of Cora's dress fell off her shoulder and Sam kissed the place it had been. He fixed the strap, then kissed the part of her neck one inch below her ear.

In reality, Sam was shouting about school registration, how you had to go visit this eighty-year-old woman Rose in her office full of dying plants and make a case for why your kid should be assigned your school of choice. Wasn't that quaint and the reason all of them had moved out there?

"That was our vision all right," said Cora.

She got up on the pretext of grabbing the cobbler. Eliot glanced at her: there was no cobbler. She went in and climbed the stairs and stood in front of the bedroom window and watched the three of them talking and laughing. Where their affair was going on, Cora and Sam had adjourned to the bedroom to try to shock each other with their respective depravities.

She found that she was chewing a toothpick herself and spit it out onto the floor, then picked it up and threw it away in the bathroom trash. She checked on the baby and the baby and the other baby and the other baby. Two slept and two played sweetly with a train that linked up using magnets. She sat down on the rug with them and made up a story about how the train had left the land of chores and rules for the land of toys and candy. The children were easy to delight.

She heard footsteps on the stairs, and Sam came in and stood behind her, resting his hand lightly on her head. Even this level of contact elicited a full-body reaction and he must have known that. With effort, she kept her neck very straight and resisted looking up at him.

He said, "It's going well, right? Jules likes you. I told you."

Another admirer. How their ranks swelled. They could erect a monument to her in the town square. An extremely fucking likable woman—that's what the plaque could say.

"Great," said Cora. "I like her too."

Here was how it worked in the world of the affair: there was a big, anonymous hotel one town away. The hotel serviced business travelers. It was not pretty, but it was not lifeless, either. It was arranged around a man-made lake, and the lake and its scrubby landscaping drew great blue herons, American kestrels, house sparrows, Northern cardinals, five species of warblers. Inside, an appealing blankness: you could fill it with whatever you wanted.

The first time Cora and Sam went, they contrived to stay overnight. This was not hard. Cora told Eliot she had a work event in the city and Sam told Jules the same. It didn't make sense to come home late only to turn around and take the train back again in the morning. The questions that followed were logistical only. What would happen with the kids and what needed to go in their backpacks? Was there enough food in the house and should they call the sitter to help with pickup? Neither Eliot nor Jules suspected anything, and the ease of the deception added to its pleasing sordidness. Because they had both been trustworthy up until now, they would get away with it without friction or elaborate falsehood.

On the prearranged day, Sam beat Cora there. She knocked and he threw open the door harder than he meant to. It slammed against the wall, and way down at the end of the hallway, a housekeeper looked up. Then she was in his arms. He pulled her into the room, down onto the bed. They undressed each other, tearing fabric, apologizing breathlessly. He got her bra off, moved her underwear aside, pushed into her. She had her hands in his hair, on his back. He bit her lower lip like he had that time in the real world.

When it was over, they lay in bed looking at their reflections in the large mounted flat-screen.

I hope that was all right, he said.

She assured him it was.

He got up and ran her a bath, called downstairs for room service. She liked to see him like this, taking care of things in his underwear.

The sun set over a building in the distance. The clouds were pink and streaky. They ate French fries and traded a bottle of champagne back and forth. Before they went to bed, they had sex again. They moved slower this time and he got her off first, going down on her at length, pulling her toward him and grinding his mouth, his stubbly jaw, into her as she came. She slept in his shirt, which was too large and had his cinnamon smell. Outside, the waters of the man-made lake shimmered darkly.

They were all friends now, so why didn't the tension dissipate? She ran into him at a birthday party for a child named Frances.

This occurred in mid-spring. Sheets of mist enveloped the mountain, sliding past each other. In Frances's backyard, a six-foot inflatable cactus shot water out of its head and arms. Kids hurtled through the spray, screaming "Cold!"

On the deck, she and Eliot talked to Frances's mother, Anita. They knew her slightly from Happy Tree, where they kept the same schedule. They saw her in the morning at drop-off and again at pickup. Cora would wave, and Anita would wave back, shrugging at how impossible Frances was being. Now she stood under blue and green streamers, fanning out water crackers on a board, redoing it when the results displeased her.

Frances was adopted, she explained, and the transition had been rocky. He'd had a tough early life, suffered extreme neglect. She mouthed the word *drugs*. He'd been born into poverty in rural Mississippi. When they'd gone down to pick him up, he'd been this skinny little thing. Getting him to trust them had not been easy. They were still working on it. It wasn't like a biological child who loved you implicitly, who was hardwired to love you. It was much more complicated than that. It was day by day, she told them, but so rewarding.

"Good for you," said Eliot. He wore Miles in the carrier, swaying side to side. "That's really worthy."

"And of course, the race thing is a hurdle."

Frances was black and Anita was embarrassed to admit they didn't know many black people. You were supposed to fill their lives with adults who looked like them, but where were she and Brandt supposed to meet such people? Were they supposed to put out a personal ad? It was a little weird, wasn't it? A little calculated? Seeking out friendships with black people for the purpose of having them help you raise your child.

Cora said, "That sounds hard."

"Did you ever think about adoption, when you were deciding to have kids?" said Anita.

"We didn't think," said Cora. "Like at all."

They had been newly married. Cora had been twenty-seven and Eliot twenty-nine. Elsewhere these ages were average, but in New York they were shockingly young. You're a baby yourself, her mother had said. Take care of it and try again in five years. But it hadn't been an accident. They had done it on purpose to fast-forward to the next phase of life, to make some stakes appear. They knew it was reckless; that was part of the appeal. They'd gone through with it not in spite of this, but because of it.

"We always wanted to adopt," said Anita. "There are so many unparented kids out there. So many kids in crisis. We couldn't justify having our own. Brandt had a vasectomy right after we got married. I recommend it. I haven't had to mess with birth control in years."

Cora and Eliot nodded. People would reveal anything about themselves. Anything. They would tell you the status of their husband's vas deferens unprompted. Then you were forced to picture sperm, unable to enter a urethra, being reabsorbed into the body of someone named Brandt.

Brandt climbed the stairs to the deck and they all looked at him.

Anita said, "I was telling them about your vasectomy."

"Best thing I ever did," said Brandt. "AMA."

Later, Eliot went upstairs to change Miles's diaper, and Cora found herself alone in the kitchen. It had recently been remodeled. The lighting fixture was shaped like a lantern. The floors were made of pale gray wood. Someone had pinned a large bundle of herbs to the wall. It resembled a farmhouse, if you'd never seen a farmhouse before.

Cora was crouched next to the oven when Sam found her.

"What are you doing?" he said.

"Oh, hey. I was just . . . looking in the oven."

"Why?"

"I guess I got curious about whether they keep their pans in there when they've got nothing in them."

"How do you know Anita and Brandt?" he said.

"Daycare. You?"

They had moved to town around the same time, Sam explained. They had been neighbors for a while, before Anita and Brandt had bought this place and renovated it. Back then, there weren't as many city people around. Jules had started a book club with Anita and it was still going. There were eight or ten women in it now. They'd recently read *Middlemarch*.

"Cool," said Cora, pointlessly. "*Middlemarch*."

"Have they told you about Brandt's vasectomy?"

"They just did."

"That's their thing. They're very into Brandt having had a vasectomy." He crouched down next to her. "What do you think about that?"

"I might not personally lead with it."

"How have you been?"

"Fine," she said. "Regular."

He put a hand on her knee to steady himself. She noticed the rolled-up sleeve of his shirt, his wristwatch, the dark hair of his arms. Certain people's hands only made you think of them touching you. In the world of the affair, this was the prelude to a breathless encounter in a child's playroom, Sam kneeling on a nubbly multicolored rug to take off her underwear as a row of stuffed animals looked on. But in this world, if she accepted what he said about wanting to be friends only, then his physical attention meant nothing and would come to nothing, and she should remove his hand. She didn't.

"Is Jules here?" she said.

"Home. Penelope has hand, foot and mouth disease. Have you had that one yet? It's brutal."

They hadn't. So far this year they'd had RSV and four different stomach bugs, but not hand, foot, and mouth.

"What do feet have to do with it?" said Cora.

"That I don't know. It's a fever, but highly contagious, and you get these sores around your mouth. Inside your mouth too. It gets hard to swallow. Poor Penelope. We'll all have it in about five minutes. I'm probably giving it to you right now."

Cora said, "Thanks."

"You should call her soon to hang out."

"Can't Jules call me?"

They were quiet, listening to the sounds outside. Kids screamed and adults talked and music played. Someone who wasn't at the birthday party mowed a lawn.

"I want things to be normal," he said. "I want you to be normal."

"I'm being normal. Are you?"

His hand still rested on her knee. He looked at it then took it away. On the other side, he had turned a stuffed Pikachu to face the wall. When she started making noise, he covered her mouth with his hand.

"Jules could use a friend."

"I thought she was friends with Anita. Aren't they in a book club together?"

"All that means is they've both read *Middlemarch*. Or part of *Middlemarch,* as the case may be."

Cora didn't understand why it was her job to forge a relationship with Sam's wife. Couldn't they let it unfold naturally, if it was going to unfold? She and Jules had the rest of their lives to become friends. Assuming they both continued to live in the town and achieved the average life span for women, they had forty, fifty more years. Why was his intervention necessary?

"I don't trust you two to make it happen," he said.

They regarded the oven. Through the smudged window, they could see Anita and Brandt's sheet pans and cupcake tins, stained red-brown and stacked untidily.

"They do keep them in there," said Sam.

"Eliot thinks it's a bad habit. He wouldn't approve."

"Wouldn't approve of what?" said Eliot.

He'd entered the kitchen and stood at the island. He held Miles on his hip and the straps of the baby carrier hung off his front. There was something feminine, mammalian, about the way the empty pouch was sitting. Cora and Sam stood up quickly.

"Storing pans in the oven," she said.

"Oh yeah," said Eliot. "You have to take them out every time you want to cook and pile them on the counter. Unsightly. I've never understood why people don't keep them in a cabinet."

He opened the fridge and took out a beer.

"Do you want one of these?" he asked Sam.

"What about me?" said Cora.

"Oh, sorry. You, too."

He handed each of them a can. Brandt entered and informed them it was time to pin the tail on the dinosaur. Cora thought again about what happened when he ejaculated. His wife was so enamored with the process that she told everyone about it. She bragged about her husband coming in his own body. Cora thought: Good for him, maybe. They followed him outside.

Summer began and it got hot. In the big, anonymous hotel, the air-conditioning kicked on with a startling clank. It worked beautifully, making the room almost too cold. You could enter from the humid, oppressive world and stand in front of it while your lover showered. Outside, everything was too bright. The white lines of the parking lot, the windshields of the cars. But if you drew the curtains, the room became a dark, chilly cave, beyond time.

They went on Thursday afternoons. Cora invented a recurring meeting. In fact, she invented a whole new coworker. She invented a young woman named Morgan, whom she had to meet every week as a part of a new company-wide mentorship program. Morgan was a recent college graduate and needed a lot of help negotiating the workplace. She was stymied by everything from email etiquette to how to enter a sick day into the system. This new generation did not exactly want to work, and who could blame them?

Cora prepared a backstory for Morgan in case Eliot asked. Morgan had grown up outside of Philly and attended UPenn. Morgan was gluten intolerant. Morgan had a dog, a Newfoundland named Beau, who she had raised from a puppy. Morgan sometimes fought with her parents, whose politics differed from her own. But Eliot didn't ask. Why would Eliot doubt Morgan's existence? He accepted the recurring meeting without question. The details of another person's recurring meetings were beneath consideration. Cora had, for instance, never asked about one of his.

On Thursdays Cora parked her car beside the man-made lake and took stock of the birds. They were usually hidden away, wherever birds went to keep cool. But once she saw a heron sitting in the shallows, bending and straightening its graceful neck, shaking its feathers, and felt herself close to tears. The affair had made her susceptible to things like being moved by a bird's neck.

Up in the room, she stood in front of the AC holding her shirt away from her body. The parking lot blazed below. She heard Sam get out of the shower, and then he was behind her, lifting the sweaty hair off her neck. She turned and kissed him. He told her to undress and she did. He said, Sit on the edge of the bed and spread your legs and watch yourself in the mirror, and she did. He said, Touch yourself and tell me how wet you are. She was very wet and she told him this and he said, Good girl.

In the hotel room, she let Sam tell her what to do. He watched her make herself come and then he had her brace herself against the headboard while he fucked her from behind. The things he whispered into her ear made her come a second time. Afterward, they had beers in their underwear. She found a laminated sheet of TV channels and put on an old movie. They touched each other lazily in the flickering light of Paul Newman's face.

In reality, Cora's friend Isabelle came up from Brooklyn. They mixed Negronis on the deck and drank them out of mason jars. Roses had begun to bloom along the fence in four different shades. They had not known what they were until now. Cora researched how to care for them, and what you had to do was mostly nothing, water them once a week if it was dry out, prune them back, and fertilize them. She did these things with relish, in gloves gifted to her by the children, and then they were hers to feel proud of.

"So you're a gardener now?" said Isabelle.

"I'm just watering plants."

"Very upstate of you."

"We're not upstate," said Cora. "It's the Hudson Valley."

"No one cares about that distinction but you."

Isabelle was from L.A., the daughter of Korean immigrants. They had met at Sarah Lawrence, where they'd both majored in media, marketing, and communications. Now Isabelle worked in television and practiced polyamory. She had a boyfriend, a boyfriend, and a girlfriend, and managing the three of them was like a second job, she said. They sometimes had group sex, but mostly they had conversations. She found Cora's life quaint and old-timey. A marriage and a couple of kids outside the city, like the pilgrims at Plymouth Rock.

Eliot was barbecuing, jamming fish and vegetables onto skewers, dressing a salad, mixing more cocktails, listening to music on a speaker he'd brought outdoors, pausing when Opal called to him from the swing set to watch her do a trick.

Isabelle accepted a cocktail. "Where do you guys go up here?"

"Go?" said Eliot.

"Like when you go out."

"Out?" said Eliot.

"Like to enjoy yourselves."

There was nowhere to go and no reason to go there. There was no enjoyment, not in the sense that an unfettered person understood the term. They had a baby and a three-year-old. The most they could hope for was gratification. Occasional reprieve. One day the baby and the three-year-old would be older, and maybe things would change. But currently every moment was spoken for.

"We don't go anywhere," said Eliot. "Where would we go?"

Over dinner, Isabelle and Cora talked about college. They had been roommates for three years. Afterward, they lived together in an apartment in South Williamsburg, at eye level with the BQE. You could see individual drivers; that's how close they'd been. Sometimes they looked right at you. Their lives in those days had been precarious. They waitressed at the same bad Italian restaurant; they were often a week late on the rent; most of their furniture had been found on the street. They had been living like this when Cora met Eliot.

"Remember that night?" said Eliot. "That thing hit you in the head."

It had been a dowel holding up a tie-dye tapestry. They had been at a party at the twelve-man loft. The dowel had not hurt her badly, but it had caused her to stagger back two steps in confusion. Why had something come swooping out of the air to hit her in the head? After it hit her, the tapestry had fallen to the ground in a coarse heap. Eliot witnessed this and made her sit down on a nearby futon, covered with yet another tapestry.

She was embarrassed, but he'd been funny about it. "Does that happen to you a lot?"

Cora said, "It's everywhere I go."

He looked at the tapestry they sat on. "What's with these anyway?"

They were all over the apartment. They had tie-dye patterns or splotches or elaborate swirls. They looked like they had been purchased at Urban Outfitters. Some of them hung in the air as room dividers, but most were covering surfaces.

"You just know that whatever they're covering is so much worse," said Cora.

They talked awhile longer and people started moving instruments into the area of the apartment that was regarded as "the stage." A band with two of everything began to play. Two drummers, two lead vocalists, two guitar players, two bassists.

Eliot said, "Oh Jesus. Not this."

He asked if she wanted to go somewhere with less clanging. They'd gone to his apartment and pretended to look at his records for five minutes before having sex. When they'd married two years later, they knew it was fast and that they were young. But they had been sure. Cora had no doubts and Eliot had no doubts. They had moved into the first of many apartments, barely caring that it was ugly. That's how happy they had been. Barely caring that the fake-tin ceiling was peeling off in one corner and had to be shoved back up once or twice a week with a broomstick.

"I remember," said Cora now. "It was a tapestry."

It had been the most important thing to ever hit her in the head.

After dinner they walked into town for ice cream. It was humid, thickly overcast. Isabelle pushed Miles's stroller. Opal rode her scooter. Hand-drawn chalkboards advertised drink specials and artisanal ice pops. Strawberry basil, lavender lemon. The storefronts were open to the evening, their louvered shutters pushed aside, and people ate and laughed, spilling out onto the sidewalk.

At the ice cream place, Eliot went in with Opal, and Cora and

THE TEN YEAR AFFAIR

Isabelle sat on the bench outside with the stroller. Sam happened by, pushing Penelope. He took out his earbuds and explained he was going to meet Jules and Jack at the taco place up the street. The taco place was bad and slow, but there was no alternative, no second taco place. Had Cora been there? Cora hadn't, but she'd heard. She introduced him to Isabelle.

"Up from the city?" said Sam.

"Just for the weekend."

He remarked that the first summer everyone came to see you. You became their country friend. Never mind that this was not the country. It was a town of fourteen thousand with a metropolitan sensibility. It had an indie movie theater, a boutique hotel. It was seventy minutes from Grand Central Station. No one chopped their own wood. Even keeping chickens would make you an outlier. People back in Brooklyn thought you were Henry David Thoreau, but then they came to visit and saw that you lived in a vinyl-siding house. It was only rustic in that you could not get good Thai food.

"That sounds pretty rustic," said Isabelle.

"Anyway, it wears off. Word gets around that it's not the woods and they stop coming," he said. "You'll stop coming. Sorry, you will. You won't come back for years."

Then he had to run. He was needed at the taco place. Before he left, he reminded Cora that she still hadn't called Jules. They watched him recede down the street, drop his earbuds, wipe them off, stick them back in his ears.

"Who was that?" said Isabelle.

"I know him from a baby group I joined when I was on leave," said Cora. "You'd have found it interesting. Eight women and that one dude sitting around talking about perineal tearing."

"He seems eager. What does he want with you?"

"To be my friend, I guess."

"That can't be it. Why?"

"I don't know. I'm cool?"

"You're not cool. You have two kids."

"Out here I'm cool. I know this is hard for you to believe. Different rubric out here."

"What's the wife's deal?" said Isabelle.

"She's normal. She's a lawyer."

"Stay away. You'll thank me."

"This is going to sound dumb, but Sam and I had an instant closeness. You know when that happens? When you feel like you already know the person?"

"Oh boy."

They sat watching the street. Families walked by, couples holding hands, a little kid and his dad with a dog. People came out of restaurants in groups. The women wore sundresses, the men wore shorts.

"I think you should be careful with any man who purports to want to be friends with you," said Isabelle.

"I thought you were for nontraditional relationships. Isn't that your whole thing?"

"For me. I'm in favor of them for me. For you, no. You can't handle it."

Eliot came out, juggling ice cream. Mint chip dripped down his wrist, and he licked at it, turning his head sideways. "Can you grab these?"

They took their cones and turned uphill for home. Eliot carried Opal's scooter over his shoulder. Opal skipped along next to him talking incessantly. Miles had fallen asleep in his stroller.

"Want my advice?" said Isabelle. "If you have to get involved, be friends with the wife."

They went home and Cora made up the pullout in her office. She got Isabelle a glass of water and a set of clean towels. Eliot cooked French toast in the morning, which they ate on the deck as the sun shone yellow-green through oak leaves. The kids were adorable, well rested, not too clingy.

"You know, it's actually kind of great here," said Isabelle.

She did not visit again for years.

Cora invited Jules for a drink at the restaurant overlooking the falls. The early evening sun made rainbows in its spray. They sat on the deck as waiters in long white aprons traced figure eights between tables. The place served small plates, flatbreads, dips in shallow vessels. Blistered this and that. It was the season of blistering in the town, something of an eternal spring.

Jules was petite, with sleek brown hair, olive coloring, and an armful of gold bracelets. She wanted to do the ordering, so Cora let her. She debated out loud which three dishes to get. When the waitress arrived with their bottle of wine, she tasted it and pronounced it "good enough," then asked her to adjust their umbrella, which was not casting sufficient shade.

They talked about their children and husbands in a friendly, impersonal way. Jules asked her questions and seemed to listen to her answers, and Cora asked questions back. Jules had grown up in Vermont. Jules had gone to Columbia, where she'd met Sam. Jules practiced bankruptcy law in the city, and the commute was psychotic. Jules skied and ran semiseriously to stay fit.

"I run too," said Cora. "Or I used to."

"Oh, yeah?" said Jules.

So that provided thirty seconds of conversation.

They discovered they had a mutual acquaintance in Cora's coworker Lily. Jules knew her a little through a friend. They talked about Lily at length, saying the blandest, nicest things about her, exhausting the topic completely. Lily was funny and smart. Lily was studying Japanese at night, not for a particular reason, but just to learn something. They had to shout to make themselves heard over the rush of water.

"She's great at Photoshop," Cora heard herself saying, and almost laughed.

On the other side, this was a rendezvous with Sam, and they were scared of being seen by someone they knew. They debated meeting inside, at the dimly lit bar, where antlers hung over the fireplace and animal pelts covered the floor. But the day was glorious and mild, and so they risked it and sat outside in their sunglasses, whispering over their wine, the toe of his sneaker on her calf, his thumb and forefinger absently encircling her wrist.

Meanwhile, Cora was actually running into someone she knew. It was Dr. Sperling, the kids' pediatrician. Dr. Sperling asked Cora how the children were, and Cora said, "Great." Dr. Sperling said are they gaining weight, and Cora said, "I think so." Dr. Sperling said are they getting enough vitamin D, and Cora said, "We try." Dr. Sperling said be careful of head lice this summer, it's rampant at summer camp, and Cora said, "Always."

"Tell your kids not to share hats," he said.

"Right."

She introduced Jules, and Jules said hello. Dr. Sperling's wife stood slightly back. She was elderly, like him, in a beige cardigan set. She informed him that they had to be going and handed him his cane. He gave Cora an encouraging nod and departed with his cane and his wife and his dignified old man's gait.

"Is Opal going to camp?" said Jules, once he'd gone.

"No. She's too young," said Cora.

"Does she have a problem with sharing hats?"

It had never come up. Opal had never mentioned sharing a hat. She hardly ever wore hats. In winter, it was difficult to get her to keep one on.

"What is he talking about then?" said Jules.

"He must be thinking of someone else, or maybe he goes around town issuing blanket warnings about head lice. Dr. Sperling is ninety-three years old, so who knows?"

"Ninety-three? Jesus. How do you know that?"

"He's proud of it. He talks about it all the time. He tells my kids if they eat their vegetables, they'll make it to ninety-three like him."

"You take your kids to a doctor who was born in"—she did the math—"nineteen twenty-two?"

"He's seasoned," said Cora.

"You should use our pediatrician. She's a woman, our age."

"He's a regular modern doctor. He doesn't do, like, bloodletting."

"Even so . . ."

Jules insisted on paying at the end. She put down a credit card in a jangle of bracelets.

"Don't tell Sam."

Sam didn't know the credit card existed. Jules kept it for splurges, drinks with friends, expensive cocktail dresses, purchases she didn't want to answer for. Otherwise, they pooled their finances. This was a good way to pretend they brought in equal money, though of course she made much more than he did.

"Maybe he has a secret card, too," said Eliot, in bed that night.

"I get the feeling he doesn't."

"I think it's smart for her to have some independence. Don't you?"

"Yeah. But why keep it a secret?" said Cora. "Why not have separate accounts, like we do, and leave it at that? Why the illusion of transparency?"

She started undressing. He lay on top of the covers reading a manuscript and intermittently looking at his phone. He wore no shirt and had trained a box fan directly at himself. It was odd, remarked Cora, how some of the couples they knew had flipped the gender roles of the past without improving on them. Now the men were disenfranchised and dependent rather than the women, when actually no one had to be.

"Don't you think?" said Cora.

Eliot scrolled on his phone. "Hm?"

The fan fluttered the pages of his manuscript.

She said, "Let me ask you a question. Do you find her attractive?"

"No."

He always said no to this question at first. He would not admit to being attracted to women other than Cora without coaxing.

"Come on."

"Not my thing."

"You're lying."

"I'm not."

What about her wasn't his thing? Her slight build? Her glossy hair? Her understated sense of style? The economic grace with which she moved?

"Yeah," he said. "None of that's my thing. I hate that stuff."

"You hate nice hair?"

"Yeah. Gross."

"You could pick her up and carry her around if you wanted to."

"Like in an emergency? I suppose that's an asset."

He had looked up from his reading, half stoned and amused with himself, his default state. She was always surprised to find she still found him funny.

"I only like you," he said. "You're the sexiest woman on Earth."

That made them both laugh. But what if it was true?

Three

Years passed in both worlds, in all worlds. In the time line of the affair Cora's affection deepened and she admitted she was in love. The heat between them, the wildness, did not abate. Sam quit the toothpicks. In late summer they walked in the park and a doe with white-tipped ears came over and nuzzled Sam in the leg and laid her soft snout in Cora's hand. They drank too much wine that night and conceived a baby, oops, and this led to weeks of wrenching conversation. He said he wanted a baby with her, of course he did, but was it ethical or responsible, was it cool to ruin the lives of six existing people to produce one new person with their shared genes? Maybe not cool, she said, no. But she wanted it and you could want something bad enough that you needed it. You could want something so bad it became indivisible from your survival.

You'll survive, he said. They decided to terminate.

Over on the other side, their kids got older. They haggled with Rose to keep them in the same class. Cora enjoyed Jules's company. They made each other laugh. Jules was better than her at most things—sports, cooking, career advancement—and this felt good to Cora, the way it felt good to tongue a canker sore.

Occasionally, the vectors veered closer together. She was walking home from the library one day when Sam pulled up beside her in his car.

He said, "You're always walking around town. You're the lady who walks around town."

She got in and they drove up the mountain.

When she asked where they were going, he said, "Not sure."

She felt a shiver, the brush of the uncanny against her cheek. This exact thing would happen in the other time line. In fact, it was happening over there, with minor differences.

Sam stopped at an overlook. A breeze came in the open windows that smelled sweetly of the ground. The town spread out before them, red and brown and gray rooftops sloping down toward a river slashed with sunlight. It seemed like a make-out spot. Cora turned to Sam. Sam put his head on the steering wheel.

He said, "Read to me from that book you have, whatever it is."

It was a book that she'd gotten for Opal, *Butterflies and Moths of North America*.

She opened to a random page and read, "In the second stage of the life cycle, the larva hatches from the egg . . . "

"Okay stop," he said.

"Well, what were you expecting?"

"I don't know. Poetry or something."

Did he think she took romantic strolls down to the library to check out books of poetry? Was he picturing her doing that, when he pictured her?

"It's for homework," she said. "Insect unit."

"You're a great mom," he said.

"Eh. It's pretty baseline. It's picking up a book."

He gave her the kind of look that usually precedes a passionate gesture. His hands were shaking. He rubbed them on his jeans. Since the time they'd kissed, there'd been no incidents of sexual contact between them, though the restraint this required was itself quasi-sexual.

"We should go," he said.

He started the car and they left.

The families began to dine together regularly, maybe once or twice a month. In a quiet town like theirs, it was what there was to do. You had friends and saw them for dinner. One party hosted and the other brought wine. You discussed current events while the kids watched a movie in a distant room. At the end of the night, you lay in bed talking about the other couple.

Sam and Jules lived a few blocks north of Main Street. Their house was larger than Cora's without being nicer. None of the houses in town were grand. It had been a factory town in the late nineteenth and early twentieth centuries, hat factories mostly. That was why it looked the way it did, with its weathered brick warehouses down on the creek, its remnants of signage painted right on the sides of buildings.

The factories had closed, perhaps when hats fell out of fashion, or when manufacturing moved elsewhere. There had been a region-wide period of depression, then, decades later, a rapid rebound initiated by the construction of the modern art museum in an abandoned warehouse near the railroad tracks. The homes that had once belonged to workers now belonged to the professional class. To trace the downward trajectory of the American empire, Eliot liked to say, one only had to look to real estate.

"Let's not drink too much," said Eliot on the way over to Jules and Sam's.

"Let's have one each," said Cora. "Max two."

"And we'll get out before the kids lose it."

They said this every time and always believed it. Eliot parked, pulling their used Subaru in behind Jules's new Volvo. None of the houses in town were grand, and yet if you spread out the particulars on a slide, cranked up the magnification, the class distinctions were there. They got out and boosted the kids down, locked the doors, unlocked them again when they realized they'd forgotten to grab the wine, the card game Opal had brought to play with Jack, the cookies. The cookies were already open and two were missing. In the course of the drive—four minutes—the kids had begged and Cora had acquiesced.

Sam greeted them on the front porch. He shook Eliot's hand, kissed Cora on the cheek. He said to her, "You look nice," and she glanced down at what she was wearing, jeans and one of Eliot's oxford cloth shirts. Sam was dressed similarly. His hair was wet from the shower and pushed back off his brow. Eliot had three inches on him but Sam was broader and gave an appearance of solidity. By contrast, Eliot had a willowy build, looked easy to knock over, and in fact had been knocked over so many times in his youth that his mother had to go to his school to meet with the principal.

"Jules is finishing something up for work," said Sam. "She'll be right down."

He took them on a tour of the house's latest problems, which was customary. Few people their age could afford homes, so when they did, they were at pains to disavow them. If the house was riddled with flaws, a teardown, if it had a puzzling layout, a persistent smell, if it needed a new roof, a sump pump in the basement, if it had one or more uninsulated rooms, then you didn't have to feel special or chosen among your peers for owning it. You didn't have to forfeit solidarity with modern history's most shafted generation.

"Check this out," said Sam.

They were outside regarding a piece of loose siding up near the roof.

"Our handyman won't repair it. He doesn't want to go up that high. He said he's got no love for extension ladders. I asked him what that means and he said extension ladders fall over. He's seen it happen. He's seen a guy's arm shatter in sixteen places. I asked if he had any friends that would do it and he said no. No one has any love for extension ladders. No one wants to pay eighty thousand dollars to fix an arm he shattered doing a job for forty bucks. The math doesn't work out."

"So now what?" said Eliot.

"It's just going to be like that. On windy days it flaps against the house and also sort of whistles."

He shushed them so they could hear it. It was breezy out but Cora couldn't detect any whistling. Jules came out onto the deck.

"What's happening here? Oh, the whistling. Can you hear it? Drives me nuts. Do you have anyone who will climb an extension ladder? Our guy is afraid. Cora, come inside and help me. I haven't even gotten the chicken in the oven yet. I'm having a crazy day."

The fact that the chicken was still raw was not promising. It meant another hour of hanging around before they even sat down to eat. Cora went inside and Jules put her to work. She told her to find a pretty bowl for the pistachios and Cora opened a cabinet to an array of pretty bowls. She chose one that was mint green inside and dark green outside.

"Not that one," Jules said, without specifying why, and Cora chose another.

Opal came in and said, "I'm bored. What am I supposed to do?"

How could Opal have been bored already? Cora wondered. Though she herself was also bored.

"You can help us," said Cora.

She lifted Opal onto the counter and showed her how to pour pistachios into a bowl. Cora could see the men out in the yard through the window above the sink. They gazed into what seemed to be a large hole. Sam chewed a toothpick and held a trowel. They looked like gentlemen farmers, but ask them to climb an extension ladder and they demurred.

Opal pointed at Jules, who was spatchcocking the chicken. "Does it hurt them?"

Her face was grave. She had clear blue eyes and freckles on her nose. Her two modes were grave and impossible. Opal was going into first grade now, and at a parent-teacher conference the previous spring, her teacher had told Cora that Opal could basically teach the class if she wasn't so impatient with her peers. This had made Cora apologize, while also feeling flattered. It was accurate, ultimately. Opal had the sort of poise that seemed like a reprimand.

"No," said Cora carefully. "If that's happening to them, they're already gone."

"Gone where Grandpa is?"

"We hold people in higher esteem than chickens so maybe not precisely where he is. Like maybe there's a tiered system . . ."

Jules glanced at her.

"Yes, where Grandpa is," said Cora.

Opal pointed at the chicken again. "Can I do that?"

"You want to spatchcock the chicken?" said Cora.

Opal nodded. It was in Cora's nature to just go ahead and let Opal spatchcock the chicken. Did Opal know how to do it? Of course not. Children did not intuitively know how to butcher. Cora had never heard of anyone being a prodigy at that. And yet maybe Opal was. Opal's intelligence was a spring that ran cool and brisk. Cora didn't fully know its depths. If a child could figure out how to spatchcock a chicken, it was Opal. But you couldn't propose that to another mother. You couldn't say, let's let this six-year-old take over, yeah?

"I think Jules has it covered."

Jules said, "I had something else to ask you. Should we join the PTA?"

Penelope and Miles were about to start pre-K and she was being recruited by the woman who wore shearling boots to drop-off. Had Cora seen her? Cora had. She had a tight ponytail and twin boys she pulled in a wagon. Every day, up the hill to school with two kids who must have been in second or third grade, and down again with an empty Radio Flyer. The kids were capable of walking—when they got to school, they leaped out and charged inside. So why did she do it? Maybe, like Sisyphus, she'd cheated death.

"Definitely not," said Cora.

Jules rubbed the chicken with butter. "See, my instinct is yes. Don't our kids need an advocate at every level?"

"We didn't do it for the other ones and they're okay."

Opal arranged pistachios in the shape of a heart on the cutting board. She'd touched every nut, but it didn't matter as long as she was occupied. With Opal, it was not just that she was okay but that she was beyond, or outside of, what you might imagine for a child. How did you help someone who was already so self-contained? It wasn't by joining the PTA.

Miles, on the other hand, had been calm and easy until the moment he turned two, and then he'd become what they called "spirited." Spiritedly, he drove them all insane. The ways he could be helped did not involve the PTA either. They were more about running him to exhaustion in a safe outdoor environment or learning the symptoms of a concussion.

"I need you to make a case against joining," said Jules.

Shearling Boots had been persuasive. She had made Jules feel a degree of guilt, a degree of ineptitude. Jules didn't like feeling that way.

"We don't need to justify it," said Cora. "But okay. You work. You're a lawyer. You have a career. Maybe you're a partner? I don't know."

"I'm not yet."

"Still. You're home late enough as it is. You'll soon be partner. If you want to be partner, I have no doubt you'll be partner. What do they do at PTA meetings anyway? The fall fest?"

"The fall fest is cute."

The fall fest took place on the field behind school every October. The PTA set up booths and high school kids ran the games. You could buy baked goods to support the soccer team. You could win a goldfish playing ring toss. Orange leaves spun down from giant oaks overhead. It was always beautifully executed, so Cora assumed it must have represented a hassle for the people who put it together.

"But annoying to organize, I'm sure," said Cora. "You have to rent a popcorn machine. Order cider donuts. Call a clown."

"None of that sounds hard to me."

This was why Jules was more successful than Cora: because she was not daunted by the prospect of calling a clown. It would take Cora hours to work up the energy to call a clown. She'd have to block out a whole day for it. It would involve confronting the choices she'd made in life up until that point, the entire chain of events that had led to calling a clown.

"It's too tedious," said Cora. "Think of what one of those meetings is like."

"It could be endured."

Jules was right that it was technically possible to get through a two-hour meeting. Cora sat in many of them each week. The hardest part was arranging your face and body to appear engaged, then holding them that way much longer than you wanted. Cora's most common thought as she sat in work meetings was Why? Why did they have to talk in person about digital marketing? Why did they have to waste their time this way? Because surely everyone else—or everyone excluding the freaks—was faking interest just like she was.

"You should make Sam join," said Cora. "He'd be great at it. He'd be handing out toothpicks. Make Sam order cider donuts. Make him call a clown."

"It's not a bad idea," said Jules. "But what are we punishing him for?"

Sam and Eliot came inside. The screen door slammed behind them.

"Oh wow, the chicken's still not in the oven," said Eliot.

He exchanged a look with Cora that said the one-drink plan

was out. They were going to have many drinks, probably too many, so they should decide now who would drive home. Cora always felt responsible in these moments for the disarray of other people. This case was particularly glaring. She had brought them into Eliot's life, and so it was her fault that Jules had not cooked the chicken in a timely fashion, or even laid out sufficient snacks.

"I'll drive," she said.

Sam opened a beer and handed it to Eliot. Eliot began eating pistachios out of the bowl. They were the shelled kind and he remarked that he didn't know Sam and Jules were millionaires.

"Cora has an idea for you," Jules said to Sam.

Sam said. "Tell me."

They told him about the PTA, the persistence of Shearling Boots, the pros and cons of joining. On the pro side, it would be good to make themselves useful. On the con side was everything else. They finished talking and Sam said, "I'll join, sure." He sat on the counter next to Opal with his legs dangling, playing with a fancy corkscrew.

He pointed it at Cora. "You join, too. It's probably the right thing to do."

Eliot looked up at her from his handful of nuts. "Tell them you don't want to."

He addressed Sam. "She doesn't want to do it."

But did she not want to? She definitely hadn't when it was going to be her and Jules. That sounded like a chore. But now Sam was on board, she kind of wanted to. It would still be boring. It would still be sitting in a school cafeteria for two precious evening hours instead of doing anything else, but Sam would be there as opposed to Jules.

"Don't speak for her," said Jules.

"You don't understand," said Eliot. "She's eminently persuadable."

Sam stopped messing with the wine opener. "Is that right?"

She said, "Unfortunately."

Her compulsion to be game was the overriding theme of her life. People could sense it. They detected in her a patsy, someone who would fold under minimal pressure, and felt emboldened to do things like ask her to join the PTA. They all looked at her now.

Sam said, "Say yes."

"Well," said Cora. "Maybe it wouldn't be so bad."

"It's everything you hate about having a job minus the one thing you like," said Eliot.

He was talking about money. She did not feel she liked money more than the average person. The average person liked money a lot and so did she. This was because she and Eliot never had enough of it. This made her squarely normal, not avaricious, and anyway it wasn't like she had ever done anything outlandish to pursue it, other than sit in meetings about digital marketing.

"Well," Cora said again.

Cora and Sam joined the PTA. Meetings took place on Wednesday nights in the school cafeteria, which smelled like every food at once. On a backless stool, too low for an adult, Cora endured. Shearling Boots was cheerful and hyperorganized. She brought brownies and kept everyone on topic. She'd pull them all in a wagon, Cora felt, if she could come up with the slightest reason to do so.

At the first meeting, they brainstormed ideas on a whiteboard, priorities for the fall fest. Sam whispered jokes in Cora's ear, and she laughed and shushed him. In the parking lot afterward, they leaned against his car. The nights were getting shorter, though it was still warm. They were both needed at home, where bedtime was taking place. Miles required a lot of attention at that hour. He had an intricate routine. He liked to be read books in a certain order, with certain flourishes that only Cora could execute. When Eliot didn't do it right, he lost his mind.

But they lingered anyway, discussing the other people in the meeting, saying nothing much about them. They had seen most of the parents around but did not know their names. The other man in the group had gotten up to use the bathroom twice and they named him Pisser. What did it say, they wondered, that Pisser and Sam were the only dads there? The structures stood, it turned out. Despite everyone's good intentions, the structures stood.

Shearling Boots had long ago locked up and gone home, waving to them as she went.

"She's not bad," said Cora.

"It's surprising, but she's not," said Sam.

"She should be president of the United States."

The current president was Donald Trump. They stood imagining a world where instead of Donald Trump, Shearling Boots was in office. She could unite a divided nation, they agreed. She could heal, with her gentle-firm affect, what seemed irrevocably frayed between countrymen.

"Why do you think she pulls her kids in that wagon?" said Cora. "They're too big for it and they don't seem to care about it either way."

"I think it must just be that she loves them."

They thought about this. The parking lot was strewn with

yellow leaves in the shape of teardrops. A sudden wind blew the leaves onto their sneakers.

In the world of the affair, they often skipped PTA meetings. They used the time to meet at a bench near the trailhead and talk. Hiking season had peaked and the trail was abandoned. They sat with the mountain at their backs, looking out at traffic. Something had changed between them since the abortion. They had entered a new phase of seriousness. What might have made them closer had put a wedge between them. This was what happened in affairs, and what hastened their conclusions. If the conclusion was being hastened, Cora wanted to know.

Are we winding down? she said.

He said, I don't want that.

The way he saw it, nothing had to change. She'd gotten the abortion for this reason, hadn't she? To keep their relationship the way it was? Maybe it would push things, he said, into a new realm of maturity. Relationships came of age, and this was what was happening. It meant they would have the full menu—camaraderie, desire, indiscretion, pleasure, pain, and loss—and they would discover the limits of their feelings for each other.

Cora watched a car pass bound for the city. She said, Do you think of me differently now?

Sam said, No.

He was offended she'd ask. He'd handled it sensitively and treated her like the modern woman she was. Hadn't he? They had decided together. They had been in agreement that they could not have a child, that it would upend their lives completely.

Anyway, he went on. It was too late now. You couldn't unabort a baby.

You told me it was fine, said Sam. You said the place wasn't depressing.

It was fine, said Cora.

It wasn't the abortion itself that was the problem but the tension it created. Because it stopped being fun once someone had to make an appointment at a clinic. Even a nice, normal place, which they all were in New York State in the twenty-first century. Secretly, Sam and Cora each held the other responsible for the loss of fun. It had made her think about mortality, she told him. What place did mortality have in an affair?

He said, It's the very crux of it.

It was getting dark now. Streetlights came on, illuminating the parking lot of the convenience store across the street that sold sandwiches and Gatorade to hikers.

I don't want to talk about this anymore, said Sam. We made the decision and I don't regret it. Do you?

Probably not.

He said, All right then.

She began to look forward to PTA meetings. At her desk at work, she thought about them. Sometimes when she sat next to Sam, they played hangman on a legal pad. Sometimes they wrote each other's names in different fonts. At work, Lily caught her zoning out and asked what was on her mind. Cora was embarrassed to say, "The PTA," so she said, "Lunch." Lily said "Okay," and they went and got tacos from a truck and ate them at a rickety plastic table in Herald Square.

Cora's mother came over to the house and told her it was unusual she had joined the PTA at all. It was an unusual choice.

"That stuff is for moms who don't work," she said.

They stood in the yard. Her mother wore black trousers, a cashmere shell, and tiny pointed shoes. She was two inches shorter than Cora but otherwise looked like her. Now that her hair had turned gray, she'd dyed it platinum. She was an accomplished gardener and was there to help Cora figure out what to do with the yard.

"No one doesn't work," said Cora. "Your generation created conditions where everyone has to work and even two incomes aren't enough."

"Great, I'm getting a lecture," said Cora's mom.

In her day, the PTA was make-work for bored women. So they could feel confident and involved, and have something to do once a week. It was for the kind of mother who stifled her children with good intentions. Oversteppers. Brittle women who tried hard but in the wrong places. Women whose faces fell when their husbands did not like the dinner they cooked.

"Fathers do it now too," said Cora, though it was only a couple of fathers.

"Do they? We'd have called a man on the PTA dickless. Brave new world, I guess."

Eliot came outside and handed Cora's mother a glass of chardonnay. It was all she would drink and they kept it on hand for her.

She said, "Thank you, sweetheart."

Cora's mom loved Eliot. She loved Eliot's mother, an education consultant in New Jersey named Shirley. They had both grown up in Jewish Brooklyn and had been disappointed by Cora and Eliot's courthouse wedding. They had mutually imagined a large-scale Gathering of the Jews with a chuppah and a rabbi and an exuberant lifting of chairs. But Cora and Eliot could not justify the expense and were embarrassed by a lot of the traditions. For instance, Cora did not want to wear white or be delivered to Eliot by her father.

Instead, they'd had the immediate families to the courthouse and lunch at a restaurant in Tribeca. The two mothers had persuaded Cora to at least register and get her KitchenAid. They'd made her choose a Le Creuset color, and she'd chosen yellow, or actually "quince," which they called a classic choice. Now she and Eliot owned the full run of quince pots, the Dutch oven, the enamel skillet, even the spoon rest, purchased for them by friends of their parents, and okay, they were nice. They'd been right about that.

"I just think maybe you could be using the time and energy for your own pursuits," said her mother. "The PTA time and energy. Like didn't you want to start freelancing?"

This was an idea Cora had been kicking around before Miles was born. Expanding her editorial portfolio by freelancing. Cora's career disappointed her mother, who had hoped she'd follow her into medicine. She thought they'd launch an epic dynasty of ob-gyns. But Cora had been daunted by the focus that would have required, the difficulty of med school, the years of residency. How her mother would then always be counseling and criticizing her, every moment the quince pots.

Instead, her stated goal had been to work in television news. It was what she'd studied in college. Then she'd done an internship at a major network and saw that, like medicine, it took a supernatural amount of drive. She was intimidated by the idea of having to push so hard. So she downgraded her aspiration to print journalism, downgraded again to any job where you got to sit at a desk. To do something you believed in or enjoyed, you had to throw yourself at it like Eliot or Jules. You had to really want it. Cora's mom had envisioned her as a no-nonsense lady, like Barbara Walters or Gayle King. It had hurt her to learn that Cora was, in fact, nonsense.

"I might still do it," said Cora. "It's not one or the other."

They took a lap around the yard and her mother made suggestions about what she should plant based on factors like shade and precipitation. They were in growing zone 6a, she told Cora, but that was shifting because of climate change. She might actually be able to plant figs in the next few years, a silver lining to the eminent death of the planet.

"All of this is crabgrass," said her mother.

"Is that bad? It looks like regular grass."

"If it looks fine to you, it looks fine to you. But you probably want to get sod at some point. When Dad and I did it, it cost a fortune. But it's so small back here that it won't even be expensive."

They'd never be able to afford sod, though it was indeed "small back there." They had enough money for basic necessities and nothing else. She refrained from bringing up the housing crisis, interest rates, childcare costs, the reason people lived in smaller houses now, the fact that most of her friends would go to their graves as renters, the disaster of healthcare, the credit card debt she personally carried, the slowly closing aperture of the American dream.

"I just don't want you to become one of those hovering parents," said her mother, talking about the PTA again. "Who thinks more is better. Who's constantly volunteering. You know what I mean? I always found that pathetic."

"That isn't what's going on," said Cora.

They went inside and Eliot was making a shrimp salad with cilantro and lime.

Her mother hugged him. "Shirley knocked it out of the park raising you."

"Let's call her," said Eliot.

They facetimed Shirley, who screamed with delight. Shirley would not believe the meal her son was cooking, Cora's mother said. The lime thing they liked. The shrimp lime thing. She had told Shirley before, but she really ought to write a book about parenting boys. Who better? Cora's mom kept repeating. She had her thumb partly over the camera for most of the call.

Wet leaves papered the windshields of cars and the fall fest loomed. The members of the PTA stayed late on Wednesday nights finalizing details. Was it satisfying? It was a concrete goal they worked toward together. They'd see the results of that work. The day would come and they'd stand at their stations watching children in bright jackets zigzag across the field, eat junk food, pet a goat, throw a ball to dunk their gym teacher.

In this way, it differed from what Cora did every day and what Sam did too. Their work was abstract. They sat at computers sending emails. They edited text that said nothing. At the end of the day, they closed their computers without having accomplished anything concrete. The next morning, they opened them again for more of the same. But with the fall fest they would see what they'd accomplished. Maybe it would make someone happy. Then it would be done and they wouldn't have to think about it again for a calendar year.

Eliot smoked on the front porch, which meant Cora had missed her window for sex.

He came upstairs and asked her, "How is it going with the fall fest?"

Cora lay in bed reading. "I'm not going to have to call a clown after all."

In the end no one had to. Shearling Boots had a relationship with a clown from the past two fall fests. Otis was his name. Otis the Clown. She texted Otis and that was it. A clown you could text.

"That's great news," said Eliot. "Should I shower? I kind of feel like showering."

He stepped out of his pants. She always found this part of the night erotic. The eroticism of the evening debrief. One of them tended to be undressing during it. Then they sprawled out on clean white sheets to criticize people they knew.

"Can we fuck?" said Cora.

Eliot said, "I'm stoned as you can see."

The real issue was that Eliot was on an antidepressant that killed his sex drive. They had fucked a lot as young people, beginning the night they'd met. It had been at the core of their relationship. He was more assertive in bed than he was in normal life. Cora's willingness to acquiesce, a nuisance to her in the light of day, was different in bed too.

But he'd been depressed on and off his whole life. It had surfaced in college, worsened when they had Opal. They hadn't considered—and this was kind of hilarious—that life got hard with a kid. That money would always be an issue. They could imagine only that they'd have fun and love their child very much and be good at it. It made her throat hurt to think of it now. In the first years of Opal's life, Eliot was tired all the time and developed a short fuse. He yelled at Opal once, when she was one. "You need to fucking stop," he'd said to her, and Cora had said, "You're yelling at a baby." Then he was ashamed: He'd yelled at a baby.

He got a prescription. It took a while and made him even more tired, but it worked. They left the city, and this helped too. Opal was no longer right on top of them. But he didn't want sex anymore, it didn't seem to occur to him, and when it did, he often couldn't finish. He thrust and thrust until she offered him her mouth, and then he'd fuck her mouth endlessly until her jaw hurt too much and she had to call it.

"Does Shearling Boots have a real name?" he said.

She said, "You need to get in the shower. You can't stand there with your dick out like that."

"Tell me her name."

"It's Marjory."

"Hot."

"Why are you trying to talk to me about school matters if you're fully nude?"

"Tell me more about the meeting."

"We were assigned stations. Marjory wrote on a whiteboard what we'd each do. I'm running the face-painting booth."

This amused him. "Why you? Do you know how to paint faces?"

Cora had asked Shearling Boots the same question. She had said outright, I don't know how to paint faces. Almost anyone else would do a better job. Sure, you do, Shearling Boots had insisted. It wasn't that hard to draw a hibiscus on someone's cheek. You just pictured a hibiscus and then drew it.

"I guess I give the impression of being vaguely arty," said Cora.

"No, you don't."

He moved a step closer. She took his cock in her hand.

He said, "I'm telling you I'm stoned. It's not going to work."

But maybe she could get it to work? Was she supposed to give up? It was half-hard. She worked to make it fully hard. She did the thing he liked with one hand, while continuing to read. Then she set down her book to give it her full attention.

He said, "Don't look so determined."

He pushed her shorts aside and stuck two fingers in her. He was appealingly rough.

She was making no progress. "I guess I don't understand. Because isn't part of it simple friction?"

He took his fingers out. Then it became a conversation about medication. Should Eliot stop taking it? Should he try a different kind? Sometimes if you stopped taking one kind and tried another kind, it didn't work, and then the first kind would stop working too. A famous author published by his imprint had killed himself because of it. This never happened in the other world. Never had practicalities distracted anyone from fucking.

"I can try to step down the dose," he said.

"Don't do that if it's working."

She didn't want him to stop taking it. She didn't want to see him yell at their baby and hate himself. She wanted him to be healthy and present. His life should first be bearable.

He said, "But I want to be able to . . . " He gestured at the length of her.

THE TEN YEAR AFFAIR

He could have gotten her off. There was nothing stopping him. And he used to. But then the lack of reciprocity began to bother them both. She did not want to be the sole receiver of pleasure, to cast him as the sole giver. The obvious solution was for him to stop smoking pot. Would that not at least help? An erection was useful after all, even if it never fully resolved. He did not have to smoke pot. He could commune with the moon, or whatever it was he did out on the porch every night, without it.

He said, "But the pot's fun."

It would only be (he was joking now) eighteen to twenty more years and the kids would move out of the house. Then he could wean off the meds no problem.

She said, "In the meantime I, what, fuck someone else?"

"Let's not lose our heads."

"You're like the guy in the thing," she said.

They had been married long enough for him to know she meant the main character from *The Sun Also Rises* who'd had his dick broken—blown off?—in the war. The book was poignant because he could not fuck his girlfriend. At the heart of their interactions was their inability to have sex. This was accurately positioned as the most tragic thing that could ever happen.

"Don't compare me to Jake Barnes," he said. "This isn't like that."

Among other things, the metaphor was grandiose. What, for instance, would be the equivalent of the war?

"Don't say capitalism," he said. "Don't say weed."

He left to get in the shower.

* * *

Her train was delayed one night, stopped on the tracks in the no-man's-land of northern Putnam County. Outside her window: a sheer wall of rock. She called Happy Tree, where Miles went for aftercare, and told them she was running late. They reminded her it was ten dollars a minute after five o'clock. She sat on the train willing it to move. Then it did move, but at a crawl. By the time she got there, he was the last one left. The lights were off and the place smelled like cleaning product. They had to run straight to Opal's school, where Opal was the last one left.

She was late getting them dinner, late getting them into the bath. Miles threw a toy and hit Opal in the head. Opal shoved him, which was out of character. Cora yelled at them both, also out of character.

Eliot came home and said, "Why is everyone so frazzled?"

Cora explained and Eliot was annoyed at Miles melting down. Miles's tantrums were often directed at him, and even when they weren't, he took them personally. If Miles was aggressive, full of rage, did it not point to some defect in his father? Did it not say something about Eliot? This was what he decided to rant about instead of helping her get the kids into pajamas.

"What if I let myself be quietly pushed out of the workforce?" she said.

"As if you'd go quietly," said Eliot.

She went to the PTA meeting that night and waited around in the parking lot for Sam. She had walked there to try to shake off the evening. What if she quit her job? But no, then she'd be home with them with nowhere else to go. Parental leave forever. One of the brittle, overstepping moms. Sam pulled into the lot with his windows down. She let him park and get out of the car.

"What's wrong?" he said. "What are you doing out here?"

Cora said, "I don't feel like going in."

"Where do you feel like going?"

Anywhere besides the town, she told him. She felt oppressed by it. She actually felt oppressed by other things, but the town was a useful stand-in. They got into Sam's car and drove to a bar farther down the Hudson Line. It was the train station bar, red brick, on the same level as the tracks. The express arrived from the city every twenty-six minutes, rattling furniture and glassware, sending the light fixtures swinging.

"Is this better?" he said.

"Yes."

It was a good setting for the affair as well. You had the romance of rail travel. The anonymity of people coming and going. The briefcases and trench coats and hats. From where she sat, she could see out across the train tracks, out across the river. A mountain on the other side made a dull swell one shade darker than the night.

"Do you think the PTA is a suitable substitute for sex?" she asked him.

And here the conversation went two ways, depending on which world you were in.

In reality he said, "Don't say that." In the world of the affair he said, Of course not.

In reality she said, "Is that not what we're doing though?" In the world of the affair she said, Okay then.

In reality he said, "It is but." In the world of the affair he said, So we'll quit the stupid PTA.

In both reality and the other world, she said, "Thank you!"

The bartender came by and set down two cardboard coasters with beer logos on them. Cora picked hers up and began peeling its fraying edge. Sam ordered beers and they arrived in pint glasses. In the world of the affair, he was down to quit the PTA, but in the real world, they had committed to it and had to see it through. Never mind that he had just confirmed they had only joined to spend time together.

"Did something happen today?" said Sam, in both worlds.

Cora said, "No. I had a five-hour meeting about migrating our content management system. Then the train stopped on the tracks in that dead zone where it always stops."

"Do you guys not use WordPress?" said Sam.

"It's too boring to talk about!"

"Sorry."

"Are our lives circumscribed?" she said, and here the time line split once more.

In reality he said, "Yes." In the world of the affair he said, No.

In reality she said, "Does that not bother you?" In the world of the affair she said, Explain.

In reality he said, "Sometimes it bothers me and sometimes it doesn't. I'm kind of used to it." In the world of the affair he said, My relationship with you has opened me back up to the world.

They finished their beers. He ordered another and the bartender asked whether his wife would like one, too.

"Let's call her and find out," said Cora. "She's probably still at the office."

The bartender held up his palms. "Whoa, sorry."

He moved down the bar to get their beers.

"Don't be mean to him," Sam said. "I like this place."

"Why would he assume I'm your wife?" said Cora. "Am I so wifely?"

"Don't overthink it. You're a woman of the correct age. Do

you want me to call him back over and tell him you're my mistress?"

The word "mistress" made them look at each other. He was being facetious in at least one time line. A train pulled into the station and there was a moment of mechanical screeching. Commuters got off and passed the windows of the bar. They heard a muffled announcement, information about the next stop, followed by more screeching, and then the train was gone again. Sam reached up to steady the light above them.

"Yeah, maybe," she said. "Actually, yes, I do."

Sam signaled to the bartender, who returned warily.

"This is my mistress," Sam told him. "This woman is much more perverse than my wife. We're supposed to be at a PTA meeting right now."

"Hm," said the bartender.

He gave them their second round on the house.

They left the bar and walked to Sam's car. The main street had a steep gradient and the same kinds of stores as their own town. Driving back along the river, they briefly raced a train. Sam accelerated, keeping pace for a while. The train was silver, each window lit up yellow, each person in each seat looking at a phone. Then it overtook them, and rounded a rocky outcropping, its lights disappearing into the darkness.

The fall fest took place the next weekend and Cora manned the face-painting booth. In a burst of last-minute inspiration, she ordered a set of stencils online, and these indeed made painting a hibiscus flower no big deal. She painted hibiscus flowers on the children of the town, and tiger stripes, and butterflies. She watched Otis the Clown get out of his Prius and put on his big red shoes. Eliot brought her a cider donut and made fun of her for being good at face painting.

Her booth was on the hill at the back of the field, which made her feel like an oracle. The kids trekking up to see her, shielding their eyes against the sun. At the end of day, when the people had left, she stood and looked down at her peers. They cleaned up in the distended shadows of hundred-year-old trees. She felt sorry for them, suddenly, and for herself. On Wednesday nights, they attended PTA meetings instead of having illicit affairs. Their secret lives—because everyone had one—had been brought to heel.

Four

The mountain that saw everything turned from green to rust, from rust to brown, from brown to green again. It was spring. Snowmelt filled the creek. Opal began piano lessons on an upright purchased by Cora's mother, Miles learned how to ride a bike, Cora got a small promotion at work, they finally got the stove fixed, and Eliot's parents died, one after the other. His father of colon cancer and his mother of a stroke two days later. They went down to New Jersey to bury them.

What happened after you died? Nothing happened. You weren't there anymore. A rent-a-rabbi in a cheap tie said kaddish and regurgitated facts your loved ones told him about you. He was a family man who liked his golf. She was a good friend and excellent baker. They were devoted to each other for five decades. Then everyone threw a handful of dirt on the casket and went to eat bagels.

Eliot took a leave of absence from work. He wore sweatpants and moved an indoor chair out onto the porch. He'd recently switched from a bowl to a vape, a silver cylinder resembling a ballpoint pen. All day every day, he sat vaping on the porch. Cora left him alone. She went up to her office, worked for hours at a time, came down again, and still he'd be vaping. He went to bed before the kids got home, woke up at two or three a.m., unable to fall back asleep. He'd prowl around downstairs or go for walks in the early morning, returning as Cora made breakfast. Once, he came home damp and disheveled, sticks in his hair.

"Why are you dirty?" Cora said.

"I was up near the mountain."

"You mean like hiking?"

"Kind of."

"In the dark?"

"It was getting light."

"Is that safe?"

He poured himself a cup of coffee. Miles sat on the counter watching Cora scramble eggs. Opal leafed through a book. Eliot was not outdoorsy; neither of them was. The mountain existed to them as a pleasant landscape feature. It was nice to glimpse out the kitchen window or while driving on Main Street. They'd hiked it once when they first moved to town, with Opal in a carrier on Eliot's back. Four miles to the top and they had forgotten to bring water. Cora had been pregnant at the time. Afterward, they'd decided they didn't have to be like that. They could enjoy the mountain without interacting with it, the way they enjoyed the river but never felt compelled to go for a swim.

"It's probably fine. I lived."

"Your knee is bleeding," said Cora.

He glanced down at his torn sweatpants. "Oh, shit."

He'd slightly fallen. No big deal. He'd caught himself. It was not that dark out. It was not like being locked in a trunk. It wasn't as dark as one's eternal grave.

"Why those comparisons?" she said.

"Just painting a picture. I could see, is my point. For the most part."

"Your forehead is also bleeding."

He looked at his reflection in the surface of the microwave. He had a series of five or six scrapes. She ran warm water over a paper towel and handed it to him.

"That's from a branch. Not the times I fell."

"'Times' plural?"

"I was not exactly wearing the right shoes."

They looked down at his shoes. They were slip-on Vans. One slip-on Van to be precise. The sock without a shoe was drenched. She noticed that he'd been leaving muddy prints all over the floor. Cora didn't ask about the other shoe. She put eggs on a plate for Miles. She put eggs on a plate for Opal, knowing Opal would not eat them. Eliot peeled off his dirty sock and left the room.

"What happened to Dad?" said Opal.

What happened was Eliot had watched his father deteriorate over the course of eight months. Eliot's dad had taught him to do a layup, given him records to listen to, moved him into every place he'd ever lived, including their current house. He'd died in hospice, as they knew he would. Eliot had gotten to say goodbye, at least. He'd returned from that ordeal and two days later they'd gotten a call that his mom had a stroke. Until then she'd been in good health. Cora's own mother had seen her a few months before for their annual shopping trip in the city.

Shirley still worked, kept active, took Opal on outings to museums and Broadway shows. Attended every occasion involving the kids, all the minor graduations and holiday performances.

She'd died instantly, maybe from the strain of caring for Eliot's dad. Eliot was an only child, much loved and doted on, and they were his whole family. Responsibility for him now fell squarely on Cora.

"He misses his parents," she told Opal. "He's sad."

"And now Grandpa and Grandma are with other Grandpa in heaven," said Opal.

Eliot shouted from the other room, "There is no heaven!"

Opal shouted back, "But Mom told me!"

"Stop shouting from room to room," said Cora.

Eliot returned in his single shoe. Blood trickled from his temple.

"Why did you tell her there's a heaven?"

"I didn't," said Cora. "What I said is there's not not a heaven."

"That means there is one."

"No, it means we don't know."

"There isn't one," he said to Opal. To Cora he said, "I'm not comfortable with her believing in heaven."

"Is it your choice?" said Cora.

"Is it yours?"

Eliot said to Opal, "When you die you go in a box in the ground, and that's it. Like how a dog dies. Like how a bird dies. A flower. A blade of grass. It's a kind of solidarity between every living thing. We all share it, so we're not alone with the sadness."

It was poetic, but Cora had already decided to be annoyed with him.

"You expect her to understand that? Oh, what does solidarity mean?"

"It means when you're hungry," said Opal.

Cora laughed. "That's correct."

"It's not correct," said Eliot. "It means unity among people with a common interest. Like how in my business—not at my work but at another one of the places where they publish books—they have a thing called a union. All the workers get together and if they don't like how they're being treated, they go on strike. They say, We're not going to make books anymore unless you give us more money or better working conditions, and they all march in a line shouting out their demands and carrying signs. And because management relies on their labor, they usually meet some or all of those demands and things get better for everyone. Sticking together like that is called solidarity."

Why was he explaining labor unions to their seven-year-old? The question had been about heaven. A piece of leaf fell off his arm and fluttered to the floor.

"Stuff's falling off you," said Cora. "Why don't you go up and rest?"

He continued to mutter to himself as he left the room. They watched him climb the stairs holding his sock.

What did grief do to the world of the affair? At the big, anonymous hotel, Cora tried to end things. She and Sam paced the room as if in a play. He got up from the bed, crossed to the window. In a wave of feeling, he pounded his fist on an end table. The table wobbled and fell, upsetting a lamp. The objects on it—hotel stationery, their wedding rings, a small gold pen—slid to the ground.

An affair should end, Cora thought, in a burst of passion. The man should object, the woman should be the one pulling away. It should get physical, or nearly physical, so she would see that he was a brute. He should tear an article of clothing or grab her hair.

We can't end it now, said Sam. We've been through too much.

He was referring to the abortion. They had already come through that trial and now they were going to stop, why? Just because Eliot's entire family had died? She explained that, yeah, that was the reason. Eliot was in trouble. She had never seen him like this. Not even at the peak of his depression. He had functioned then, exerted effort to appear normal. Now he'd stopped trying.

Don't talk about him so much, said Sam.

He held a glass of whiskey and he threw it at the wall. It hit with a clunk but did not shatter. It left a divot and a brown splash. Ice scattered across the carpet. He went to the tray that held the glasses and took another and hurled it. It left a second divot, a triangular puncture in the drywall. Cora put a hand on his arm before he could throw a third.

He said, Admit you don't actually want it to end.

He grabbed her wrist and held it against his chest. It hurt, and she attempted to pull away and he wouldn't let her. He pushed her back onto the bed and fumbled with his pants. She stared at the ceiling listening to the rattle of his belt buckle. Then he was ready and she guided him in with one hand. He thrust twice and came inside her, shuddering.

Oh god, he said. Shit.

She said, It's all right.

He kissed her and told her he couldn't lose her; his life would be over. He couldn't go back to however he'd been living before. He begged, which was correct. A lover should beg. This was maybe the most important qualification: that the man should be willing to make himself pathetic. That he should grovel at the feet of the woman's excellence.

I know, she told him.

So, it's not over?

She could not end it because to do so would be to dwell in the moment. To do so would mean living with Eliot inside his grief. He was being crushed by it and she would be too. In the real world, as in between the sheets of the big, anonymous hotel, she found she didn't want to be crushed.

Later that summer, Sam came to the front door on a Saturday afternoon with a covered dish. It was a veggie lasagna made by Jules. It had eggplant in it, he told her. No one in Cora's house was allergic to eggplant, right? He wore silky red running shorts and a gray T-shirt. At some point, he'd gotten fit. He told her that he'd seen Eliot loping uphill toward the trailhead around dusk the day before.

"Loping?" said Cora.

"Yeah. Running sort of buoyantly."

He'd followed him for a couple blocks. Eliot had not looked like himself. He looked skinny and haunted. He wasn't moving like he usually moved. Other passersby had seemed unsettled. Cora knew about the weight loss and the hauntedness. These were features, like the vape chair, that Eliot did nothing to hide. But the loping was new.

"How can I help?" asked Sam.

There was no way for Sam to help, unless he could raise the dead. A therapist could help, or a grief counselor. Sam could take the kids for an afternoon, bring them to the park with his own kids, give her a short break, but this would not change the fact of her husband loping around the trailhead at odd hours, freaking people out.

"I think it has to run its course," said Cora.

Sam sat down in Eliot's chair. The view from the porch faced away from the mountain. Across the street were the homes of their neighbors, the friendly clutter of their porches, their recycling bins and shaggy front gardens.

"Has this chair always been here?" said Sam. "It's kind of nice."

"That's where Eliot sits to be depressed. It used to be in the living room."

"You should think about leaving it out here permanently."

"Maybe."

She had to get inside. Miles could not be left alone for more than a few minutes. In the past while unattended he had thrown a pair of Eliot's jeans in the garbage, cut himself on a soda can, eaten a washer left over from an Ikea build. The washer had sent them to the emergency room, where after a three-hour wait, an exhausted doctor had told them to do nothing.

"How are you?" said Sam.

Cora knew she looked gaunt. No one had been eating except Miles. She was grieving too, but it was not like her to vape for nine thousand hours a day or develop a new style of running. She had about two more minutes before Miles reduced the house to rubble. She leaned against the porch railing and stretched out her legs.

"I'm always the same."

"What if we all got out of town? Change of scene."

"Somewhere with no hiking," said Cora.

"The beach."

Sam's parents' friends had a place on Cape Cod. They lived in Florida now and rarely used it. They had been trying to persuade him and Jules to take the kids for years. He'd been there once. Big old house with access to a pond. Gray shingles, driveway made of crushed oyster shells. It was a long trip, was the issue. Interminable with the kids at their current ages. Four and a half hours and then you hit the bottleneck. But once they got there it would be easy.

Sam said, "I'm so good at being on vacation. You have no idea."

"Is that right?"

Why were they flirting? Two people had died tragically. Cora had loved them both. One of them had suffered until the end. The other might have lived for twenty more years. The kids had lost a set of grandparents. Plus, Eliot was unraveling. They should not have been having a cute conversation on the porch. They should not have been having fun.

"I'm Mr. Vacation," he said.

"We'll see about that."

Eliot needed more than a vacation. He needed a nineteenth-century Swiss sanitarium. He needed a stern-faced woman to give him a water cure, roll him up tight in flannel blankets, whip him with switches cut from a special tree. Let him wander around in the Alpine air writing inscrutable poetry. In one or two years' time, he could be allowed to rejoin society. This was not possible, so she agreed to the Cape.

They left the next weekend. Cora did the packing while Eliot sat in his chair. Opal hung around asking questions. Why are you packing for Dad? Why are you packing Dad's underwear?

Can't Dad pack his own underwear? Cora explained that people needed help sometimes. If Opal was ever in a bad place, Cora would pack her underwear too. Opal made a face and said that was never going to happen. Cora told her she hoped so, but Opal's life had just begun and there was no telling what she might need help with.

Opal said, "*Not* underwear."

Eliot moved the chair back into the house before they left, which signaled a minute amount of progress. The drive was as bad as Sam had said and she did all of it so Eliot could stare out the window at nothing. The highways of New York State gave way to the highways of New England. The kids played on their tablets for the first hour and then Opal initiated a game of Mad Libs.

"Noun," she said.

Eliot said, "Morgue."

Cora told him to pick something else and he said, "Chloroform."

He'd put on a bandanna before the drive, biker style, which Cora tried not to find funny. When her father died, her mother had acted odd too. She refused to take bereavement days from work. Cora and her brother, Drew, attempted to persuade their mother that it was normal and necessary to take some time, but she insisted she did not need to. She maintained an eerie composure, dressed immaculately every day. She delivered a baby the morning of his funeral. Cora found this scary and sad. It was not exactly like wearing a bandanna biker style, but they both fell broadly under the heading of unusual behavior.

"What if we listened to a podcast?" said Cora.

They put on a science podcast for children and learned about tapeworms. Miles fell asleep contorted into an awkward position in his booster seat. In Rhode Island, they stopped at a rest area and she pumped gas while Eliot wandered into the store. She worried that he would not emerge again, that he'd slip out the back and into the woods, keep going until he found a mountain to inexpertly hike. She was about to send Opal in after him, but then he returned with gummy bears for the kids and a coffee for her, and they were on their way again.

The drive in the other time line was an hour shorter. Cora and Sam rode together in a Mustang convertible. They stopped for lemonade at a roadside stand and he drained his cup and ran an ice cube along the length of her arm. Then it was back into the car, where she tied a silk scarf around her hair for the wind. It was how she wanted to live, and nowhere in it existed a man in mesh shorts and a bandanna, intermittently crying in the front seat.

In reality, they arrived at the house at sunset. It was large with clusters of blue hydrangeas on either side of the door. The shells of the driveway crunched under their wheels. Sam and Jules pulled in behind them. Cora nudged Eliot, and he unfolded his body with incredible lethargy. The kids got out and ran for the front door. Sam's kids were running too. Sam jogged to the porch and let them in. Eliot had drifted around back, and Cora followed him just to be sure.

There was a shed behind the house with two old beach cruisers, a tire swing, a peeling deck. Inside, the kids sprinted from room to room. The beach house recalled every beach house Cora had ever been in. The couch was damp, the theme was ocean. Upstairs, a long hallway with many bedrooms to choose from, two bathrooms, and a den with an iridescent sailfish mounted above the couch. The kids wanted to sleep together in the same room. Jack requested a sleeping bag on the floor. Opal asked to share with Penelope. They let it happen. They were Mr. Vacation and Mr. Vacation and Ms. Vacation and Ms. Vacation.

That night, they ordered a pizza and took it out onto the deck. Eliot ate a whole slice, and Cora hated that she noticed. She hated to monitor him like he was one of her children. He told them about the Laurentide Ice Sheet, how it had descended out of Canada to shape the region's geology. That had been thousands of years ago, back in the Pleistocene. It made Cape Cod Bay and Martha's Vineyard and Nantucket. It made the fine yellow dunes of Provincetown.

"Laurentide," he said. "Pretty word."

He went upstairs right after dinner. The rest of them put the kids down, then stayed up talking. They sat on the floor around the wicker-and-glass coffee table, drinking beer and playing cards. Sam had remembered to bring a Bluetooth speaker and they took turns choosing the music. It felt good to be out from under the shadow of the mountain. It was not necessarily quieter, but it felt that way. They went to bed before midnight.

At the beach the next day, they laid out a blanket. Cora had bought new beach toys and the kids carried them down to the water's edge. Sam took his shirt off and Cora took her shirt off and Jules took her shirt off and Eliot took his shirt off. Cora almost laughed at this momentous stripping down. She stole a glance at Sam. He was tan already and had a tattoo on his pec of the famous Citgo sign in Kenmore Square in Boston.

"That's been there the whole time?" she said.

"I got it with my high school friends after graduation. We were really into being from Boston."

"Isn't it awful?" said Jules. "I keep telling him to get it lasered off."

She had on a red two-piece and a large straw hat. She wanted help setting up a tent. The kids were going to need a break from the sun in about an hour. She made Cora feed poles through polyester and drive them into the sand. Cora could not believe Jules had found a task for her to do at the beach. The fabric kept catching in the wind and almost knocked her over. Then the kids came back and asked to bury her feet.

"Why not my feet?" said Jules, and they shrugged.

"Okay," said Cora.

They told her where to sit and dug a hole. Opal gave directions and Jack did most of the digging. They had her climb in and filled it back up. Cora stood, buried to the knee. Now you're short, they told her. They called various adults over to compare her new height. She was nearly Opal's size now, smaller than Jules. Smaller than Eliot, smaller than Sam.

"Do you like me like this?" she said to Eliot.

He said, "Don't be a freak," and she saw a glimmer of his old self.

When everyone else was occupied, Sam asked her to put sunscreen on his back. Jules had gone off looking for shells with Penelope. Eliot stood down near the water. This happened in real life. She shook the bottle, then squeezed some lotion out onto him. Actually, it happened in the other world too.

"Are you writing your name?" he said.

She had been, but she said no. She could smell his skin and the sunscreen. Her breast grazed his back. The sensory details were overwhelming, almost suffocating. She did his neck and his shoulder blades and the flesh was warm and the muscle was firm. She rubbed and he made a groaning sound and then said, "Sorry."

Cora sat back. "I think that's enough."

She lay down next to him and opened her book.

He said, "I like your bathing suit."

It was a white one-piece with a plunging back. What he seemed to mean was he liked her body. She could not decide if all this pretending was fun or stupid. Opal came running from the water and the two of them sat up again. She told them Miles had scratched her and showed them a welt on her arm. Miles appeared and said he had not. Someone else had. Opal said, that was ridiculous, of course it was him. He was a known scratcher. Who else could have done it?

They looked alike, Opal and Miles. They were tall like their father, freckled like their mother. The resemblance irked them both.

"Would you two like a snack?" Cora said.

The other kids came back and made use of the tent. Cora handed out sandwiches. The adults had beers, except for Jules, who had a hard seltzer. Eliot read a magazine behind his Ray-Bans. He seemed better in this environment. Cora had only seen him loping once, way down the beach. Where had he been going, moving like that? She rose to play Frisbee with her children.

In the other time line, there was bedroom swapping. The doors on the long hallway opened and closed. It was calibrated for discretion, so no one got mad or asked too many questions. Cora had integrated the idea of Sam's Citgo tattoo, and maybe she liked it. Maybe she liked the idea of something ugly on him, an artifact of his youth. She met him on the couch under the sailfish and put her mouth on the tattoo, while Jules slid into bed next to Eliot.

But then Cora tried to imagine Jules and Eliot fucking and couldn't really get there. They'd have differing ideas about what constituted pleasure. He'd lift her up and put her on a high dresser. She'd tell him what to do and he'd inevitably get it wrong. Like this? he'd say. And she'd say, Jesus, no. Then he'd apologize and she'd say, Take me down. Why am I up here? Who puts another person on a dresser?

In the real world, Cora and Jules went running together through the woods. The trail was shaded and cool, with a designated lane for bikers. Whenever they streamed past ringing their bells, Cora and Jules would fall, momentarily, into single file.

Jules said, "You're actually pretty fast."

Cora said, "That's surprising?"

"Just because you said you don't do it much anymore."

Jules wore black running tights and a black sports bra. Cora wore navy running tights and a navy sports bra. They were racing, Cora realized. Jules stayed a pace in front of her. Cora was at the limit of how fast she could go. Her throat burned with acid and she thought she might throw up.

"You can go on." She gestured vaguely ahead of them. "I can meet you down there."

"That's okay," said Jules. "You set the pace."

Cora had run cross-country in high school, mostly because it was the one sport where no one bothered her and she could think. Moving her legs helped pull the thoughts along. That she had been good at it, made varsity her freshman year, sometimes placed in races, had barely mattered. It was not about proficiency but a kind of free-range solitude. Now she mostly walked. You still got to think but didn't sweat out your clothes.

"Do you want to do a half marathon next spring?" Jules said, maybe to demonstrate she could speak.

Whatever the activity, Jules would make it a competition. Cora had a college roommate, before Isabelle, a horsey girl from Virginia named Millie, who'd wanted to compete over everything. One day Millie suggested they race up from the lobby to their dorm room on the fourth floor. Cora tried to protest, but Millie had already launched herself into the stairwell. Why did she agree to these things? Cora wondered as she jogged up four flights. Millie had won, of course. She'd stood in front of their room panting and gloating.

"God no," said Cora.

Some women wanted to compete and others, like Cora, wanted to lie down in the road and let traffic roll over them. If it was a competition with Jules, Jules would win. How aware was Jules of this aspect of her personality? Probably she knew and found it gave her an edge.

They continued running for another half hour, then returned to the house. Sam sat in a lawn chair in the backyard watching the kids play badminton. He wore a linen shirt unbuttoned and open to the sun. He drank a beer and held a bag of Tostitos in his lap. He sized them up, their bare midriffs and sweat-drenched ponytails. Cora was still breathing hard.

"Who won?" he said.

"She's actually pretty fast," said Jules.

It was the same thing she'd said on the trail. Cora hated when she caught people rehearsing a remark on her to use later. Like whatever they said was practice for the real person they wanted to say it for.

"No, I'm not," she said and jogged up the back stairs and into the house.

In the evenings, Eliot cooked dinner, and Jules took a cocktail to her room. She did this at home too. No one was allowed to bother her. You could make rules like this, she told Cora, and after a certain breaking-in period, your family would obey them. The kids were tired by then, sun-drunk, thrown by the change in routine. They watched TV in the living room in various attitudes of sprawl. Upside down on the couch, in a pile on the floor.

Cora and Sam would retrieve the bikes from the shed and ride them around. They brought beers along, steering with one hand. The streets were paved, but sandy. Trees arched above them. People walked dogs, waving as they rode past. One night, in the winding backstreets of the neighborhood, they found the pond. It was shielded from the road by a stand of pines. They leaned their bikes against a picnic table and sat at the water's edge. The trees had dropped pinecones and Cora picked one up and felt its ridges.

Sam said, "How are things with Eliot?"

Things with Eliot were the same. He was out of his mind. The night before, she had discovered him using a shoe as a bookmark, one of her strappy leather sandals. She'd worn the heel paper-thin over the course of two summers. Cora had never seen anyone put a shoe in a book before. That shoe had been to a farm. She'd worn it on a trip with Opal's class to the fish hatchery. The ground had been covered in fish food. She'd worn it into the city. Tompkins Square Park. She'd taken the subway a couple of times. She'd transferred at Canal. They had been lying in bed, so the shoe was in bed with them. Eliot saw no problem with this.

"I don't want to talk about Eliot," she said. "How are things with Jules?"

"It's not that there's a problem . . ."

He played with the laces of his sneakers.

"Maybe the nonproblem is that Jules drinks alone in her room every night," Cora suggested.

"No."

"You sure?"

"The booze isn't what that's all about. It's more about getting away from us."

"Oh, okay."

"You know what I mean. Alone time. It's healthy. Don't you think? She deserves a break."

"I like getting a break, but I don't drink in my room every night."

"She's under a lot of pressure at work. It's all she does. And then she comes home and the kids are more work."

Cora didn't want to argue, but everyone with kids faced this. It wasn't exclusive to Jules. The workday ended and the second workday, the harder workday where irrational people threw tantrums and demanded endless snacks, began. The sun was setting. They looked out at the water, orange and slightly rippled.

"Let's go in," said Sam.

"I don't have my suit on."

"I won't look."

THE TEN YEAR AFFAIR

They faced away from each other to undress. The pond was surrounded by houses, backyards, sun-bleached docks, but no one was outside. She took off her sweatshirt and shorts and stood in her underwear, hesitating. It would happen in the world of the affair. It was happening. But the rules were different there. The rules were "Do whatever you want and don't worry about it."

He went in first and she caught a glimpse of his bare ass. She'd imagined it many times, and there it was for real. She felt too close to the other world, weakened by her proximity and her desire. After a moment, she followed him. The bottom was mucky, the water warm. He disappeared and reappeared in the center. She swam out to him and he turned and smiled, his hair slicked to his head. He was not chewing a toothpick and this made him seem doubly naked.

Her leg slid against his by accident and he said, "You're smooth."

She went under and came up again.

"It's hard to fuck in water," he said.

She said, "What?"

"There's no traction. Water should be wet, but it's somehow dry in the context of sex."

"Why are you saying this?"

"Just thinking out loud."

She drew away from him, swam farther out. Her body cut easily through the water. Their spouses were back at the house. Eliot had announced his intention to make a chowder. He was worried about getting all the grit off the clams. He hated the feeling of grit in his molars. When Cora and Sam left on their bike ride, he'd been rinsing with unhinged fervor.

"Which one of these houses would you want?" said Sam.

Cora turned in a circle, looking at them. They were family homes, on the large side of modest, with kid gear outside, swing sets, T-ball tees. Inside, they'd have the same mass-market paperbacks and fish-shaped tongs as the house she stayed in.

"Maybe that one," said Cora.

It was yellow with a play structure and a dock piled high with red and orange kayaks. Now that it was getting dark, she could see fireflies in the yard blinking at random.

"I would choose that one, too," he said.

This opened the door to the idea of living together. Like maybe the Sam and Cora of the other world would swim back to their own dock and sprint into their house. Otherworld Cora would turn on their shared shower and let it fog up their shared bathroom mirror and they'd both get in. They'd fool around or wash each other's backs, take turns rinsing off. Afterward, they'd wrap themselves in their shared threadbare towels, open a bottle of their shared wine, and Sam would start a fire in their shared fireplace.

"We should go," she said.

He said, "Already?"

"It's getting dark."

They swam back toward shore and climbed out, walking next to each other. Their modesty had fallen away. Stars had appeared, and a couple of the nearer planets.

"It's Edenic," he said.

They reached their clothes and he looked at her naked body for a fraction of a second before averting his eyes. She looked at his, too, and saw he was half hard. It was almost too dark to tell, but she was pretty sure. She felt a shift between them, plates sliding over each other into new configurations.

"Here," he said.

He tossed her his shirt so she could dry off. She used it on her legs and torso and face and hair, threw it back to him when she was done. He put it on, wet from her body, and they returned to their bikes. They had not taken note of how they'd gotten there, and they got lost on the way back. All the houses looked the same, with their hydrangeas and salt-eaten shingles. They turned around, and turned around again. They retraced their path, finding themselves back at the pond. It was black now and reflected the moon.

Sam said, "We're less than a mile away. We'll find it."

"They're going to yell at us."

"They won't. Why would they?"

They got back on the bikes and tried again, followed a different series of streets past a different series of houses. This time they succeeded in finding it. Cora was stirred by the jewel box quality of the house at night. Its windows were lit up yellow and leaked music. Over the music, a kid shrieked at a remarkable register.

"One of mine?" said Sam.

He was halfway up the back deck.

Cora said, "It sounds like Miles."

Sure enough, Miles was displeased with his mac and cheese. No, he would not accept anything else. No, he didn't want nuggets instead. No, he could not be persuaded to apologize to Dad for scratching his neck. Cora hustled him upstairs and into the bath and out of the bath and into bed in under ten minutes. This triage provided cover for their lateness.

They sat down to dinner, which had taken longer than expected anyway. Eliot had wanted to be thorough with the clams.

The remaining kids had asked to eat with the adults, and there was a flurry of activity getting them situated, finding an extra chair, pouring cups of juice. Jack insisted on pouring his own juice, so Cora found herself pouring berry punch back into the container so that he could do it himself.

Jules said, "How was your bike ride?"

Sam didn't look at her. He served himself salad and passed the bowl. "It was nice. You should have come."

"There are only two bikes."

"I would have stayed back," said Cora. "We didn't know you wanted to."

"You didn't ask."

"You were already in your room," said Cora.

"Sometimes I need a break. Is that okay? Don't you ever need a break?"

"Of course. All the time."

Jules squinted at Cora and then at Sam. "Why is your hair wet?"

"We found the pond," said Sam.

He said this with innocence, reaching for the bread basket. Maybe he was innocent. Nothing had happened except for the accidental collision of their legs.

"So, you're sitting there in wet trunks."

"No," said Sam. "We were skinny-dipping."

"Funny," said Jules.

"I'm not kidding," said Sam. "Tell her, Cora."

Cora looked at Eliot, bent over his chowder.

"I'm not getting involved," said Cora.

Jules said, "So, you guys are what? Having sex now?"

"Stop it," said Sam.

"What is sex?" said Opal.

Eliot looked up from his bowl. "The simple explanation is it's how adults make babies. Sometimes. Sometimes making a baby is more complex and medical interventions are needed. That's called in vitro fertilization. A doctor helps with that. It's miraculous. They take eggs out of a woman and fertilize them in a lab. Any way it occurs is miraculous. Think about it: from nothing, a person. You and your brother were both made by sex and you're both miracles. Sex can also just be for pleasure, and some kinds of sex can't result in a baby at all. For instance, sex between two men."

"Can we talk about this later?" said Cora.

"But what *is* it?" said Opal.

"I'll get you a book when we get home," said Cora.

"There's nothing wrong with her knowing," said Eliot.

"No, I agree. But maybe not right this second."

"You know a penis?" said Eliot. "Like what boys have?"

Jack put down his spoon and stared into his lap.

"It's not necessarily about a penis," said Jules. "And a penis is not always what boys have."

Eliot started over. "You're right, sorry. Okay, let's see. You know genitals?"

Cora went into the kitchen for more wine. It was dark except for the light spilling from the dining room. She opened the fridge and looked at their vacation groceries. Juice boxes and shandies and half a watermelon and cold cuts and yellow mustard. A package of hot dogs they'd open tomorrow when they barbecued. Zero percent yogurt belonging to Jules. She found a bottle of wine in the bottom drawer. The wine that year was cloudy, with bits of matter floating in it.

From the other room, she could hear Eliot still trying to explain sex. How aware was he of what was going on? He was not observant in general, not tuned in to subtext. He was smart, but dumb. Or not even dumb, but pure, so fundamentally incapable of deceit that he sometimes forgot that others weren't. His grief had pushed him further into oblivion. He was beyond clouds now, in some obscure layer of atmosphere. He was gazing down at Earth from on high and he couldn't make out many details.

He must have said something funny because she heard Sam laugh. She found the corkscrew and opened the wine. By the time she returned to the table, everyone was in a good mood again. Jules sat back in her chair and her shoulders shook.

"That's technically correct," she said.

But then an uneasy silence fell. The kids climbed out of their seats and sat under the table whispering. Cora refilled everyone's glass. Jules gazed off across the room. Sam chewed slowly with a neutral expression on his face. Eliot looked at each of them and asked if the clams were gritty.

"Is anyone getting any grit? Any sand?"

No one was getting any grit or sand.

"You guys would tell me, right?" said Eliot.

They said they'd tell him, yeah.

He caught Cora's eye. "What about you, Cora? Anything to report?"

"Nothing," she said.

He made her swear to it.

Later, there was heated conversation in Sam and Jules's room. Cora could make out their voices but not what they were saying.

THE TEN YEAR AFFAIR

Eliot didn't seem to understand that there might be something for Cora and him to fight about too. They watched *Twister* on TV and he passed out after ten minutes with his glasses on. Cora tried to sleep, but the mattress felt spongy. Both sides sloped inward. She kept finding herself right next to Eliot, pressed up against his arm. At home, a whistle blew twice an hour, announcing the train's arrival from either direction, and the absence of this, she realized, was why it seemed quieter here.

She got up and went to check on the kids. They had rearranged themselves in the double beds according to age. She checked that Miles was breathing and Penelope was breathing and Opal was breathing and Jack was breathing. The room felt stuffy, so she turned on the ceiling fan and watched it blow their hair. As she was leaving, the door at the end of the hall opened and Sam emerged.

"Still out?" he said.

"Yeah."

"They had a big day."

They had gone to the go-kart place in the afternoon, then gotten ice cream. Plus, there had been all that talk about sex at dinner. Sam wore boxer briefs and a T-shirt. In the moonlight, he appeared monochrome. She thought about how he'd looked at the pond the second before they'd gotten dressed. There were so many empty bedrooms. All they had to do was choose a door and slip inside.

"Everything okay?" said Cora. "I heard raised voices."

"Do you want to sit for a minute?"

She followed him into the den. Above the couch hung the sailfish, with its bayonet-like snout. Racks of DVDs flanked the TV and the couch was plaid. They sat on opposite sides and he put his feet up on the coffee table.

"She wants to leave early. She said I'm embarrassing myself."

"Embarrassing yourself how?"

Jules had told him he was acting sexy with Cora and he should be mortified. She had seen him looking at her at the beach, doing nothing to hide his desire. Gaping like a cartoon character. She said how could he even joke about skinny-dipping with Cora? Who did that? Cora was her friend. What must Cora think of her, being married to someone like him?

Cora listened with shame fanning out over her body. "Maybe she has a point."

"It's harmless."

It embarrassed Cora that Jules was embarrassed for Sam. It embarrassed her that Eliot was not with-it enough to be embarrassed. It embarrassed her that this was happening while Eliot was grieving. She had her arm up on the back of the couch and Sam drummed his fingers on her forearm, raked his nails gently from her wrist to her elbow. This turned her on, which made her most embarrassed of all.

"Is it though?"

They had gotten close to something happening. They were close now.

"I think we should pull back," she said.

"*You* want to pull back?"

"Yeah."

It could not continue. They could not go on bike rides together. They could not swim naked in a pond. They could not be in any situation that could be described as Edenic. They couldn't be like Adam and Eve in an old painting with an apple and a snake hanging from a tree and the blush of creation on their skin. They couldn't continue seeking out closeness. Even the platonic closeness he'd insisted on. It was too complicated.

He said, "I think you're overreacting."

"Eliot's parents just died."

She could not carry on with Sam during the worst of Eliot's grief. Perhaps it was late for this revelation, but you had to take revelations as they came.

He said, "We'll just watch it a little. Nothing has to change."

He reached to his mouth for a toothpick that wasn't there.

"It's the middle of the night," she said. "You were sleeping. You don't chew one in your sleep, do you?"

"I don't chew one in my sleep. Unless I can't sleep, and then I do chew one."

She pictured gnawed remains on his nightstand and shuddered.

"We should discuss this some other time," he said. "It's late."

"No. We're talking now. This is the talk. What is the point of postponing it?"

The only solution was to not know each other at all. The next day, they would begin the work of becoming strangers. They would go back to their lives and reorient their friendship along gender lines. She would be friends with Jules and he would be friends with Eliot. They would continue to see each other in passing and behave normally. They would obey boundaries. Gradually, they would come to feel less. No one would know except the two of them that things were different.

"And that's what you want?" he said.

She stood up to go back to her room. This took enormous determination. He sat with his arms crossed over his chest, his boxers riding up a little. What she actually wanted was to drop onto her knees, ease them off over his hips. But she wasn't going to get what she wanted. Not now and maybe not ever.

"It is," she said, and left the room.

Five

She deleted his number. She walked around town, down by the river, past the old brick factory, the new solar farm. She enrolled Miles in karate. She took him to class in a basement studio on Main Street. He wore a gi and a serious expression. She migrated her company's data to the new CMS. She did not think about how Sam had bitten her lip that one time. She did not think about his Citgo tattoo. Six months passed without checking into the big, anonymous hotel. If the birds there still beat their wings, she didn't want to know about it. It was over.

She ran into Sam at school pickup and chatted with him like she'd chat with any parent of her kids' classmates. They talked about what they'd done over the long weekend, the new restaurants in town, the coming weather. They did not touch each other or stand close. At first, it felt fake, like they were performing indifference, but in time it came to seem genuine.

"It's cold today," he said.

He breathed a white cloud into his cupped hands for emphasis.

"Worse tomorrow," she said.

"Oh yeah?"

"Cold front, I think. From Canada."

"It's always Canada."

What did any of it mean? It was polite nonsense. They gathered their kids and took them home. The winter went on, and yes, you could by force make yourself stop wanting something. She got Miles to karate on time. She bought Opal a new parka because her old one was beat. She thought about what she might plant when the ground thawed. The creek filled with snowmelt and threatened to flood. She looked out at the mountain from her kitchen window.

Maybe they'd have gone on like that. Maybe the virtuous picking up and dropping off would have worked. The swapping of trivialities. Maybe they'd have grown more distant until they didn't know each other anymore, until they looked back on their many loaded exchanges with embarrassment and even curiosity: *What was that?* But in the fifth year of the affair, a global event almost ended both of their marriages.

They heard about the virus weeks before it reached them. They saw it on the internet. They turned on the news to footage of empty streets and shuttered restaurants. They learned its name: Covid-19. What had happened was not clear. A man had eaten a bat? But no, how could that cause a plague? The word "plague" suggested wood carvings and ships full of rats. Though history kept happening to them, they never felt prepared.

"It'll only last a few weeks," said Eliot. "Then everything will be back to normal."

He was on his laptop at the kitchen counter.

"What is that?" said Cora. "What are you looking at?"

He turned his screen toward her. It was an infographic about how the virus spread. Two figures stood facing each other. They spewed red and blue particles, drenching each other completely.

"Are they both sneezing?" she said.

"I'm not sure. We should try to avoid this."

It was March. There was nothing to do but wait. Uneasily, they bought hand sanitizer. The kids were five and eight that year. They said, is it coming? It's not coming, right? Cora told them no, it wasn't coming. Nothing bad would happen to them. She talked on the phone to her mom, and her mom said, you should worry. Cora asked if maybe it was a little overblown, and her mom said no, the panic was justified.

"I cannot believe this," said Cora.

Eliot said, "Maybe the experts are wrong."

There was an unusually warm weekend—the air smelled humid, like spring. They took the kids to the Guggenheim and had to yell at them for trying to roll down the ramps. It seemed quieter than usual, but otherwise normal. Afterward, they went downtown and ate at a famous brasserie. Miles had an eight-dollar orange juice. Opal would not touch her burger. They got slices on the way home and Cora wondered if these were the last slices they'd have in New York City for a while. Everywhere was a feeling of unease, though nothing was different.

Then it arrived and proved her mother right. For about five minutes the world came together and said work is not important. Cora was too miserable to be vindicated. An email from her company informed her they were going fully remote until further notice. Cora logged on to a town hall to hear the CEO, a man she'd never met before, talk about how everyone's safety was their first priority, but their second priority, or maybe they should call it priority 1.1, was keeping the company afloat. He was a blond guy with a forgettable, corporate face and a smooth side part.

Lily texted her, *His hair looks like it snaps on.*

"We are all in this together," he said.

Later, Cora heard the same speech from her own boss. Maybe it was a script. "We're all in this together," said Ryan. He even used the same emphasis, hitting "all" too hard, maybe to stress that management could catch a virus too. In the background, Cora could see a bed with a light gray duvet, an orchid on his nightstand. The door to the bathroom stood open and his bath mat was striped and his hand soap was generic brand.

"Follow the advisements. Stay inside. Be with your families. That said, we still have to think of the bottom line. We still have publications to put out."

A man walked behind his chair without a shirt on. He was young and ripped, in sweatpants that said DARTMOUTH up the leg. These days you saw a lot of people being accidentally nude in professional settings. She'd watched a CNN clip where the newscaster's husband had gotten out of the shower in the background. Briefly, the steam had cleared and his bare ass had been on live television.

"Oh shoot, sorry," said Ryan. "That's . . ."

Abruptly, the meeting ended. Later, they got an email apologizing for the presence of Ryan's partner, Edward. Ryan was still getting used to the technology. They all were. It was a big adjustment to have their colleagues right there in their homes. Incidentally, in case anyone was wondering, there was a way to choose a background other than wherever they were. You could choose a beach or a library, or even somewhere famous. The Taj Mahal, for example. That one was neat. He'd attached a screenshot showing them how to do it.

In bed at night, Cora and Eliot discussed the children. They were supposed to supervise remote learning. They had picked up a thick packet of materials at a table outside the elementary school. The assistant principal, in a surgical mask, had crossed their kids' names off a list. Classes were held online every day and there was work for them to do independently. Opal wouldn't be a problem, but Miles was in kindergarten, and this alarmed them. It was the year he was supposed to learn how to read.

"How can they expect a five-year-old to sit still for a Zoom?" said Cora.

"He's going to have to. He'll adapt," said Eliot.

They could bribe him with snacks. They could offer a reward. A toy, or more screen time. More of the kind of screen time he liked. They could sit next to him and encourage him and make sure he didn't get up.

"You're going to sit next to him for three hours every day?" said Cora.

"One of us."

"You mean me."

"It's a busy time for me."

Eliot's work had not slowed down. In fact, it had picked up. The world needed more books. It needed more content. Why it needed these things was not clear. There was a lot of entertainment in existence already. But it felt better to continue working at some frenzied pace than to listen to the news, or look at the numbers, or study the infographic of people sneezing.

Cora said, "I don't have the energy to make him sit there or discipline him for not sitting there. I don't even think he should be disciplined. They're not naturally inclined to sit in front of computers. They want to run around. They want tactile experiences."

When Cora watched over Miles's shoulder, she could see his teacher struggling. Kids talked incessantly, interrupted with non sequiturs. The teacher tried to refocus them, but nothing got done. Miles interrupted along with the rest of them. Cora would remind him not to and he would get discouraged. Every day like this. What was the solution? She didn't know how to teach him to read herself. How did one go about that? It was why teachers existed and why they had to go to grad school. He would just not learn for a while.

Eliot said, "He has to learn how to read."

"You do it then."

"You know you have less to do. Your day is less rigid. You have fewer meetings. Your job is . . . "

He stopped before he said "less important."

Cora got out of bed. Now that he was around all the time, she saw he was untenable. His crime was being too near and too himself. His personality never abated. The issues that had previously seemed small and forgivable now seemed large and egregious. How he ate all the time. How he got stoned every night, rendering himself useless. He did the cooking, but this was the only task he did and he'd selected it because it was creative. No laundry, no vacuuming. He had never once cleaned the bathtub.

"Where are you going?" said Eliot.

She had picked up her pillows. She *would* teach Miles to read.

They both knew that. She would end up doing it. She would google "how to teach someone to read" and make the flash cards and order the special books and email his teacher for tips. She would not even resent it in the end. It had to be done and so she would do it. But she hated that he took it for granted.

"I'm sleeping upstairs."

They never slept apart, even if they were fighting. He remarked that it was drafty up there, which was true. It was drafty and it smelled like an attic. A metal bar bisected the pullout. They called it the deathbed because sleeping there made you long for death. The last person to sleep on it all night had been Isabelle, and she had been the one to coin its nickname. She said she'd felt like she was being tested, or awaiting her execution. Like in the morning she'd be beheaded.

"Don't go," said Eliot.

But she'd already made a show of it, so she had no choice.

She would divorce him. She woke up thinking it. When it was over, she would retain a lawyer. She couldn't do it right then because they needed each other and didn't know how long the pandemic would last. Maybe they'd find themselves in a situation where they had to flee or forage or both. She'd want Eliot around for that—more hands would be better. Though how useful would he be? She got mad imagining the two of them in the woods, trying to survive. He'd be strolling around looking for chanterelles as she washed clothes on a rock.

She called Jules and said, "I'm losing my mind."

Jules said, "Me too."

Sam had been laid off. His stupid content job had been dissolved, along with the stupid content company. It wasn't that people didn't want mortgages. They wanted mortgages more than ever. It was that they didn't want mortgages from an app that looked cute but had some bugs. They didn't want a purple rhino telling them whether or not they'd been preapproved and then making them reenter their password over and over because they'd been mysteriously logged out.

"It was going to fail anyway. This just made it happen faster," said Jules.

"How is he?"

"Not good."

He seemed oddly happy, which could only indicate he was not. He kept saying he was going to teach himself how to fix cars. He wanted to convert a diesel engine to biodiesel. He was obsessed with the idea. He ordered a book about it and read it during what used to be his workday. He kept telling Jules their lives would improve if they had a car that ran on biodiesel. Didn't she want to move closer to a completely green existence?

"It does sound pastoral," said Cora.

"He's getting fat," said Jules.

"And that matters?"

"I guess we can pretend it doesn't."

"Is it his fault? We're all eating pasta."

"Everything is his fault."

"Come on," said Cora.

"I'm not attracted to him. Is that not important?"

"It might not be right now. I think the focus has to be on getting by. It's a crisis. We're on the deck of the *Titanic*. I'm not sure you need to find your husband hot. It's not salient. It's not going to help you get in the lifeboat."

"How about this: I'm going to murder him."

"Stop."

"I'm barely kidding."

She'd had some ideation. It would probably be easiest to kill him by suffocating him with a pillow as he slept. It wouldn't leave any marks. The thrashing of his dying body would be the worst part, but she'd look away and count to ten. She'd go elsewhere in her mind, back to her childhood in Burlington. She'd picture herself cross-country skiing through a quiet wood. Her only worry was if he woke before she finished, he'd be able to fight her off.

"I don't think you should kill him," said Cora.

"He doesn't help. He has no job and he still doesn't help. He thinks he's helping but he's completely incompetent. He can't log in to a portal. I have no idea how he worked at a tech company."

"What if we formed a pod?"

This was something Cora had seen on the internet. Jules had seen it too. You found another family you could tolerate and agreed to only see each other. That way, you could divvy up the childcare and the kids could play together. Cora's kids were not handling isolation well. Miles had begun to regress; he'd been putting up a fight at bedtime. Opal cried easily now, out of frustration, boredom, anything.

Jules said, "Penelope has been sleeping with us. It's a disaster. They're becoming babies again. They're going to ask to go back up inside me to live in my uterus. Mom, can we live in your uterus? they'll say. You never let us live in your uterus anymore."

"I bet you're good at supervising remote school," said Cora.

"You mean because I'm a fascist?" said Jules.

They laughed. But yeah, it was because she was a fascist.

"We might as well try," said Cora.

Jules agreed that at the very least, it would bring some structure to their days. She didn't like her kids anymore, even as she loved them, and this alarmed her. She offered to make a spreadsheet with everyone's schedules and figure out what would work best. This will be good, they assured each other. The kids would be less lonely. They themselves would be less lonely. Less murderous. More generous.

"Maybe we could reframe it as an experiment in collective child-rearing," said Cora. "Put like that, is it so bad?"

"Yes," said Jules.

And of course she was right.

They were lucky. Everyone kept saying this. They could have been dead. Millions were. So many were dead in New York City that bodies were being stored in refrigerated trucks. What was happening to them was bad but they were alive. So the restaurants had closed. So they were forced to be around their families all the time. So they couldn't get toilet paper. So they dreaded running errands. So fury and exhaustion were the only two feelings anymore. It was bad, yes, but they were alive.

"We're very lucky," said Sam.

He and Cora had the kids together three afternoons a week. Cora front loaded her days, so her meetings occurred in the morning, and then she was free to make children do schoolwork or, more often, to make them do nothing. Once flights had resumed, her boss had decamped to Chiang Mai with Edward, the shirtless boyfriend. Important missives tended to arrive during the night and be waiting in the morning. I AM WORKING ASYNCHRO-

NOUSLY AND MAY NOT RESPOND RIGHT AWAY, said his email signature in all caps, and then referred people to Cora if they needed an immediate response.

"At least we don't have to be on the PTA anymore," said Cora.

They were sitting on her deck while the kids ran around the backyard. She had gotten them bubbles, a new soccer ball, a jump rope, paddleball, activity books, lawn bowling. The yard looked like a birthday party had taken place—toys everywhere—but it was only the four of them.

"Her email was cute," said Sam.

Shearling Boots had written that they were pausing for global chaos, smiley emoji, but she hoped to see them soon. It was one of many responsibilities that had ended wholesale, leaving them with both too much and not enough to do. Now they hung out in Cora's or Sam's yard most days. The steps they'd taken to become strangers had been for nothing.

"Sorry about your job," she said to him.

He made a dismissive gesture. "I wrote copy for a mortgage app that didn't work."

"So you're not down about it?"

"Hard to get too upset."

She didn't believe this. It was not hard to get upset about your employment situation. It was compulsory to be stressed out. Certain jobs contributed nothing to your sense of self, but losing them shattered you anyway. She looked at him and tried to determine if he'd been shattered. Was he getting fat? He'd put on weight but it looked good on him. He had that stocky build. It was impossible for her to find him unattractive.

Down in the yard the kids screamed at one another. They screamed at one another about every fifteen minutes. Sometimes the boys grappled too roughly and had to be separated. They were grappling now. She heard Jack call Miles a name and it sounded like he'd called him a ho. Cora asked Sam if he'd heard it and Sam confirmed. An eight-year-old had called a five-year-old a ho.

"What are we going to do?" said Sam.

"I guess we could tell them to stop fighting and then, I don't know, take them to ride bikes?"

But he'd meant generally. What were they going to do now that this was life? There was no pleasure left. There was nothing for them. Nothing to look forward to. He'd go home at the end of the day and Jules would be on her computer and she'd be mad at him. Then she'd cook dinner while mad at him. She'd work more after dinner while drunk and mad at him. Later, in bed, she'd be drunker and madder at him.

"What is she mad at you about?"

"Specific things. Things I'm not doing or doing too much. Am I looking hard enough for a job? Am I doing sufficient drudgery? Am I too interested in turning a diesel car into biodiesel? But lately also big picture stuff. The fundamental flaws of my personality. She thinks I should have matched her stride, as if that were possible. She keeps telling me I was raised rich. I am a handsome white man who was raised rich. All I had to do was exert the minimum effort and I hadn't."

"You'll get another job," said Cora. "I'm sure there are tons of openings for a . . ."

She'd forgotten his title.

"Chief storytelling officer," he said.

They both shook their heads at that. Everything was so humiliating.

* * *

Sam was right that pleasure had been reduced to almost zero. There was nothing for them. In this environment, the affair returned. It pushed through cracks in the sidewalk. Its green shoots sought the sky. It shyly climbed a chain-link fence. They spent more time together in the real world and it grew stronger. Nurtured by their proximity, by their misery, by the time he pulled her into a room by her belt loop, by the time he accidentally called her honey.

By summer, it had returned in full force. Sam wanted a threesome and she allowed it. He wanted a foursome and she allowed it. He wanted to watch a woman who looked like Jules eat Cora out while a man they'd never met before fucked her mouth, and then he wanted to do those things to her himself while the two other people politely excused themselves.

They got toys, props, costuming. They watched porn together for ideas. The big, anonymous hotel was not enough anymore. Familiarity had diminished its appeal. It had begun to seem like a place you'd go under duress. Not by choice, but for lack of better options.

They stood naked in front of the windows one Thursday and noticed the man-made lake had been drained. It was a pit now, full of mud. A backhoe had been abandoned at the bottom. Why had they done it? Was there some kind of bacteria? Had someone fallen in and drowned? Sam called the front desk and asked. The concierge told him she didn't know. She apologized and called him sir.

No need to apologize, said Sam, for not knowing why a lake had been drained.

THE TEN YEAR AFFAIR

They flew to Paris. Forget the logistics—they managed it. Sam rented them an apartment in the first arrondissement. Windows stretched to fifteen-foot ceilings. Paris was cold and overcast. They sat at outdoor cafés in their coats and scarves. They huddled over espresso, speaking intently about art. They walked arm in arm to the Louvre and encountered no crowds. The galleries were hushed, the staircases empty, the treasures theirs. Sam dared her to scream and she did. He dared her to touch a fresco by Botticelli and she did. She brushed the face of one of the Three Graces with the tip of her pinkie. It felt rough and dry. They ran as if a guard was chasing them, but no one was. Through the airy rooms, sliding on parquet. They were untouchable by authority, possibly invisible to it.

That night they went to a club and did cocaine and brought home a French guy named Baptiste. His English was perfect. Baptiste gave them more coke and told them about his erotic adventures in the capitals of Europe. He had seduced an opera singer in Vienna, an Olympic equestrian in Monte Carlo, a young Romany girl in Athens. All three he'd made his wives, and all three he'd lost. They'd died one by one: no fault of his. His favorite had been the Romany. He'd met her selling roses down near the seaport. She had put one in his hands and demanded two euros. He'd given her fifty and whisked her off to Mykonos. She was witty, brash, missing a front tooth. She wore jeans and flip-flops like an American college student. She could sing and play the guitar. She wrote songs about the two of them, the most romantic story ever told. They spent seventeen consecutive days in bed to commemorate each of her years. She had been his great love, but she had died of tuberculosis.

TB? said Sam, in surprise.

Yes, said Baptiste, true story. People still got it and they still died of it, although it was treatable with antibiotics.

How did she even get it? said Cora. Why didn't she take the medicine?

Is there not a clinic on Mykonos? said Sam. There must be. There must be a small, permanent population of people who work at the restaurants and hotels. Or do you have to go to the mainland for healthcare?

Baptiste said, Let's not get bogged down.

He had worshipped her body, he told them. He looked at Cora as he said this. He was packing a bowl with hash so they could come down. Cora sipped champagne out of a coupe. A cream-colored candle was jammed into a wine bottle. Otherwise, the room was dark. Show us how you worshipped her, said Sam. Baptiste led Cora to the bath. He undressed her and helped her in. He bathed her gently and compelled Sam to bathe her. Steam rose from the surface of the water and the mirror above the sink fogged over. Baptiste packed another bowl and held it to Cora's lips while Sam ran a sponge over her feet and arms and neck and breasts and between her legs. Then they helped her out of the bath and into the bedroom, where the sheets were crisp and the windows open to the night. There was nothing for her to do, no tasks, no obligations, except to be worshipped like someone's teenage wife, who'd died improbably of TB.

Online, they found an outdoor meetup. "Covid-safe," it boasted. "Educational," "masked," "distanced." It met in the park down by the river with native wildflowers and too many geese. The meetup was called Victoria Platt's Pandemic Parenting. It sounded unappealing, but who cared? They packed snacks and a blanket to sit on. They begged the kids to give it a chance.

This was how Broccoli Mom reentered their lives.

She looked the same as she had, though she'd grown out the bob. Now her hair was long and witchy. She wore clogs, high-waisted jeans, a light blue mask printed with cherry blossoms, and rubber gloves. Some people seemed to be relishing the pandemic, and she was one of them. She'd set up a card table near the kayak launch. Cora and Sam both recognized her instantly.

"You're Victoria Platt?" said Cora.

They had never known her name.

"You two," she said, as they laid out their blanket.

Sam had a toothpick in his mouth, idly chewing.

"Can you put a mask on?" Victoria said to him.

"We're outside."

"It's to teach the kids. Pandemic Parenting, remember?"

Sam complied, pocketing his toothpick.

"What are your qualifications to teach this class?" said Cora. "I just wonder because it's all pretty new. How do you know what to do?"

Victoria recited a number of résumé items, including a master's in dance. Her only real qualification seemed to be that she'd successfully browbeaten Hoby into using the bathroom way back when. Hoby was now a moonfaced five-year-old, with his hands in his pockets and a swoop of dark hair falling onto his forehead. Victoria called him over to say hello. He didn't remember them, which was good, because the last time they'd seen him he'd been sitting on a toilet.

"Say hi to Hoby," Cora said to Miles.

Miles said, "Who?"

"One of your first friends. You knew each other when you were babies."

Miles looked at Hoby. "Okay."

"Hoby is a student at the Meadow Project," said Victoria. "Do you know it?"

"You mentioned it once," said Cora.

She and Eliot had toured it, actually, when they were thinking about kindergarten for Opal. A woman in a long madras skirt had shown them around. In fifth grade, the students did a week where they were not allowed to go inside. Class was held all day in the meadow. They encouraged the students to stay out there. Eat lunch out there, do class out there, even if it rained. If they wanted shelter, they had to build it themselves. If they needed the bathroom, they were to use a wooden outhouse in a nearby glen. This was to teach them resilience, survival skills, oneness with nature.

"He was thriving," said Victoria. "You know, before."

Cora said, "Mine were too. At the elementary school."

It seemed they were on the verge of finding common ground. Maybe this was the purpose, cosmically, of the pandemic. That you might bond with your fellow man. That you might lay down your arms. But Victoria said, "Don't they make them walk in lines?"

"I don't know," said Cora, though they did.

It was public school. They stood in lines for everything. There was even a specific order they stood in, alphabetical by last name, and Opal knew that G for Green made her sixth in line, and often talked about it, and felt pride at being number six, and rattled off her friends' corresponding numbers as a party trick. Alasdair was first, Madison was second, Dante was third, and so on.

"Does it harm children to stand in a line?" said Sam.

"I saw a study," said Victoria. She noticed he was unpacking a cooler. "You're free to snack, but don't eat peanuts around Hoby."

"Oh, is he allergic?" said Cora. "That's a tough one."

Hoby wore a purple fabric mask and he pulled it down to wipe his nose with the back of his hand.

"We don't know if he's allergic but we want to be really safe. We like to keep him away from potential food allergens as much as possible. The immune system is constantly changing, especially when they're young, and we want to be careful."

"So he preemptively can't have peanuts?" said Sam.

"Right," said Victoria. "Luckily, there are lots of nut-free alternatives these days. He loves biscuit spread, for instance. We put that on a sandwich for him."

"But he goes to school in a field," said Sam.

"Sorry, I don't follow," said Victoria.

"I'm just wondering, does it cohere? He can't have peanuts just in case but he goes to school outside like he's Jack London or something."

Sam was doing it for Cora's benefit. If he was alone with his kids, he would not antagonize this woman. He'd say okay, you got it, no nuts. But he was trying to amuse Cora. She remembered something she'd forgotten, which was that their attraction existed in opposition to this woman and everything she stood for: self-righteousness, rigidity of spirit, the need to control.

"It coheres," said Victoria.

They corralled the children onto the blanket. Victoria's presentation began, She told them they had to wash their hands for a long time to kill germs. They had to sing "Happy Birthday" twice and use a lot of soap. They already knew this. The children already knew this. Everyone on the planet already knew this.

"What are we doing here?" said Opal under her breath. "Can we go?"

They ignored her. They turned their faces to Broccoli Mom. Sam crossed his legs and his knee touched Cora's. It felt familiar, exhilarating. In the world of the affair, she dabbed perfume into the hollow of her neck. He bought her something filmy and asked the shopgirl to wrap it up.

Eliot's grief had ebbed. He had woken up to the situation they were all in. Now he seemed full of anxiety like Cora, like everyone, but at least he'd stopped loping. He turned himself intensely to the business of work-from-home. He'd set up a desk in the dining room and gotten himself a Bluetooth headset. When she ducked in to ask him something, she didn't always notice he was wearing it. He'd hold up a single finger and keep it in the air, continuing to talk. This gesture alone seemed like grounds for divorce. She would divorce him, she thought, as she drank beers on Sam's deck. As she argued with Opal about whether Jack was "random." As she held up flash cards for Miles and he looked at her blankly.

They went back to Victoria's class. They sat on their blanket and listened to her talk. She had run out of pandemic tips and moved on to general child-rearing. She wore her floral mask and half the time they couldn't understand what she said. But it didn't matter. Buds had appeared on the trees and the mountain grew greener by the day. Crocuses had come and gone, making way for better flowers.

Victoria taught them about the Dirty Dozen and the Clean Fifteen. The Dirty Dozen were the twelve fruits and vegetables with permeable outer layers that absorbed pesticides. It was imperative to buy organic when partaking of the Dirty Dozen. Side effects of consuming pesticides included cancer, type 2 diabetes, skin irritation, dizziness, limp, coma, death, and/or irritability. She was reading off a piece of paper.

"Irritability?" said Sam. "Limp?"

"That's what it says," said Victoria. "The point is, you should buy organic whenever possible unless you want your kids to get cancer. I'm not saying it's definitely going to happen, but even if the odds are slim, don't you want to do everything you can to prevent it?"

She moved on to the Clean Fifteen. A banana, an avocado, an onion, and so on. It was not necessary to buy these organic, she said. But you might want to anyway. If you were trying to consume ethically, if you cared about the future of our planet, organic everything was the way to go.

Afterward, as she was packing up her materials, she beckoned Cora over.

"Are you two together?"

"Sam and me?" said Cora. "We're friends."

"Oh, okay," said Victoria.

"For real."

"I only ever see you together, so I thought it was a blended family situation."

"It's a pod. Because of the pandemic? We're married to other people. The four of us trade off. You see us together because our days coincide. I promise you I'm just as frequently with his wife."

She wasn't though. More and more, it was Sam and Cora with the kids, Sam and Cora at the playground, Sam and Cora inventing an activity to occupy a couple hours, a couple minutes. Let's make masks. Let's make slime. Let's go on a picnic to the park. Let's ride bikes in the church parking lot that was recently resurfaced.

One afternoon during a video call with Cora's team, Miles came in and climbed into her lap.

She said to her coworkers, "Sorry, hang on."

Then Sam swooped in and got Miles out, waving sheepishly as he went. She knew he seemed like her husband. The way he'd been gentle and playful, effective, an expert swooper.

Lily texted her, *Is that the famous Eliot?*

But it wasn't. The famous Eliot was off somewhere else being famous. He was working from the dining room in a headset, eating his third sandwich of the day. There was effectively no Eliot anymore. It was her and Sam now. They were a unit. Even Broccoli Mom could see it.

Cora caught the virus and had to quarantine. She didn't know how she'd gotten it. Someone had rained red or blue molecules upon her, but who? Where? The grocery store? Victoria's class? No one else tested positive, not Eliot, not the kids. No one in Sam's household. A man had eaten a bat on the other side of the world, so they said, and now Cora could barely hold herself upright.

"What are we going to do?" said Eliot.

He stood downstairs in a mask. Cora was on the other side of the house, also masked. She felt weak, disoriented. She'd leaned heavily against a table. He'd have to take some time off, she told him. Maybe Sam and Jules could help. Maybe they could call her mother.

"It's not a good time for me to be out," he shouted. "There's a lot going on."

Nevertheless, the kids needed to be taken care of. They couldn't be around her. The virus didn't hit kids hard but you kept hearing the phrase "long-term neurological effects." They should try to keep them from getting it if they could. By the way, wasn't he worried about Cora's health?

"Yes," he said. "Sorry. That's implied. I'm concerned for you always. You can assume I'm concerned. Get better. That's the most important thing."

She moved to the pullout in her office, the deathbed. The bar cut into her back. She felt the dread of a beheading in the morning. She ate nothing, watched streaming shows on her computer, self-tested every two days to track her progress. Dimly, she registered movement in the house below. Sounds of her family reached her, the crystalline voices of her children asking too much of their father, but none of it meant anything to her.

That week, in the world of the affair, she and Sam wheeled through a bazaar in Marrakesh. A collage of sights and smells. Fabrics, colors, spices, voices. Cora turning to the sound of tinkling bells. Then they were disembarking on a dock somewhere as sailors unloaded wooden crates and cursed and spit and sang to each other. Someone tried to coax a cow down a gangplank as flies circled its head. Creatures in the crates reached through the slats with their paws, their tongues, their tails. Then they were in a night market eating street food. They were in a parade and people were costumed. Feathers, humidity, the smell of glue, the smell of sulfur, the smell of roses. Open mouths. Limbs like tentacles. A nude body in an owl mask. A nude body in a goat mask. An alleyway with a cat giving birth at the end. Indoors somewhere, citrus rotted in a bowl. A debutante bleeding from the nostril wielded a riding crop. Men in heavy makeup and powdered wigs fed each other grapes. A back room led to another back room that led to another back room, each smaller and darker and closer than the last. The final room contained a fortune-teller with a missing eye, who said, your lover will betray you. Cora said, what? And the woman lifted her eye patch to show her the empty socket. They had descended into a smeary underworld. Pigmen and brothels and broken taboos. Ceremonies with oil. Ceremonies with fire. Ceremonies with flesh. Pagan symbols scratched in the dirt. Then they danced furiously in a town square as a volcano erupted. Death was certain but no one stopped. Worms wriggled on the ground. Livestock screamed. Virgins rent their clothing. Drums beat all around. Ash rained from the sky and coated their skin. You could not breathe, she could not breathe. She woke in real life and she could not breathe.

"I can't breathe," she called down to Eliot.

Her sheets felt damp. Her fever had broken. How long had she been up there?

He came up the stairs. "You're talking. You can breathe."

"It doesn't feel good, though."

"No," he agreed. "It wouldn't."

He asked her if she needed anything and she said maybe some water. He looked wrung out. She could hear Miles calling his name and after a while Opal joined in. There was some kind of problem with the TV. It was frozen on the menu again. He shook his head and said he'd better go.

"How is everything down there?" she said.

He told her everything was normal.

"What?" she said.

He'd begun descending the stairs already.

He shouted again, "Normal!"

Sam bought an old Mercedes off a guy in the Catskills for three hundred bucks. He was going through with the biodiesel car. He kept pitching it to them as a STEM activity for the kids. He would teach them about combustion engines. They'd all learn together. On a Friday afternoon, Eliot went with him to pick it up. Cora and Jules sat on Jules's porch, waiting for them.

"It'll keep him busy," said Cora.

"For how long?" said Jules.

Down on the sidewalk, the kids drew a map of the town in chalk. The mountain was in the right place, and the river, but they'd taken some license with the other landmarks. The library was purple. The waterfall had an angry face. The school sat right next to McDonald's. Miles came over and touched Cora's legs with chalk hands.

"Oh god. Don't do that."

He departed again and Cora rubbed at the handprints he'd left on her jeans. "He's going to get a job."

"I keep thinking—and this is uncharitable—who would hire Sam to do anything?"

"Plenty of people," said Cora.

"Really? What are his skills?"

She had a point. Even his interests were scattered. Before the pandemic he'd been playing pickup basketball with some of the other dads in town. He listened to music and watched movies, but did those count? Those were entertainment. He liked to hang around and drink, but they all liked that. That didn't qualify as a hobby.

"He's got a lot of skills," said Cora. "He's an excellent father."

"Workplace skills."

"He's charming? That sometimes helps you get a job."

"Okay, so he's charming. What else?"

"He's probably talented at what he does. What he used to do."

"I'm not sure that's true."

"But he was competent enough to stay employed for a while."

"So, we've got dad, charming, and competent enough."

"It's more than most people amount to," said Cora.

She knew Jules disagreed. Jules found him underwhelming. Earlier that year, she had made partner at her firm, expanding the gulf between their accomplishments. She'd succeeded and he hadn't. He was not a deadbeat dad. He contributed. But the jobs he held never paid well, never added up to a profession or had dignity attached to them. He wasn't singular: there were many men like this now, who held supporting roles in family life. Maybe it was the natural result of the ascent of women in the workplace. So, in a way, victory? Yet up close, it was disconcerting. A man who had no idea what to do with himself.

"I always thought he would get it together eventually," Jules said.

When they'd met during their final year at Columbia, she'd liked his rudderlessness. It was a good way for a young person to be. He'd grown up wealthy, which had dazzled Jules. He'd had a Jeep Cherokee at his disposal, and many functions to attend. His five siblings all went to East Coast schools, graduated from them constantly, and his parents paid for their educations free and clear. Guys with that background failed upward. They became lawyers or politicians or worked in finance. Their fathers helped them out, and their fathers' friends, and their mothers' cousins, and their mothers' friends. But then the time had come to do something, to make a move, and he hadn't. She'd never understood why.

"He wouldn't have had to try that hard, is the thing," said Jules.

Jules was the daughter of a schoolteacher and an alcoholic housepainter and had exerted an unbelievable amount of effort to pay for college and law school. Sam hadn't had to do any of the things she'd done—work in restaurants, get scholarships, take on loans. His future was handed to him and he still didn't take it. For reasons unknown, he had said no thank you. Instead, he let Jules mostly support them. He let her solve their problems. For a while, he'd talked about going back to school, and Jules had encouraged it. Then he hadn't because you had to take a test and fill out a form, which was too much for Sam. Anything was too much.

Cora said, "I can't give you a pep talk about this if you won't allow that he's good man."

"Who mentioned good? Whole separate issue."

Eliot returned with psychedelic music pouring from the open windows of the car. He got out and examined the chalk map. The kids screamed, "Dad!" and threw themselves at him.

"The school is right next to McDonald's," he said and joined Cora and Jules on the porch.

"How was it?" said Cora.

"Fun errand."

He sat on the railing with his long legs hanging and told them the story of the guy who'd sold them the car. He was an old hippie in a raccoon cap. Ten, twelve dogs roaming around. He'd showed them his pedal steel guitar, played them a couple songs. He'd been a roadie for some big bands. As they were leaving, he'd tried to give Eliot a handful of pot. He'd thrust it at him, no container.

"You didn't take it," said Cora.

"No, I took it," said Eliot.

He pulled it from his pocket and showed them. Loose buds fell on the porch. He was living a different life than Cora altogether, though in theory they shared a life. He was accepting shwaggy bush weed from a magical hillbilly while she watched their kids. Sam pulled up, a dramatic moment. The car was long and custard yellow, glamorous in a way that things were not anymore. He got out and they came down from the porch and the kids instinctively lined up on the curb.

"What do you think?" Sam said to Cora.

"Don't you want to ask Jules?" said Cora.

Sam shrugged, and Jules turned away. She stood back from the rest of them with one foot on the bottom step of the porch. Cora looked at Eliot, who had absorbed none of this.

"It's pretty," said Cora, carefully.

Sam kneeled and spoke to his children. A diesel engine could be easily converted to biodiesel. All it needed was a separate fuel tank and separate fuel lines. Then it could run on recycled vegetable oil. You could go pick up grease that local restaurants were throwing out and it would power the car. You could get it from school cafeterias.

"Transesterification," he said to Jack. "Do you know what that is?"

"No," said Jack.

"It's the chemical conversion of triglycerides into biodiesel. It lowers the viscosity of oil. You'll learn this. We're going to learn it together."

Night fell and they stood in front of the car. The streetlights turned on. The kids climbed into the back and played Driving to Grandma's (and Mom Forgot the Snacks). The adults sat on the curb and drank beer from cans. All except Jules, who had gone inside without saying good night to anyone.

Summer became fall and Sam got the car up on blocks. He opened the hood and showed his kids the engine. Eliot helped with this; they borrowed the necessary tools and spent a lot of time in the driveway. They sourced used oil from restaurants in town. The Chinese place, the restaurant on the falls.

But then the pandemic ended. It ended by degrees, like the loosening of a blood pressure cuff. It took many more months, but the world came back. There was no more need for a project, or the parenting class, or any of the other diversions they'd drummed up to fill the time. Sam moved the car farther back into the driveway. Beautiful and inoperable, a souvenir from the worst era of their lives. You could begin to see why Jules hated it. You could begin to understand her frustration. It had all this potential but it just sat there.

Six

Normal life resumed and the town became busier. Tourists were drawn to the mountain, to the main street, to the modern art museum in the old cracker box factory down near the river. The train disgorged them in their weekend hats. They smelled the air and saw no garbage on the street and thought they were upstate. They wandered around in clumps, spending money on soy candles and hand-dyed clothing and sour IPAs.

Did Cora divorce Eliot? She did not. The kids were back at school, back at their activities. Cora's company returned to the office, at least for part of the week, and Eliot's did too. Most days he rode his bike downhill to the train, let it whisk him off for a full eight hours, returned in the evening, red-faced and starving, having ridden home directly uphill. They ate dinner with the kids and met in their bedroom, where they had new things to talk about.

"Let's be ourselves again," she said.

He said, "Absolutely."

Ourselves: what did it mean? Bravely, they would attempt to find out. They would reacquaint themselves with themselves.

Cora wanted to laugh and drink and move on. She wanted to stop feeling bad and start feeling good. They lay in bed and made plans, joked about how brutal it had been. The idea of divorce, sustaining during the pandemic, got pushed under a piece of furniture in a remote corner of her mind.

She cut her hair, shorter, breezier. They painted their bedroom sage green, sanded the deck railing that gave everyone splinters. She started taking a yoga class at the gym, and sometimes Eliot would join her. A guy came by to look at the mushroom, which had continued to grow out of the bathroom wall. He yanked it out and studied the crack in the tile.

"It's a moisture problem, not a fungus problem," he said. "What you should focus on is making the room less wet."

Cora said, "But how? People shower in here."

The guy said, "I'm not a shower expert."

Over and over, you had to commit to the task of living. You had to insist on resilience, spring back from defeat. Once a week they'd hire a sitter and go out to dinner or see friends. This was the plan. They'd rediscover interests, hobbies. They'd read again and talk with their peers about topics of global import. Fervently, they'd interrogate the issues of the day. They'd be themselves, the same as always, different each moment, ever-constant, vastly changed.

New people had moved to town during the pandemic, doubling the price of real estate. They had media careers or hybrid arts careers or taught college. They too wanted to shed the heaviness of the recent past. Their hunger to live was almost teenage. It was a second adolescence, tinged with weariness, susceptible to hangover, less elastic. But more innocent somehow, more embarrassing.

The new neighbors over the back fence were called Richard and Celeste Hood. They had three kids, a dog, and a multifarious workforce fixing up their house.

Cora and Opal went over with a pan of brownies to meet them. Richard was Ecuadorian on his mother's side, big and sweaty in short shorts and a linen shirt. He worked in advertising but gave the impression of having real money, not job money, but money built in a mine or a factory or on real estate. Celeste had recently left her job at an auction house.

"I'm worried I'm going to die of boredom," she said.

But she didn't look worried and she didn't look bored. She looked happy and pretty. She had auburn hair and lots of cleavage and wore a peasant dress with bare feet. They called to their daughter, Sarah Beth, who was Opal's age, and the two girls sized each other up and disappeared upstairs.

"Tell us about the town," said Richard, and Cora told them the town was as it appeared. The people were who you'd expect. They thought they were better than New York City and they thought they were worse. They were conflicted, overeducated, somewhere between modestly prosperous and completely broke. The Hoods laughed at this, then Richard put his hand on Cora's lower back and took her on a tour of the renovations. Two men were heaving the fridge out of its nook. Upstairs windows were becoming dormers. Beige carpet was being pulled out. They'd discovered Douglas fir underneath, which would require sanding, staining, and a two-week period of off-gassing.

"So can we stay with you guys during that?" said Richard. Then he rubbed her back and said, "Kidding."

In the master bedroom he showed her the corner where a new bathroom was being built.

THE TEN YEAR AFFAIR

"Now are you still working with American toilets?" he asked her.

"Working with?"

"Using."

"We're using the toilets the house came with, if that's what you mean."

"See if you ever want to upgrade, you have to go Japanese. We're going all Japanese this time around. We visited Kyoto recently. Ask Celeste. They're way ahead on toilet technology. Heating elements. Different strengths of jet. It anticipates what you want. And it can save settings for each person in your household so you never get the wrong thing."

When it was time to leave, Opal and Sarah Beth hugged like old friends. Celeste told Cora to come back for dinner on Friday and to bring people, to bring anyone. This was how they began to spend their weekends in the backyard of the new people. In their kitchen and on their deck and down on their lawn, where they'd set up a long dining table of scarred wood and surrounded it with mismatched chairs. They integrated the Hoods instantly, or the Hoods integrated themselves. Maybe they'd needed a third couple.

Sam and Jules came with them to dinner that first time. Richard sat Cora next to him, which made Celeste roll her eyes. Sam sat at the other end of the table, observing Cora and looking away. Eliot poured wine for everyone. The wine was orange that year and tasted like shoes.

"It's better. Things are better. Not perfect, but better," he said.

"Better not to think about it every second of the day," said Jules.

"But not that different," said Cora.

"Effectively identical," said Sam.

They were talking about the new president, Joe Biden, who'd taken office that winter. He was less bad than Trump, less of a buffoon. He was stately and vacant, prone to mild gaffes. You didn't have to feel bad laughing at his jokes because he made no jokes. The joke was his age, but you couldn't say that.

Jules said, "Remember how you'd be clenched for disaster, glued to your phone? But somehow it wouldn't come in the way you were expecting? There'd be a long delay, or it would never arrive. No one was held accountable. Everything was this big stressful blur. And you'd scroll and scroll and scroll and scroll. The scrolling didn't help. But not scrolling didn't help either. Sam got addicted to cable news."

"You did?" said Cora.

Sam had a toothpick in his mouth. "No."

"He'd watch Fox News and rant," said Jules. "His face would get red."

"My face would not get red. She's exaggerating."

"It would get a little red. Anyway, I'm grateful all that is over, and we've got a respectable person in there," said Jules.

"His Botox is tasteful," said Celeste.

They laughed, though it was. This concluded the evening's political discussion. They moved on to gossip of a swingers' scene in town. Apparently, it centered on a figure drawing class. The class took place on a rotating schedule at different people's houses.

Celeste passed around a tub of chocolate chip cookies. "The people are nude, the models. Then I guess it goes from there."

Cora said, "The models are involved?"

Celeste said, "No, I don't think so. I don't think it's that straightforward."

"So, the nudity, what? Sets the mood?" said Cora.

"Something like that."

"And the models slip out or . . . ?"

Celeste said, "I only heard about this thirdhand. Our sitter works at the coffee shop and hears everything."

Sam interjected that he'd done a semester as a studio art major, and figure drawing classes were not actually sexy. They were awkward and the models tried hard to do a good job and so did the artists. Everyone at the table shouted him down. This was obviously not that kind of figure drawing class. No one was trying hard to do a good job.

"I can't imagine a horde of local people fucking in my home," said Cora. "Who goes to these things? The mailman? The city clerk?"

"Probably not the mailman or the city clerk," said Richard.

"Mail carrier," said Jules.

"Imagine you're at an orgy and you look over and the city clerk is there," said Cora.

"I'm not sure I would recognize him on sight," said Eliot.

"Or her," said Jules.

"It's not an orgy, I don't think," said Celeste. "I don't think it's some big fleshy group. I think it's more like swinging. I think everyone disperses into separate rooms and does whatever they want."

"Swinging," said Sam. "Retro."

"I don't know," said Eliot. "Seems a little corny."

It made you picture bell-bottoms. Free love. Cora could see herself there, with the city clerk or whomever, the mail carrier, on a shag carpet. She was curious about how the segue occurred, the moment the host signaled to the nude model that the time had come to put her robe back on and discreetly collect her fee. But she didn't tell them this. They chewed their cookies and agreed: it sounded retro and a little corny.

They were living now, attempting to live, so the need for the affair lessened. Maybe it was time to give it up altogether, to face material reality, exile other selves. A radical thought: to reside in a single time line. To do only what she was doing and not a second activity as well. To respect the laws of time and space. She boldly imagined a future where she didn't imagine anything.

But still, they returned to the hotel, and everything was as it had been. The lake sparkled, though she could have sworn they'd drained it. An otter played out in its center and birds sang to each other from the reeds. Inside, the AC ran, dripping water on the rug. The TV had every channel she didn't have at home. They fucked, but it took more now to seem exciting. It took effort to think of acts they hadn't tried.

Foot stuff? she suggested.

He said, I guess.

So they did foot stuff, and ass stuff, and light choking. Bondage. The stuff that was left after you exhausted the obvious. Role playing. Professor and student. Inappropriate masseuse. Stewardess and unruly passenger who needed to be restrained. They pretended they didn't feel foolish, but they felt a little foolish. If you had to try so hard, it wasn't a good sign. It pointed to a larger issue and the issue was repetition. The issue was that sex got old, even if it was illicit.

* * *

Meanwhile in the real world, she was back at the office three days a week. Her company had downsized to a smaller space in the same building. Despite efforts to get everyone back in person, the room was mostly empty. This time, Cora's plants really had died. She threw them into the trash can under her desk. But nope. There was no trash can where one used to be, so she dumped dried dirt onto her feet. She went and found the actual trash can and threw them out and sat down again and did the same work she'd done at home for over a year. The new office had a snack machine but not the updated snack machine. So it was back to the keypad, a humiliating comedown.

She said to Lily, "Everything is a little worse now. Have you noticed that?"

Lily said, "Yeah, and you need a code for the bathroom on this floor. The code is 1234."

They worked and they went to lunch. They worked and they went to lunch. Ryan rounded them up for a meeting in the conference room. It was windowless, carpeted gray like the rest of the space. He wore three necklaces made of wooden beads and Thai fisherman's pants. He was the kind of Western man who went East and became keenly interested.

"I wanted to check in with the two of you to see how it feels to be back."

It felt fine, they both said, though how did it really feel? It felt like the world should have ended and hadn't. It felt like coming down from Everest and checking your bank balance. It felt like seeing the situation for what it was, in a flash, and then having to pretend for the rest of your life that you hadn't.

"It's nice to get back into a routine," said Cora. "And to see you both in person."

Ryan said, "That's great."

They discussed the projects they were working on, and this was where meetings became difficult. The chitchat up-front wasn't so bad. You could do it with your brain off. But the agonizing discussion of what had already been agonizingly discussed was intolerable. Cora was launching a newsletter aimed at people trying to get a footing in marketing careers. She had talked about this at their last three meetings and now she talked about it again.

"I wanted you two to be the first to hear," Ryan said as they wrapped up.

He was headed back to Chiang Mai to get married. He showed them the ring, a big oval-cut diamond in a platinum setting that made no sense with his fisherman's clothes. He'd met someone new, a prominent Thai national who owned restaurants. This was how he described his fiancé: a prominent Thai national.

"That's wonderful," said Cora and Lily.

"I can't bear this life anymore." He paused. "I'm probably not supposed to talk like that."

He was not a bad guy or a bad boss. He had chafed too. Everyone chafed and pretended they didn't. Everyone had to suppress their personality, to act like the job they had was the one they'd chosen. Now he'd be free, or perhaps trapped in a different way, which could feel like freedom at first. They asked him what he would do and he told them he'd travel and eat and climb and relax.

"They're going to be hiring for my position. Just a heads-up. Maybe you want to try for it, Cora. I gave them your name. Or maybe, I don't know, maybe they'll hire from outside."

They went back to their desks and worked in silence. What

did it mean to try for it? Was she supposed to email the head of HR? Since she'd worked there, they'd given her raises and title changes often enough to retain her, but never had the promotions marked a real shift in responsibilities. Maybe they'd give it to her, and she'd be marginally more challenged. More fulfilled. Was it possible to be fulfilled working at the digital marketing job? Probably not, but it was worth a shot. She would do it and see, she decided, and felt an unexpected wave of hope.

At the urging of Celeste Hood, they joined the local pool. The women started taking the kids on weekends. There was a bar where a college student, home for the summer, mixed cocktails and poured draft beers. The gin and tonics were so weak you could barely taste the booze. They were tonic and tonics. Which was good, because you didn't want to get drunk, just loose, and you wanted that feeling to abate by dinnertime.

The kids swam and mostly self-governed. Occasionally, they came over and pestered Cora in particular for snack money. The clouds overhead were wispy. The sounds of tennis drifted over from the court, which was medium well maintained. Cora and Celeste and Jules sat in deck chairs with unopened books in their laps.

One day the topic turned to infidelity.

"I don't know if I care about it," said Jules.

Celeste said, "What do you mean?"

Jules had on a black bathing suit and large sunglasses. Her hair was slicked back from taking a swim but refusing to play with her kids. Recently, she had begun getting subtle or not so subtle work done to her face. Her forehead was tight and reflective as a billiard ball. She'd gotten the undereye filler that made you look refreshed, well rested, but ran the risk of blinding you.

"I'm not sure I'd mind if Sam cheated. It seems silly to let that ruin things. Don't you think?"

This was surprising coming from Jules, who never struck Cora as a libertine. She had always seemed uptight, exactly as bourgeois as the institution of marriage. Cora knew instantly that something was up.

Celeste said, "I don't know. You've met Richard. It's not a secret that he likes to flirt. It's never gone too far, that I know of. It's harmless. But I think I'd probably be upset about a real thing. If he, I don't know, fell in love. Maybe I'm old-fashioned."

"What about you, Cora?" said Jules.

"Not theoretically. I don't have a moral objection."

The prospect of Eliot cheating seemed far-fetched. Though, this wasn't fair, was it? Eliot worked with many smart and attractive women who probably found him smart and attractive too. He *was* smart and attractive. It was not inconceivable that something could happen with one of them. If it did, would Cora be fine with it? She'd be impressed, possibly turned on. Definitely sad. It would especially hurt if the woman was very young. It would hurt if she was too beautiful or not beautiful enough. It would hurt if it was someone they knew, someone in their lives.

"Look, there he is," said Celeste.

Eliot had arrived at the pool. It was early evening. He often worked for a few hours on weekend days and drove over afterward. He had on a black Lacoste shirt and his Ray-Bans. The fit of the shirt made his arms look more muscular than they were, which was why those shirts cost what they did.

Jules said, "He looks different. Did he do something?"

He hadn't done anything but let three days of stubble grow on his jaw and show up at magic hour. Still, he looked good. Cora saw for a second how an affair might be viable.

She said, "He doesn't usually look so handsome. He works in publishing."

Jules said, "Do you two have sex?"

They had never talked like this before, and Cora thought again, something is up. She didn't want to tell Jules whether she and Eliot fucked. Mostly they didn't—Eliot was still on the medicine. But it felt wrong, too personal, to talk about Eliot's prescription with Jules or explain why he could not go off it.

"Do you and Sam?" said Cora.

Eliot shielded his eyes from the sun and waved at her. The kids ran to him and he picked them up, slung Opal onto his back, held Miles upside-down, staggered along that way for a while. Then he dumped them off into the grass bordering the pool deck. He shucked off his shirt and the women watched.

"God no," said Jules.

"Are you having an affair?" said Cora. "Is that what you're trying to tell us?"

"This guy has been DMing me."

"Who? Does he live in town?"

"He doesn't live in town. He lives in the city."

They'd gone to law school together. They'd reconnected in the early pandemic. Did Cora and Celeste remember that time? Jules's impression of it was blurry, similar to how she remembered giving birth. It had been that unpleasant, that dehumanizing. People from the past had gotten in touch and made sentimental proclamations. It had seemed that the world was ending or, more precisely, that it was okay to pretend it was. In this context, it had not been so odd to hear from him.

They started DMing every day. She began to look forward to it. She enjoyed the attention. He was good looking and successful and Sam had just gotten laid off. A lot of her attraction to Sam was related to his confidence, which he'd lost along with the job. Or maybe it had been eroding for years. It was hard to tell. Then had come the car. The car was almost too easy as a metaphor for Sam's whole thing.

"We're meeting for a drink in the city," said Jules.

"And you're going to . . . ?" said Celeste.

"I don't know. Maybe not."

"Don't do it," Cora heard herself say. "He wouldn't do it to you."

"He absolutely would do it to me. He's dying to do it to me, but he's chickenshit."

"Not true," said Cora.

"He's afraid of the consequences. That's the only thing that keeps him from doing it. Cora, you should know."

She said it without apparent rancor. Cora could not read her expression behind her sunglasses. The day was ending and soon they would go home and Cora would think about this conversation. *You should know*. Beyond the pool, women in tennis skirts zipped up their bags, gathered their balls. They were playing at affluence, or maybe they were affluent. They were affluent relative to somebody.

"So do it then," said Cora.

"I might," said Jules.

Eliot called out to ask what they should do for dinner. He swam over and had his elbows up on the pool deck. Everyone, at some point, would have the best-looking day of his life and maybe this was Eliot's. He said he'd make pizza, unless that was too labor intensive. Celeste sucked in her stomach. Jules took a long sip from her gin and tonic.

Cora went home with a secret. If she told Eliot, he might repeat it to someone. He would probably not tell Sam—they weren't close like that—but he might tell Klaus. He'd shout it to him over the squeak of his own sneakers on the racquetball court, or he'd tell him later, as they drank beers. He'd be commiserating about Freda and it would slip out. *You know who else is fucking up her life?*

"What were you girls talking about?" said Eliot.

He'd turned on his countertop speaker. Three men with similar voices were discussing politics. The politicians in office were not far enough left for them. In any other country they would be the center right party. One of them mentioned Karl Marx and another one, or the same one, mentioned Freud. A third one, or one of the ones who'd already been talking, mentioned Adorno. The kids flew into the room and wrenched open the refrigerator.

"We're gonna have dinner soon," Cora said to them. "Don't . . ."

But they were gone already, gripping string cheese, racing for the TV. Eliot had begun rolling out pizza dough. He had a smudge of flour on his glasses. She took them off his face, cleaned them, handed them back to him.

"I kind of have a secret," she said.

"Tell me."

"If I tell you, are you going to tell Klaus?"

"Of course not. Not if you don't want me to."

"I thought you confided in Klaus."

Opal was back, standing on one leg, peeling string cheese. She'd gotten taller that summer, complained of growing pains at night. Her room smelled of mall store perfume and she'd been lobbying for a phone. "Can I have a glass of milk?"

"Remember how we talked about getting things for yourself?" said Cora. "How we're going to try to do that now that you're getting older?"

"It's boring," said Opal.

"Pouring milk into a cup is boring?"

"Yeah."

"It takes two seconds. You're bored in that amount of time?"

"Yeah. Other people have phones."

"What does that have to do with it?"

"If I had a phone, I could look at it while pouring milk."

Eliot handed her a glass of milk and she departed again. They watched her go, the swing of her ponytail. The second she had a phone she'd be further away from them. But at least she'd stop asking for a phone.

"I won't tell Klaus. I only say that to nettle you," said Eliot. "Can you smell this?"

It was the gallon of milk he'd poured from, down to its last third.

"If you think it's spoiled, it's spoiled." She smelled it. "Yeah, it's sour."

"Shit."

He ran into the other room and returned holding Opal's cup. He dumped it down the drain, along with the rest of the gallon, rinsed the jug and crushed it under his sneakers, opened the back door, threw it in the direction of the recycling bin. It went in and then he had to gloat and shout catch-phrases from the original NBA Jam, while the Hoods' dog barked and Cora begged him to shut up.

"So, what's the secret?" he said, when he'd calmed down. "You want to tell me, so tell me."

"Jules is having an affair. Or is about to."

"Wow," he said. "That's a good secret. I'm going to tell Klaus."

"I know you're kidding, but please don't."

"You didn't keep the secret, but you want me to."

"Spousal privilege," she said.

"You're not using that correctly."

"It means you can't disclose what I told you because we're married."

"In a court of law. In testimony. If I choose not to."

The rule didn't mention racquetball or Klaus. It certainly didn't mention what you may or may not say over drinks at the strip mall sports bar near their gym.

"What is she going to do?" said Eliot.

"I don't know. Sleep with the guy probably. They're getting a drink in the city."

"Why did she tell you?"

"She seemed to want permission."

"Permission from you?"

"Yeah, or anyone."

He had finished rolling out the dough and arranged it on a baking sheet.

"But she's going to stay with Sam?"

"That's what she was implying."

"I guess that isn't surprising."

They already knew of one person, Freda, who had walked out on her family. Freda was supposed to be a worst case. Freda was what happened if you got hypnotized by abs and airplanes and hotels and money, and mistakenly ascribed to them the illusion of freedom. Two women walking out on their families would represent a pattern.

"Jules seems like the affair type," said Eliot.

"Is it a type?"

It was, he told her. Someone who was together on the surface but seething underneath. Someone whose apparent composure concealed roiling self-doubt and loneliness and fear. Ego, too. Ego was part of it.

"I'm not sure I agree," said Cora.

"She was mad about the car," said Eliot.

"The car was ridiculous."

"He still might convert it."

"He's not going to convert it!"

"No. Obviously not."

Opal came in again and asked for a glass of milk.

"The milk went bad," said Cora. "How about water?"

"No."

"How about apple juice?"

"No."

"Can you run out?" Cora said to Eliot. "I've been to the grocery store five times this week."

"I can't do anything else today. I'm completely wiped out. I read submissions for five hours."

"All right, I'll go."

"Can you get deli turkey, too? And Swiss. And, let's see . . ." He opened the fridge. "I guess you should do a big shop."

THE TEN YEAR AFFAIR

They needed everything. Whole peeled tomatoes in a can, an onion, butter. Bread. Salad greens. Anything but arugula. He was sick of arugula. Peanut butter. Opal would only eat bow-tie pasta lately? So, a couple boxes of that. Eggs. Pasture-raised, not cage-free. Last time she'd gotten it wrong, so she should make sure. The cage-free kind meant they crammed the chickens together on a warehouse floor and let them peck each other's eyes out. He'd seen a news report about it. The free-range ones got to be outside at least. When Cora bought the eye-pecking ones it was all he thought about when he was eating them. And sponges, of course. The sponge was, like, rotting.

He held up the sponge. "Here, come smell it."

This was what he was doing on the best-looking day of his life, having bad smells confirmed for him. She went and smelled the sponge and briefly retched. Sure enough, it was rotting.

She retrieved her keys and prepared to go. "You're not going to tell Klaus, right?"

"I won't tell him," Eliot said. "Unless I really want to."

What did a secret do to the world of the affair? It made her pity him. If you pitied a man, you didn't fuck him the same way. It turned you into his mother. You wanted to put him down for a nap, take his temperature, read him a bedtime story. Poor baby. At the big anonymous hotel, she found herself cradling his head.

What are you doing? he said.

She said, Huh?

You were stroking my brow.

I wasn't.

No, but you were.

Sorry, she said. I won't do it again.

He was a cuckhold, a dated word that had recently come back into fashion. But manhood was different now—less repressive, more open. They were all supposed to be enlightened and so Jules's cheating on him should not have made him seem weak. It should not have changed Cora's perception of him. He was a victim, she reminded herself. And yet.

She wanted to tell him, but he got up and went into the shower. She wanted to tell him after his shower, but he had to run home. She wanted to tell him the next time they met at the trailhead, but he pulled her back into the woods and spread his coat out on the ground. She wanted to tell him the next time and the next, but the moment was never right. He would be too playful or charming or happy. He'd have his tongue in her ear.

In the real world, she also tried. She met Sam in the city and they went to lunch. After a year of unemployment, he'd gotten a new job at a start-up that helped people rent baby gear at the airport. It was a communications job, like his last. Hybrid remote. He wrote and sent out press releases about baby gear and how the company was making it easy to obtain. Car seats, strollers, pack-'n-plays. This app, like the last, was buggy and of questionable necessity. Lunch had been his idea.

"You look nice," said Lily, as she was leaving. "Where are you going?"

Cora told her the name of the restaurant and Lily said, "Oh wow, that place is trendy."

This threw Cora. She'd thought maybe Sam knew something and wanted to talk. But why would he have chosen a trendy restaurant for this? She scanned the menu on her way and saw it had a raw bar and interesting wines. Who selected a place with a raw bar for a difficult conversation? Slurping seafood and crying. A hundred and fifty bucks a head to hear your life was ruined.

He was waiting near the door when she arrived, looking at his phone. They'd only ever interacted in town, and that once on the Cape. In this new context, she noticed physical changes that she hadn't before. She could see how he'd aged. He'd thickened through the waist, though he'd lost some of his pandemic weight, and his hair had receded. He would not be able to wear it long forever, maybe a few more years. She knew this would be hard for him, a major shift in how he saw himself.

He kissed her on the cheek and Cora wondered what she owed him. If she told him about Jules, there was a possibility that he'd think *fuck it* and make some kind of serious attempt with Cora. She wanted for this not to be her motive. Standing there, she convinced herself that it wasn't. She convinced herself that telling him was objectively the right thing to do. To save him embarrassment. To grant him the dignity of having all the information. She felt bad for him, that was it. They sat on the sidewalk in cane-back chairs.

"I have something to tell you," she said.

But the waiter appeared to explain the restaurant's modus operandi. This took ten minutes. Got it, they had to keep saying. Got it, sounds great. She felt the stiffness of her smile. Every restaurant these days explained the concept of a restaurant to you. They ordered oysters to start, his idea again, though it was decadent for a Tuesday at noon. He'd undone the top button of his shirt and she thought of the Citgo tattoo. It was remarkable that Jules had married a man with a gas station logo on his body. It seemed so far removed from what she'd find attractive.

"Are we celebrating something?" said Cora.

"No. Well, my job."

"Oh."

"And I thought it would be fun to see you here. Away from—"

He motioned vaguely north. The waiter returned with their wine. He poured a sample for Cora and she tasted it self-consciously. She remarked that it was delicious and Sam laughed. She asked him why and he said she made for an unconvincing connoisseur.

She raised her glass. "Well, congrats."

He'd invited her there to celebrate his job, not to talk about Jules. Their feet touched—the table was white marble and wobbly and too small—and they apologized to each other. Then he asked what she needed to tell him. She told him to forget it, but he insisted.

"Has Jules seemed off to you?" she said, finally.

"What do you mean off?"

"Has she not been around much?"

"I don't know."

"No, but she hasn't."

"Not worse than usual."

"Yeah, but no. It's been worse. Are you sure it hasn't been worse?"

She wanted him to come to it himself, to grasp what she was getting at without her needing to say it. He looked at her and shook his head. The city took place around them. There was a florist on the corner and people walked by holding flowers in paper cones. The ground rumbled when the subway went under them and passing dogs sniffed at their feet.

"She's never around," he said. "She's never been around. It doesn't get better or worse. She's been at dinner, hasn't she? She's been at the pool."

He was right that it was hard to pin down a specific time she'd been absent. Cora couldn't come up with a single example. Maybe Jules had been absent spiritually, but this was a tenuous claim to make. How could you know for sure what was happening with another person's spirit?

She tried it a different way. "Has she seemed unhappy lately?"

He told her they had just come out of the longest and most intense period of despair, a near universal despair, that had eaten at the fabric of most relationships. It had fundamentally broken the idea of "feeling good" to the extent that he was no longer sure it was possible anymore. Yeah, she'd been unhappy.

The waiter returned with a silver platter of oysters on crushed ice. Oysters were supposed to be sexual. These were very fresh and eating them on the street in Manhattan was, she understood, one of the pinnacle human experiences.

"I'm having fun," she said, frowning.

Sam laughed. "That's bad?"

She'd expected it to be the opposite. She'd expected a grueling interval of comforting him and advising him about whether he should leave his marriage. She'd expected to go back to her office feeling drained. To need something, and be unable to locate what that something was.

More food arrived and Sam said, "Look how good this looks."

They'd garnished the ceviche with tropical fruit. He was not going to get it, and so she gave up. The waiter brought more wine and an aperitif. It was too much to eat and drink before heading back to the office to stare at Microsoft Outlook. She felt like Caligula staggering uptown. Lily asked her how it had been, and it had been a boondoggle, a complete failure, a question mark. But it had also been the first thing she and Sam had ever done that felt like, and maybe was, a legitimate date.

"It was nice," she said, and opened up her email.

You could sleepwalk through summer and Cora was. The roses grew huge that year, vivid as children's faces. Outside watering one evening, she looked up at Richard and Celeste's house. Richard was framed by the bathroom window. He wore a towel around his waist and waved at her, smiling broadly. Then he let the towel drop. It was the hour when the sun shone orange against glass, so maybe she wasn't seeing what she was seeing. She continued to water while he stood naked gazing down at her. He had dark chest hair and dark pubic hair. He had a pot belly that was not flabby but tight as a drum. He wagged his hips, which made it unequivocal. She could see his dick in the most general sense but couldn't tell much else about it. She could not see if he was circumcised or if he was erect. Probably he was erect.

She finished watering and wound up the hose, calmly clipped back the rhododendron. When she looked up again, he was gone and the blind had been pulled down.

Later, she started to tell Eliot about it.

"I saw Richard outside just now," she said.

"Doing what? Like you talked to him?"

"No. I saw him in an upper window of his house."

Eliot waited for more, but she'd changed her mind. Not out of embarrassment, but because they'd been having a fun summer.

The Hoods had rallied the adults and now everyone hung out a lot. The atmosphere felt charged in a new way. Richard flashing her was objectively creepy behavior and if she told Eliot, he'd say, Yikes. He wouldn't offer to kick the guy's ass—that level of macho could not be found in the town—but he'd say, let's stay away from them for a while.

"He's an interesting cat," said Eliot. "I like him."

There was that too. Why not let everyone continue to like each other?

But then the next day at the pool, after three quarters of the weakest possible gin and tonic, she found herself telling Sam. They were lying side by side on deck chairs. He had gotten out of the water and flopped down next to her. He wore his sunglasses on a braided lanyard and purple swim trunks from Patagonia. Droplets beaded up on his torso, running off him. She had not seen his body since the Cape, and the Citgo tattoo had faded slightly. Its blue had lightened, its red was pink.

"You should go in," he said, "Feels nice."

"Maybe in a bit. I need to get hot first."

He took her drink, sitting between them on a low beveled glass table, and drank the rest of it. It was a Saturday and they were all there. Eliot had gone to the snack bar with the kids to procure mozzarella sticks. Two chairs down, Jules filed her nails and talked to Celeste about the med spa that had recently opened on Main Street, where you could get a procedure called a lip flip. She was considering getting one: she'd always been self-conscious about her smile. Richard Hood, who had diving prowess from a youth in water sports, took the low dive and executed a perfect jackknife.

"That's the jackknife of a younger man," said Sam.

"I sort of saw his dick the other day," said Cora.

She understood right away that she'd said this in lieu of telling him about Jules. Sam sat up and took his sunglasses off to indicate he was listening seriously. In the other time line he'd confront Richard, shove him into the pool. There'd be an uproar, lifeguards shouting, *Whoa, whoa, whoa*. But Sam was no more macho than Eliot, and no more aggressive. Anyway, did she actually want a bunch of people grappling for her honor?

Richard had gotten out and prepared to dive again.

"What do you mean?"

She told him about the roses and the bathroom window.

"What is 'sort of' about that? It sounds like you definitely saw it."

"Okay, so I definitely saw it."

"Richard has a crush on you. It could not be more obvious. He always sits next to you at dinner and touches you and refreshes your drink."

Cora doubted that flashing indicated a crush. She'd always assumed it indicated mental illness. The three to five times men had exposed themselves to her on the subway it was not because they had romantic notions. When men whipped their dicks out with no warning, it was never about sex but was about being scary. It was only ever a threat.

"You think Richard was threatening you?"

"No. Clearly not."

They watched him dive again, and it was impressive. Almost no splash. His dimensions made sense in relation to the water, his seal-like body. You could picture him balancing a red and white ball on his nose, eating a fish in one gulp.

"Is he diving for your benefit?" Sam said.

Richard looked over at her as he climbed out of the pool, and yes, he definitely was. He didn't wear a Speedo, though it seemed like he should have. He wore little orange trunks that stuck to him and he pulled them away from his body.

Sam said, "What a douchebag. Are you going to fuck him?"

She glanced over at Jules, who was still filing her nails. You could also get an IV drip at the med spa, she was saying, for a bad hangover. But she didn't know about opting in to intravenous treatments for that. Bacon, egg, and cheese sandwiches still existed after all, as did dumb television.

"I'm not going to fuck him, no."

He asked her why and there were so many reasons. He lived over her back fence and his dog barked incessantly. He was trying too hard. She did not feel any way in particular about him, not even to be darkly compelled by his strangeness. But the one she gave Sam—it was the heat, it was the flesh on display, it was the anomalous boozy summer—was "I only like you."

At the end of August, there was a feeling of coming to. Labor Day arrived and the heat broke. In the other time line, Cora went with Sam out to Montauk, ate lobster, got a little sunburned. He could sail over there, and they took out a catamaran, jumped off of it into open water, drank cold white wine, lay in the sun kissing. You could feel the first inkling of fall, that invigorating first inkling.

But in the real world, she bought school supplies and figured out who she had to pick up where on each day, and who Eliot had to pick up, and what maneuvers were required to make it on time. This necessitated constant amendments to an oversize wall calendar that had a pen attached to it with a string. Eliot had attached the pen. Tuition came due for karate and ballet and the kids wanted Sambas because everyone cool now wore Sambas. Sarah Beth wore Sambas and Jack wore Sambas. Penelope wore Sambas and many people Cora had never heard of wore Sambas.

"What are Sambas?" said Eliot, and they all screamed at him to get a clue.

The roses had gone; their petals wilted and fell. They left behind waxy green bushes, and the kids forgot what they were and went in after soccer balls and baseballs and Frisbees, and got slashed up by the thorns. It would be many months before they'd return, and in the meantime, they'd look ugly, patchy, a little sinister.

Cora went to work and it was Ryan's last week. She planned a party for him in the conference room. She'd ordered a cookie cake, his favorite. She'd planned Ryan-themed party games. In one you had to guess what his email response would be to escalating problems with the website. The winner got a carabiner.

An hour before the party he asked to meet with her in the conference room. She wondered if she was being promoted. She went in and saw he looked nervous. He sat alone with no devices in front of him. No computer, no phone. He'd begun to dress even more like a guru. Everything flowed and he was cultivating complicated facial hair. A goatee bisected his chin and met up with more beard at the very bottom of his face.

"I want you to know this wasn't my decision," he said.

She said, "What wasn't?"

He explained that they had given his job to Lily and he'd been discreetly training her for a month. It was nothing against Cora, but she seemed busy with her family—she often had to leave early or rearrange her work-from-home days—and Lily had the time to put in. It was illegal to say that, and she told him so.

"You can't not promote someone for having a family. It's discriminatory."

He looked scared. "I'm trying to do this gently."

"I emailed HR. I interviewed for it. What did I not do?"

"It's not anything like that. They just went with someone else."

"I planned your party. I got a cookie cake!"

"I'm grateful for that. How did you know I liked cookie cake?"

She'd worked for him for almost a decade. She knew he liked cookie cake and had two iguanas named after manga characters. She knew he was from Kentucky and it took his parents a long time to accept that he was gay. She knew the guy he was with before his current fiancé was named Edward and did a lot of crunches. She'd picked up details over the years, made a point of picking up details.

"I'm sorry," he said.

"So Lily is my boss now?"

"You know how our team operates. We don't use the word 'boss.' Supervisor, yes. Technically. But you'll keep working together as you always have."

"And she makes more money than me?"

"I can't disclose salary information."

He looked at her helplessly. She would have to stay at this job and have Lily be her boss. She'd have to tell Eliot and try to explain why. He would point out it was discriminatory and she'd say yeah, and he'd want her to do something about it. When she told her mother, she'd say the same. But she wasn't going to do anything about it, except continue to work there, apply for jobs with "content" in their titles, try and fail to imagine other careers for herself.

"Nothing will really change," said Ryan. "Lily is deserving and passionate."

Cora was willing to show up and do her best. She was willing to participate, fill out the annual self-evaluations. In general, she complied. But it was too much to ask her to be passionate. No one was passionate about content management. Passion was what went on in the other world. It was between two people with unwholesome fixations on each other, determined to do something stupid. It was not between a person and her desk job.

Seven

Every year felt like youth's end, until the next came along and showed you just how young you'd been. She threw a thirty-seventh birthday party for Eliot. She threw a thirty-eighth birthday party for Eliot. They were all down with norovirus on Eliot's thirty-ninth. She and Jules teamed up to throw a joint fortieth for Eliot and Sam.

She showed up early on the day to help Jules set up. It was cold out, mid-December, a true winter like they hadn't had in years. Snow blanketed the rooftops and lawns. The falls had frozen, the first time Cora had seen it. It had a furred appearance, beard-like and opaquely white. A small crowd gathered there at any given moment, taking pictures from the overlook near the restaurant. Holding up gloved peace signs, orienting their phones vertically for posting. At Jules's house, salt crystals littered the front porch.

Sam opened the door. "Oh hi."

"I thought you were supposed to be gone," said Cora.

She leaned down inelegantly to remove her boots.

He said, "Can I help you with that?"

She said, "With taking off my shoes?"

Jules came downstairs holding a large cardboard box. She had her hair up in a bandanna, which frightened Cora. Women only did that to signal they were rolling up their sleeves. She shifted the box to her hip and said to Sam, "You're still here?"

"Leaving now."

He slipped into his parka, patted the pockets for his wallet and phone. He would go to the library. Maybe he'd also have a sandwich. He asked Cora what Eliot was doing that day and Cora told him she didn't know. Both sets of kids had been sent to their grandparents' houses for the weekend and they weren't used to this much freedom. Sam said he kept thinking he was forgetting something, forgetting to make lunch or pick somebody up. Jules held the box—it was labeled PARTY MISC—and watched him impatiently.

"All right," he said. "I guess I'll see you guys later."

He mouthed *good luck* to Cora on his way out.

She followed Jules into the living room and helped her unpack the box. It held bar tools, a cocktail shaker, holders for tealights, a bag of the candles themselves. They needed to roll up the rug, Jules told her. They needed to set up a bar area for the bartender they'd hired. She wanted to know if Cora thought there was enough space for dancing. Cora looked around and noted the Christmas tree straining against the ceiling.

"Are you worried about that?"

Jules said, "Isn't it insane?"

Its bluish green needles had fallen all over the floor. It was not just tall but fat. A porcelain angel on top, a family heirloom, said Jules, pressed horizontally against the ceiling. The tree held ornaments that were half store-bought and half homemade by children at school. Cora owned a matching set of the homemade ones with different children's faces on them.

"I told Sam medium-sized, but he let the kids pick. And then they come home with this. It's not like the ceilings in here are high."

Cora made sounds of agreement, but she would have let her kids do the same. They would have worn her down, then hailed her as a hero when she gave in.

"People will dance around it," said Cora.

This was hard to imagine. Were people really going to dance? She had not been to a house party since they moved to town. She had not, come to think of it, been to a house party since before she'd gotten married. She could remember going to them with Eliot in her twenties. At some point, a bunch of their friends had been living in a condemned brownstone near Pratt. They had a lot of parties: keg beer, ten dollars to enter. The windows were boarded up and the staircase to the second floor had a stair missing. She recalled once watching the host beat a rat to death with a tennis racket. This probably wasn't going to be like that.

They rolled up the rug to bring it down to the basement. It was unwieldy and Jules made Cora be the one to walk backward. Jules was in charge in general, though they were splitting the cost. In the weeks before the party, she'd sent Cora a color-coded spreadsheet divvying up the tasks. Cora's color was blue, while Jules's was red. Their shared color was purple. This was fine with Cora; she was happy to be delegated to, but it meant that the party would have Jules's stamp all over it.

"The jazz trio is arriving early to set up," said Jules, and here was a perfect example.

A jazz trio would not have been Cora's choice. A speaker and a playlist, for instance, would have been free. But Cora was not in charge of music, Cora was in charge of alcohol.

"The booze is in my trunk," she said.

So that was the update on her end. She'd gotten a lot of midrange bottles and a few good bottles. She'd offered one of the girls who worked at the coffee shop three hundred bucks to come bartend. The caterers, selected by both of them but really by Jules, would pass food. In addition to much else, they had sprung for something called the "charcuterie ultra-deluxe."

They heaved the rug into a corner of the basement and headed back upstairs.

"How do you think turnout will be?" said Cora.

"Did you not get the RSVP list? I sent it to you."

Cora dimly remembered receiving an email attachment while on deadline at work. She had opened it, gathered that a number of people planned to come, and promptly closed it, never to think about it again. There were only so many spreadsheets one could be asked to look at recreationally.

"Oh right," said Cora, "Eliot thinks no one's going to show up."

What if none of their old friends came? he'd asked Cora. What if everyone was busy? No one wanted to get on a train for seventy minutes to fête some guy they'd known a decade ago. Cora insisted he was being silly. They did want to fête him. They would definitely come. On top of everything else, they were probably curious about where he lived. People heard the name of the town and wanted to see for themselves. But he said, I don't know.

He'd been having some thoughts about death, he told her. They were really and truly going to die one day. He'd recently begun to understand this in a new way. With the party, there was a feeling of taking measure. What had he amounted to? What if it was nothing? What if it turned out, headed into the second half of his life, that he'd wasted his time? His parents weren't here and soon he wouldn't be either. Cora had tried to comfort him. He hadn't wasted his time. He was good at what he did. He was an executive editor at an influential publishing house. He had a great family, great kids. He was beloved by his colleagues and friends. They would all come, even the degenerates.

"Seventy-five people have RSVP'd," said Jules.

They both looked around the room again. Seventy-five people. The floor was bare now and dusty in the outline of a rug. While they'd been in the basement, the Christmas tree had managed to drop more needles.

Jules said, "I need you to, and I hope this isn't insulting, mop the floor."

Cora was there to help. She mopped the floor. It was just a Swiffer anyway, not some bleak bucket with gray water slopping out of it. Jules did nothing while this was going on. She arranged flowers in a vase and stepped back to look at them. Cora could not remember clearly what they had done on Eliot's thirtieth—she vaguely recalled a bar with red light—but she knew she hadn't mopped a floor.

When she had finished, they unloaded the booze from her car. They took the bottles out of the boxes and arranged them for the girl who would come after her shift at the coffee shop. There would be a signature punch, and Jules made a sign explaining what it had in it. LEMONS, RAW SUGAR, COGNAC, AMONTILLADO SHERRY, FRESHLY GROUND NUTMEG. Her handwriting was girlish, adorned with curlicues, and Cora wondered if it was how she wrote all the time, or if it was an affectation put on specifically for signage.

"I think this is going to be really nice," said Jules.

It was definitely going to be nice. With Jules involved there was no way for it not to be nice. Perversely, Cora wondered what would happen if it somehow ended up not being nice. If the whole thing flopped. What would it look like, and what would Jules do? Would her head pop off her body? Would she simply leave, start a new life elsewhere with a wig and a pseudonym? Would she take it out on Cora?

In the afternoon, Cora drove into town to pick up the cake. It snowed again, but lightly. More people were out looking at the falls, bundled up in scarves and long coats. A man took a picture of two women in berets. If they were tourists up from the city, this single phenomenon would drive the next wave of gentrification. Half of Brooklyn would appear in town with moving trucks. We saw the waterfall and we fell in love, they'd say. It was frozen like a wizard's beard.

Main Street was decorated for the holidays and so was the bakery. They'd stowed the cake in a brown box, and the counter girl opened it to show Cora how it had come out, then retied it with red string. It was a white cake, simple and pretty, with Sam's and Eliot's names on it. Like any purchase you'd make in town, it cost five dollars too much. It had a satisfying weight as she carried it to the car. She drove with it on her lap so it would not slide, and she felt she had done well, had met the impossible standards set by Jules.

When Cora returned, two guys from the rental center had arrived to set up the heaters they'd ordered for the deck. They were out there shoveling to make space. She showed Jules the cake and Jules said it was lovely, it was perfect, and Cora wished this did not please her so much. The rental center guys came back inside with flushed cheeks and runny noses and Jules gave them coffee and Christmas cookies.

Then the band was there, stomping their boots on the front porch. The woman bassist had a long gray braid. The men wore porkpie hats. They began taking equipment out of a van, asking where they should set up. One of the guys observed the Christmas tree and said "damn" and Jules repeated the story of her children and pushover husband, but this time she played it for laughs.

In the early evening, they went upstairs to get ready. The work was mostly done. Cora followed Jules into her bedroom, where Jules pulled her sweater over her head and stood in her bra and jeans rolling a joint on the surface of the dresser. She wore two silver necklaces and they jangled against each other as she leaned in and out and told Cora about the new neighbors.

Jules had run into them the day before. They had talked over the fence while their kids played in the snow. "They're fine. Crunchy. They moved up from Brooklyn last month and they're optimistic about their fresh start. You remember how it was. *The air smells good. And you can send your kids to the local school.*"

Their kids weren't allowed to eat anything processed, which Jules had learned by tossing them fruit snacks over the fence. She'd gotten a lecture from the husband about why kids shouldn't have artificial dyes. He was painfully nice, and the next day left a tray of homemade snack bars on their doorstep, which were brown and gloopy and which no one in her household would touch.

Jules licked the joint to seal it. She handed it to Cora, along with a lighter, then disappeared into the closet. Cora sat on the bed, smoking. The room was desert colors, the bed a cream expanse. There were books on each nightstand, running shoes in the corner, a framed print on the wall faded unevenly from the sun.

"Open a window," Jules called and Cora did.

Cold air stabbed its way inside. This was Cora's first time in Sam's bedroom and he was not here. She lay back on her elbows and blew smoke at the ceiling. She'd stuck her head in this room before but never entered. This was where Sam lay worrying about money or mortality. It was where he fucked his wife. Maybe they'd conceived Penelope here. How was Jules in bed anyway? Demanding, probably. And probably good. She'd had that affair with that old friend of hers.

"What ever happened with that guy?" Cora said into the closet. "The law school guy. Is he coming tonight?"

Jules emerged and held out her hand for the joint. "You're joking but I did invite him."

"And?" said Cora.

"He said it's too far to come out and too weird anyway."

"You're not still seeing him, are you?"

"Not for a while. He kept insisting he wants to be happy. He wants something that makes him happy. Who wants to be happy?"

"Pretty much everyone."

"No. Happiness is for children. It's like when you're eight and you get an ice cream. A cotton candy. My kids are happy. They're happy because the things they want are attainable. They want something, I get it for them. Their father gets it for them. Their grandmother or babysitter gets it for them. They want a toy or an article of clothing and someone in their orbit makes it appear. Adults are after something else. They're after something interesting. Interesting is better than happy."

"Do you believe that?" said Cora.

"I don't know. I'm kind of high." She unlocked her phone. "Look. He's seeing someone."

Cora took the phone and scrolled. The girl appeared to be in her twenties with wavy hair and complicated nails. She and her friends dressed alike. Many of her posts were photo dumps of incongruous objects with the caption "Lately." A headless mannequin, a plate of dumplings, a knocked-over garbage can on a city street.

Cora handed the phone back. "She seems . . ."

What did she seem? Young and pretty, but Cora couldn't say that.

"He didn't even tell me about her," said Jules.

She had figured it out herself. He'd been distant, out of touch, and a feeling had built up in her. They'd been on and off for a few months by then. Mostly off. It hadn't been difficult to find the girl. It had taken five minutes. She'd looked at the list of who he followed, clicked on the obvious candidate, and there he'd been in the comments, three flame emojis in a row.

She went back into the closet and emerged holding two dresses. She wore only her underwear. She turned and asked Cora to fix her bra strap in back.

"It's wonky. See how it's loose?"

Cora gripped the joint between her lips as she adjusted the strap. She grazed Jules's shoulder blade with her knuckle and Jules shivered. Jules turned around and said thanks and took the joint back. She stood close to where Cora sat on the bed. A C-section scar was visible over the top of her thong, like a faint red smile. The end of the joint flared as she inhaled.

It had the texture of something that would happen in the

other time line, but the players were wrong. It only made sense if she was Jules and Sam was her. If she was naked in the closet and Sam was on the bed. If Cora was the one who wore two necklaces and licked the joint, and Sam was the one who took it and smoked it.

The pot made this thought hard to pin down.

"What are you wearing?" said Jules.

Cora had brought a garment bag with two options, and she laid them out on the bed.

"Let's see both," said Jules.

They pantomimed being women trying on dresses. They stood in front of the mirror, turned sideways, checked the angles. The radiator hissed. The windows had fogged up, but there were no children present to draw smiley faces on them, or write in dripping letters "Help Me."

Cora was sitting on the bed alone when Sam came home to change. They'd heard glass breaking in the kitchen, yelps from the caterers, and Jules had gone down to investigate. By then, the joint had been extinguished in a saucer on the windowsill and was giving off a tendril of smoke.

He stopped on the threshold when he saw her. "It's you."

He stared at her for a long moment, taking in the red dress, her bare feet.

"Sorry. I'll go."

"Hold on a second."

He went into the closet, shouting over his shoulder. Did he have time for a shower? He needed one. He and Eliot had been playing pool at a bar in town. People had been smoking in there. Definitely not legal. *He* had been smoking in there. He hadn't smoked in a decade, hence the toothpicks, but you didn't turn down an opportunity to smoke inside. Had Cora ever been to that bar? Real locals place. Everyone stood around smoking and eating fried food. They all seemed to know each other. He'd had some onion rings.

He came out holding a suit on a hanger. "Does this need to be steamed?"

It was a question for his wife. Cora should have left already. They heard more glass breaking downstairs.

"Bring it here."

He brought it closer and she looked at it. It was wrinkled. It needed to be steamed. The prospect of doing something domestic for him pleased her. He went into the bathroom and produced a steamer. They stood waiting for it to heat up. She could smell cigarettes on him and, now that he had mentioned it, onion rings.

"You go shower," she said. "I'll do it."

He looked at her again. Her shoulders were bare and so was her back.

"You don't usually wear that color."

He slid his arm around her waist. The barrier between worlds grew thin. You could glimpse figures moving on the other side. Their twins were bolder and less fumbling. They were deft with zippers and knew each other's preferences. Real-life Sam ran his hand up her back and into her hair. She moved closer so they were within an inch of each other. She felt she could reach across, as if through a beaded curtain, and touch the other Cora's hand. Then something would happen, some cosmic merging, and everything would go still.

They heard Jules on the stairs. She stopped and called down to the caterers, "Half an hour!"

Cora took a step back. Sam disentangled his hand from her

hair. His watchband caught on her necklace and he yanked. The chain broke and the charm went flying.

"We'll find it," he said.

He moved away and busied himself disposing of the roach. Cora began steaming his suit. She was crouching to do a cuff when Jules walked in.

"Why are you doing that? Don't do that." She turned to Sam. "Don't make her do that. What's wrong with you?"

Sam didn't look at either of them. He tapped ashes from the saucer out the open window.

"She offered."

Jules took the steamer away. "Go do a last sweep."

Cora was always at the mercy of these people. Being led by them or placated by them or confided to by them or refused by them. She went out onto the landing and heard the shower start. She did not want to be there anymore. Why had she and Eliot not simply gone out to dinner? Why had she not baked a Funfetti cake and let Opal and Miles decorate it?

Downstairs, she saw to the remaining details. There were no remaining details, so she saw to nothing. In a hall mirror, she caught her reflection and she looked flushed and unusually glamorous. The red dress fit well, cinched her waist, made her look like herself and not herself. She fanned a pile of cocktail napkins embossed with Sam's and Eliot's names, which Jules had ordered without telling her. Custom napkins. Given a thousand years Cora wouldn't have thought of it.

She ladled some punch into a glass and brought it out onto the deck. The heaters were warming up, glowing orange. The neighborhood smelled like other people's fireplaces. She thought about Sam and the charm of her necklace, an imperfectly hammered gold disk, lost somewhere in his bedroom. Eliot had bought it for her in Rome on their honeymoon. He had gone out walking alone while she napped one day and returned with it in a black velvet pouch.

That had been Eliot at his most charming. He'd given it to her as she was waking up. It was extravagant—they had no money—which made it even better. Early on, she had not thought much about the fidelity piece of marriage. She had not thought the person who had bought her the imperfectly hammered gold disk could be diminished by familiarity, or her interest in him could fade. That was something that happened to other people, though which specific traits distinguished her from those people she wasn't sure.

Sam and Jules came downstairs as Cora was finishing her drink. She saw them through the sliding glass door. Jules shook her head at something he was saying. Sam gestured around the house in annoyance, but what could be annoying him? The place was impeccable. They noticed her looking, Jules did, and stopped arguing. She walked away abruptly and Sam stuck his head outside.

"What are you doing out here? It's freezing."

Cora held up her glass.

He said, "I'll join you."

But then Jules shouted his name from somewhere within the house, and he said, "Hold on."

Cora tossed the dregs of her drink over the railing. The ice skittered along the surface of the snow. She went inside and Jules stood on the threshold of the living room. She wore a peacock blue dress so short it was more of a shirt. She had slicked back her hair so it looked wet. She kneeled to plug in the Christmas tree, and there was the kind of quiet, reverent moment that made Cora want to shout an obscenity.

"I think we're good," said Jules.

Eliot arrived in a black suit and skinny tie. His hair was frozen. He smelled of aftershave and cigarette smoke. He too had been smoking at the locals bar. He had walked from their house in snow boots and he looked like a kid, crouching near the front door to change out of them. But then when he stood, he was dashing. He was somewhere on the goofy to dashing continuum where tall men resided. Never fully one or the other.

"Plows are out," he said. "It's sticking."

He rose and kissed Cora on the cheek.

"You're stoned," he said, delighted.

He did not otherwise remark on her appearance. He said the place looked great and then he saw the Christmas tree and laughed. He went over to the bar and picked up a napkin with his name on it and laughed again.

"Who would write the word Eliot on a napkin?"

Then he started a conversation with the bartender about the history of moonshine. He'd edited a book about it a while back. They'd originally made it with barley mash in Ireland and Scotland, though in the new world they used maize. The bartender, a girl of maybe twenty with a blond ponytail, nodded politely.

"You probably know what maize is," he said to her.

She said, "Yeah. Corn."

He was loose, enjoying himself. It seemed he'd forgotten his anxieties about his friends showing up. Anyway, they did. The front door opened and the Eliot fan club poured in. Friends from town and friends from the city. Friends from college and their early twenties, including three former residents of the twelve-man apartment.

They all found Eliot and hugged him. They hugged Cora too, and congratulated her on the party, and were amused by the jazz trio. Eliot's boss arrived with his wife. Eliot had described him as old school and she saw that this referred to his blue suit and sandy gray hair, his striped shirt and big white veneers. His wife wore pearls and had highlights that looked like they cost five thousand dollars. They were up from Westchester, on their way to a dinner party. They couldn't stay long. Cora felt obligated to stand with Eliot and talk to them. She observed how Eliot acted, like himself with an added layer of respectability.

Eliot said, "It was nice of you to come."

His boss said, joking, "So this is how you live."

Cora realized a second before Eliot that he thought it was their house. It was a reasonable assumption. Nothing marked the house as not their own. The décor wasn't what they would have chosen—Jules's taste was a little austere—but how could an outsider know? Eliot didn't see what was happening in time to make the necessary explanation.

Instead, he said, for some reason, "It is."

He wasn't lying because it *was* how they lived. Broadly speaking. They lived in a house like this. It had a similar layout, similar vinyl siding. But they didn't, you know, actually live there. The wife leaned into a bookshelf to look at a framed picture of Jack and Penelope and remarked that they were beautiful. They *were* beautiful. They just weren't Cora and Eliot's.

"They are," said Cora.

"How many square feet?" Eliot's boss asked.

Eliot reddened as he cooked up a number. He was not an accomplished liar. He had never been able to tell harmless lies to get them out of social obligations. Now he gave his boss the number of square feet of their actual house.

The wife said, "Well, it's very pretty."

Cora said without thinking, "It's got some problems. There's a piece of loose siding up near the roof that whistles on windy days. It's been like that for, what, four years? More? We can't find anyone willing to go up on an extension ladder and fix it."

Eliot shook his head, but there was no backtracking now. Because what kind of people pretended for even a second that they lived in a house they didn't live in? Cora had claimed the children. She had behaved like they were hers, brushing off a compliment the way she did when someone said something nice about Opal or Miles.

"What about a roofer?" Eliot's boss was saying. "A roofer would climb a ladder. Get a roofer out here, kid. Do you want me to take a look?"

This was a taste of what Eliot got at work. The gentle paternalism of a man who thought he knew, and almost certainly did know, more about any given topic than Eliot did. No one deserved to have his work dynamic laid out in front of his spouse like this. She could not imagine Lily in their home—or the home they were pretending was theirs?—speaking the way she spoke to her at work. Her terrible guilt at being promoted over Cora making every interaction strained and tremulous. Cora's faultless kindness somehow only adding to the tension.

"That would be helpful," said Eliot.

He allowed himself to be led out the back door. Why was his boss leading? Cora was left with the wife, but she was able to steer the conversation onto firmer ground.

"Do you have kids?" she asked, and the woman told her about Matthew and Brit, who'd be home from college next week. After five minutes, Eliot and his boss came back inside, stomping the snow off their feet.

"It's not that high up," the boss reported. "If the weather was better, I'd do it myself."

They left, making apologies. Cora and Eliot saw them out. Their car, a gray Lexus that was at once flashy and staid, pulled away and Eliot said, "Let's do drugs."

Rafe had come in at some point during their ruse. They went and found him, a giant man with a red beard in a chunky, multi-colored cardigan. He and Eliot embraced and he lifted Eliot six inches off the floor. She had never seen a relationship like this between a man and his dealer.

Rafe said, "You're Cora. We met a long time ago."

"Did we?" said Cora.

"Yeah. Once in Prospect Park at a concert I think? Then once at y'all's apartment? It had, like, a freestanding dishwasher?"

This jogged her memory. The dishwasher. They had a dishwasher that could be wheeled around the room. She could picture him standing next to it, taking up most of the kitchen, which was three feet wide with a single barred window. That had been their worst apartment.

"Oh yeah. I remember now," she said.

He said, "What was that thing? That dishwasher thing?"

The apartment listing had advertised a dishwasher without noting that it wasn't embedded in a countertop. With nowhere natural for it to go, it had to be moved around constantly. They'd experimented with keeping it in one place, but it blocked the kitchen door, or the bathroom door, or the oven, or the table. Its destiny was to roam. When Cora wanted to use it, she had to wheel it over to the sink and manually hook it up to the faucet.

"Cora loved that thing," said Eliot.

"It did the dishes," said Cora.

Rafe looked around. "I need a surface."

They went into the kitchen, where the caterers listened to reggaeton at low volume. Rafe had brought a box of prerolled joints in Christmas colors and a baggy of white powder. A high shelf held cookbooks and he took down *Nothing Fancy* and cut up three lines. Cora had not done coke in many years. It made her too chatty, too confidential. It gave her a shame hangover that lasted three days. Eliot did a line and Rafe did a line and Cora tried to demur but Eliot said, "You made me pretend this was our house."

Rafe said, "What?"

Cora said, "It was a misunderstanding."

Eliot said, "Why did you say that thing about the siding?"

"I was trying to help."

He handed her a rolled-up twenty and stood with his arms crossed until she said "Fine" and did a line. She rose and rubbed the residue on her gums.

"Good," said Eliot.

"Punitive drugs," she said.

But then it hit and seemed like the best idea in the world. She told Rafe she was sorry she hadn't recognized him at first, that maybe she was blocking out that part of her life. She'd been lost then and wasn't proud of it. Rafe told her don't worry about it, he had a forgettable face. They laughed: he had a septum piercing and a gold tooth in front and there were rubber bands in his beard, dividing it into a bunch of tiny ponytails.

They went back out with the air of conspiracy that always accompanied cocaine use. The room was full now and everyone was drinking. It was a house party! Cora felt the swirl of it, a productive swirl. She felt it moving like a model of the solar system. Everything hanging together, orbiting, rotating. Evidence of a celestial design. People laughed and talked. They wore suits or cocktail dresses. Sam's eyes followed her wherever she went.

"Cor, come here," he said.

He had never called her Cor before. She went over to him. He'd taken off his tie and tucked his hair behind his ears. He had cut it shorter, though still not short. He stood with his siblings near the stairs. Four brothers and a sister who all looked alike. The same square jaw replicated six times as with a rubber stamp. One of them had a cigarette tucked behind his ear. The effect was overwhelming, like they were about to jump her, hustle her into a van, take her to a secret compound where there'd be even more people who looked like them. Sam introduced them one by one.

Cora asked his sister Jeanine what Sam had been like as a kid. Jeanine said he was funny and stupid. He was a middle child, deep in the middle, which made him chase attention. He took unnecessary risks and got hurt a lot.

Cora said, "Like by girls? By relationships?"

"No. He'd fall down and get hurt. He got bounced off a trampoline. He skied into a tree. That kind of thing. Dumb brother stuff."

"I have one too," said Cora, and she thought distantly of Drew.

What was he doing at that moment? It was three hours earlier where he was and forty degrees warmer. Drew was probably teaching tennis or walking his dog. Did he still have a dog? She hadn't gotten an update on Drew's dog in a while. What was the dog's name . . . it was a Jack Russell terrier . . . she searched for it . . . Brandi. She realized she was saying this out loud.

Sam's arm hung next to her leg and he ran his knuckle against her bare skin.

"What are your parents like?" she said to Jeanine.

Jeanine told her about being from a big Irish-Catholic family outside Boston. Cora was so locked in that it was like watching a film. She could see their outerwear, their haircuts. She could see their father raking leaves, their mother trying to round them up to go to mass. The boys' bedrooms would smell terrible. They'd have posters from *Sports Illustrated* on their walls. Basketball players, women in bikinis. Then Jules materialized next to her whispering in her ear that Klaus had shown up with Freda and Jonathan.

"*The* Freda?" said Cora, and Jules shushed her.

"I told him not to bring them. He asked and I was explicit. They're right behind you. But don't look. Okay, now look."

Cora turned slowly. They were talking to Eliot, who'd taken off his suit jacket. Freda had blunt bangs and wide-set eyes. She wore a short, gold-sequined dress. She was tall, even taller than Cora. Next to her, Jonathan had dressed for a different occasion, in a leather vest with no shirt under it. Seeing his abs was a minor excitement, like seeing a celebrity running errands in New York.

"Why did they come?" said Cora.

"I have no idea. Oh god, they saw us," said Jules. "Turn away. Turn away."

But now they had to go over. Freda held an unlit cigar and used it to beckon them. She was statuesque, the kind of pretty that was almost ugly, natural with a cigar, which in Cora's hand would have looked like a prop. Though they'd never met her before, she greeted them with familiarity, kissing them on each cheek. Did she wear men's cologne? It smelled like it. Instantly, Cora understood the power she had over Klaus, over anyone.

Jules said, "You're not going to smoke that in here, are you?"

Freda laughed. "Oh no. I know how you people are."

The story of her departure was famous. How she'd left Klaus in the middle of the night. How she'd taken a single suitcase and they didn't hear from her for a week. The kids had been four and seven. When she'd finally called, she'd told him that she wasn't coming back. After that, he hadn't heard from her again for six months. She disappeared and resurfaced. She called often, usually on drugs, but confined her visits to once or twice a year. When he begged her to be around more for her kids, she said no. Family life was not the antidote.

Now she and Jonathan were in from Banff, where Jonathan had been photographing pasta.

"Canadian pasta?" said Cora.

"Not specifically Canadian," said Jonathan. "It was normal pasta. Spaghetti. The shoot just happened to be in Banff."

"Right, but why Banff?"

"That's where the shoot was," Jonathan repeated.

In person, he was smaller than Cora had imagined. The leather vest looked custom, with a stallion rearing on each lapel. A necklace hung down to his navel holding a small vial of green liquid.

Freda said, "Jonathan's work takes us all over the world. We're just here through the new year to see the kids."

Jonathan scratched his chest and looked around the room. Cora searched for something else to ask about food photography. What was there to know? It was taking pictures of food.

"I heard they use glue instead of cereal milk."

He said, "What?"

"When you're shooting breakfast cereal. Don't you use glue

instead of milk? Because it's more milklike than milk when it's photographed? Like some foods don't look like what they are in a photo for some reason?"

"No," he said. "Well, sometimes, yes. Glue is viscous. It doesn't pour right. So no for a commercial. But yes, in a still photograph."

She said, "Ah. Right."

The hors d'oeuvres had come out by then. This was a good excuse to walk away and check on them. Everyone ate. Much was made about the charcuterie being not just deluxe but ultra-deluxe. People wiped their mouths with napkins that said Eliot or Sam. Lingering near the bar, she saw Anita and Brandt. Anita was pregnant, which was curious. They saw her noticing and explained that Brandt had had his vasectomy reversed.

"We figured it's our last chance, you know?" said Anita.

Brandt said, "No regrets. They just hook you back up."

Cora said, "Congrats."

They disconnected and reconnected the man's cock from his balls whenever it suited them. Brandt appeared to love it.

"Is Frances so excited?" said Cora.

Anita said, "Oh it's a horror show. Imagine being eleven years old and black and your parents are suddenly having a white baby."

What could you ever say to Anita besides that sounds hard? It was like she sought out difficult scenarios to test herself. The transracial adoption was not enough. She now had to add a late-in-life biological baby. What advice could you give her besides Godspeed and I hope you don't fuck them up too badly?

"I'm sure it'll be fine in the end," said Cora.

Then she heard herself asking why she'd never been invited

to join the book club. This startled her. She'd never consciously envied the book club or wondered why she wasn't in it. But actually, come to think of it, why wasn't she after all these years? She fit the profile. She liked to read and was friendly with the other members and what else was required? Shouldn't that be it?

"We haven't *not* invited you," said Anita. "Not pointedly."

"But you haven't invited me."

Anita looked to Brandt and Brandt shoved a piece of salami in his mouth.

"We didn't know you were interested," said Anita. "You can join."

"I mean, consult your fellow members. Do you have to vote or something?"

"We don't vote. We just decide. Jules and I decide. I'm sure it's fine."

Later when she was sober, Cora would regret this conversation. How adamantly she'd insisted they hold a vote. She'd recall demanding unanimous approval, or at least a three-fourths majority, and feel sick with embarrassment. She was joking, but they didn't seem to sense this. Anita and Brandt eventually made an excuse to slip away. The sitter, they said vaguely and disappeared across the room. After that, she'd decided it might be a good idea to get some air.

Eliot's suit jacket hung in the hall, and she put it on and went out back. The weather had cleared and the moon was sharply wrought against the night. Jules smoked, leaning against the railing. She greeted Cora and immediately fell into a snowbank. Eliot's colleague Marcus had to haul her out and hoist her back onto her feet.

"Oops," said Jules.

The back of her dress was soaked a darker shade of blue and she'd lost her cigarette. Marcus was a handsome black guy in a well-tailored suit, an editor like Eliot. You wouldn't want to fall into a snowbank in front of him: one of the books he'd edited had recently won a Pulitzer.

Marcus said, "You're shivering like the little matchstick girl."

Jules said, "The irony of that story was she sold matches but froze to death! Get it?"

"Yeah, it's well known," said Marcus.

Jules clung to Cora's arm. "He didn't come."

"Who didn't?" said Marcus.

"Our dog walker," said Jules.

"You knew he wasn't going to," said Cora. "You told me he wasn't."

"Why should that be a big deal?" said Marcus. "Your dog walker not coming?"

"He's deeply important to me. He brought my dog back to life after a long period of feeling dead."

"How do you know the dog felt dead?" said Marcus.

"It was acting like it felt that way."

"Like it was depressed?"

"Maybe," said Jules.

"What did the dog walker do to fix that?"

"He made the dog remember what was good about being alive."

"Like by motivating it to run around outside?"

It was almost impressive that a man who had edited a Pulitzer-winning novel could not pick up on subtext. Either that or he was teasing Jules.

"Sort of."

"Did you take it to the vet?"

Jules was losing the thread. "No . . ."

"Where's the dog now?"

"What dog?"

Marcus looked at Cora for help.

"I think we should get you some water," Cora said.

She led Jules into the mudroom off the kitchen and sat her on the bench where the kids took their shoes off. Sports equipment had been shoved underneath, tennis racquets and life jackets and soccer cleats. Back in the kitchen she poured a glass of water and grabbed a handful of crackers.

"You probably don't want to be too confessional with Eliot's coworkers," Cora said, handing them to Jules.

"I know."

Cora closed the door, muffling the sound of the party. This felt like a metaphor. All of life was a party overheard from the next room. All of life of was a party overheard from the next room while stuck talking to a drunk person. All of life was a party overheard from the next room while stuck talking to a drunk person who was also crying.

"Oh no, don't cry," she said.

"It's just I thought he'd come anyway."

"It's your husband's birthday. He'd be nuts to come. Has Sam ever met him?"

"No."

"Does he know he exists?"

"I don't think so."

"How would you have explained his presence?"

"Maybe as my colleague. It's almost true. It's true in the sense that people use that word to mean all people who share their profession. All lawyers." She made a sweeping gesture. "My colleagues. He's out with his girlfriend, probably. Guess how old she is."

"Twenty-four."

"Twenty-five."

"Twenty-four would be worse."

"It's the same. Twenty-five-year-olds are effectively twenty-four."

There was nothing to do about men liking younger women. It could not be eradicated through feminism. Acceptance was also impossible. The implication that women were disposable after a certain age could not be rationally integrated. Everyone was aging and a lot of people were frightened by that, and returned to the fountain, drank greedily, made fools of themselves. It would have been grotesque if it was not so common.

"So, he's shallow," said Cora.

"No, he's not."

"I'm trying to say what you want me to say."

"Say he's a dick," said Jules.

"He's a dick."

Jules said again, "No, he's not."

Cora knew almost nothing about the guy except his profession, but she knew he was not special. One day Jules would understand this. His failings would snap into focus. For one thing, he'd initiated a relationship by sending her a bunch of sexy DMs on Instagram. The day was coming when this fact alone would make Jules want to shrink down to the size of a spider and crawl into the wall.

"It's something I did," said Jules. "I'm too quick to anger. I push people away. I'm a bitch."

Who had not experienced this? Self-blame over the dissolution of a tepid and doomed relationship? If something went wrong with the object of romantic yearning, this was what the mind did. Scrounged around for personal shortcomings and found lots. Cora had experienced it herself many times (she was too much of a pushover, she wasn't sexy enough, and on and on) and it made her feel for Jules.

"It's not that you're a bitch," said Cora.

"What is it then?"

"It's the way things happen sometimes. They fizzle. They end."

"No, they don't."

There was no telling her anything. That affection ebbed and flowed for no reason was not a daring insight. Anyone who'd been alive for a while was acquainted with the mystery of interpersonal relationships. The winds blew and the particles shifted and someone who had previously liked you didn't anymore. Yet if you were in love, you could not see it. Cora had a sudden impulse to get her out of there.

"Let's leave," said Cora.

Jules said, "What?"

"Let's go. Let's go get a burger or something. Just you and me. Or take a walk. We can talk some more. I don't know."

"I live here," said Jules.

Her face was a smear. She wiped it with the back of her hand. She rose and prepared to go back out. She wanted to know, suddenly, what they were doing in the mudroom. She kicked a stray sneaker farther under the bench.

"I think you should wait another minute," said Cora.

But Jules was already gone. Out in the living room, no one

was dancing. It had gotten stifling hot, and Cora went around opening windows. People moved toward them gulping air and fanning themselves.

Jules had climbed up on a chair. "Everyone needs to dance now."

She clarified that you couldn't dance with your own spouse. The penalty was death. She climbed down again. The band struck up something Sinatraesque or maybe it was Sinatra. Cora thought she'd walk outside again for this part, the part where they were embraced by random men from the community. But then Richard Hood seized her, put his hand on her hip, her hand on his shoulder. He danced well, as louche men tended to.

"You've been avoiding me," he said.

He'd manufactured a scenario in which she was still mad at him for flashing her. This was bewildering, but funny. She had not forgotten it—she thought about it every time she saw him—but she wasn't mad. She hadn't even been particularly menaced in the moment. You couldn't rape someone at a distance of fifty yards.

"I have not," she said.

"So you liked what you saw?"

She looked around the room for help. Eliot danced with Isabelle. Rafe danced with Anita. How had that happened? She told Richard the truth, which was that she hadn't felt anything about what she'd seen, and she hadn't seen much. She knew this sounded cruel, though he laughed and pretended she was joking. Finally, the song ended and it was time to dance with a new man. Why had Jules insisted on this round robin of being grabbed?

Someone tapped her on the shoulder and she turned to see it was Sam. She discovered suddenly that she liked the idea of the dancing. He slipped her gold disk into her hand. "It was under the dresser. I'll have it fixed for you if you want."

"Thanks."

She put it in her pocket, this token of her early marriage. It seemed unlikely that he'd get it fixed, but it was a chivalrous offer.

Sam said, "I don't know how to dance. You get to adulthood and you're sometimes expected to do it, but the age of learning is long past. Look at Eliot. How did he learn?"

Eliot was showing off for Jules, doing things like dipping and spinning her. His parents had gotten him lessons as a kid, some idea his mother had about how a young man should be. Jules laughed, less bedraggled than before. The back of her dress had dried. Cora thought of her in her underwear, the frankness of her scar. She pictured Eliot on the bed, where she had been sitting. She pictured him adjusting Jules's bra strap, Jules shivering. Then she tired of imagining people in different configurations.

"You're doing fine," she said to Sam.

He was doing badly, actually. He was rigid where he should have been supple. He lifted his feet up and put them down in the same place. The two of them were barely moving. How did he dance in the other world? she wondered. Naturally, the answer was better. He pulled her closer and she felt his belt buckle slide against the fabric of her dress.

"I want to be alone with you," he said.

This was new. As long as they'd known each other, he'd never been direct. She'd been direct and he'd laughed at her, made excuses, hid what he felt. But he seemed to have changed his mind, thrown out his old ideas about who he was and what was permissible. Or maybe he was just drunk.

"How?"

They stood still now. His pulse beat in his neck. She had changed too; her feelings had become tamer. You could not sustain the same level of heat over so many years. Occasionally, she was hit with a surge of desire for him, but she had become used to not acting on it.

"I don't know."

It would recur until they did something about it or one of them left town. This was the thought she had as the song ended. He squeezed her hip and let go, then left the room without looking at her again. She sat on the couch with Isabelle, who fanned herself with a Christmas card from someone named Uncle Sid. They shared a beer from a six-pack she'd brought.

Isabelle said, "Are you okay? You seem distracted."

She asked if the guy Cora had been dancing with was the guy they'd seen on the street years ago.

"The one who really wanted to be your friend? Whatever happened with that?"

Cora told her that nothing had happened. They had become close, their two families. Through the sliding glass door, they could see Sam on the deck alone, staring out at the yard. His shirt had come untucked in back. Isabelle looked at her searchingly but said nothing else, and Cora changed the subject.

"How's Sheryl?"

Sheryl was Isabelle's fiancée. Now that polyamory had gone mainstream, Isabelle no longer wanted any part of it. There had been too many articles about middle-class women being pressured by their husbands to open up the marriage. It made the lifestyle seem dowdy and embarrassing. She'd been with the same woman for several years. Cora was happy for her but could not help but gloat a little. After all the boyfriends and girlfriends, the revolutionary ideas about love and sex, Isabelle was getting plain old married to one person.

"We're looking at country houses," said Isabelle.

"You know, I don't know about you and monogamy," said Cora. "I'm not sure you can handle it."

There was a small commotion as Jules brought out the cake with tall candles that sparked. Someone lowered the lights and they sang "Happy Birthday" to two grown men. Cora got up and stood next to Eliot, who looked happy. He kissed her with a mouthful of white cake, like at the wedding they did not have.

Around midnight, Sam's younger brother Colin knocked over the Christmas tree demonstrating a dance he'd seen on the internet. It fell in slow motion. The angel at the top smashed, sending shards of porcelain to the corners of the room. It was captured on video by Sam's sister, Jeanine. A group effort to right it commenced. It had knocked a print off the wall on the way down and spilled water on the floor. With this distraction under way, Sam beckoned Cora upstairs.

The guest bedroom was also the coatroom. Sam pulled her in after him and closed the door. They said nothing and left the light off. A desk to one side held a pristine iMac, and when Sam brushed past, it sprang to life with the pink and purple factory preset background.

"Damn it," he said and fumbled to turn off the screen.

After many years of her imagining an upstairs rendezvous, it was finally happening. She could only see him in silhouette. From downstairs came laughing and shouting, the sound of more breaking glass. Outside the windows: the finely etched night.

"Do you want to sit?" he said.

They had met in early parenthood and their older children were now preteens. In that time, restaurants had opened and closed. The overpriced children's clothing store had been turned into a florist's shop, then back into an overpriced children's clothing store. Lines had appeared around her eyes and on either side of her mouth. Time softened you, but it also made things more urgent. They would really and truly die one day, Eliot had said. Cora and Sam sat on the bed. The years pressed down.

Eight

A switch occurred. The two vectors still existed, but they changed places. In the one you might call reality, she was now having an affair with Sam. In the other, technically fictional, she was a happily married woman, had never strayed, had never betrayed the vows she'd made to a justice of the peace on a Friday morning in October in the presence of her parents and Eliot's parents and Isabelle and Drew.

So she ate with Eliot in a nice restaurant while she and Sam whispered on the phone. He tore the dress off her body as she picked Eliot up from the train station. She and Sam showered together, which became sex, and Eliot wondered aloud if he should resubscribe to *The New York Times* or let it lapse because it had become a little expensive, hadn't it?

She was still caught between worlds, that hadn't changed. But now the affair had become real and her stable life with her family where nothing ever happened had become imaginary.

After the party, she'd sent Sam a nude, tasteful, not too porny. He wrote back, *You look good.* He did not send a dick pic, which was curious. She tried not to read anything into it. Then nothing for a while. They saw each other at third-grade pickup and acted normally.

"Fun party the other night," he said.

She stomped her feet to keep warm. "A good one."

"Thanks for throwing it."

"You're welcome. Did Jules have fun?"

"I think she did. Did Eliot?"

"Definitely."

"All those glasses broke."

They'd broken half the glasses the caterers had brought. Were they extra thin? Was there something particularly slippery about them? Maybe the caterers had broken themselves. There had been that early wave before the party when one of them dropped a pallet and it hadn't stopped. She thought of the way Jules looked cleaning up glass in the shortest possible peacock blue dress. It didn't make sense for Sam to cheat on her. She beat Cora by every metric.

"Do we need to talk about what happened?" she said.

"Probably a good idea."

The kids had been released and were streaming out of the building, jumping in snow piles, dropping their water bottles and art projects and picking them back up. It was the last day before winter break. There was nothing casual about the way Cora felt, but she had to act casual.

"Drink soon?" she said.

They planned to meet up in the next few days. She doubted they'd do it, she was sure he'd flake, but Friday came and he texted her.

And so, back to the bar with too much information posted everywhere. The bitters were handcrafted; the gin was made in town. Any animal you consumed had been raised no more than fifty miles away. Sam did his trick with the toothpick, but by now he was practiced. He flipped it automatically, as he told her what was going on between them was wrong for nine different reasons.

"Of course it's wrong," she said.

"I was drunk."

"I was, too."

They were both drunk. They were both stoned. It was the drugs. It was the moment. It was a lapse after many years of resisting. They were sorry. Jules and Eliot would get hurt if they found out. Sam and Cora would get hurt. The kids would get hurt.

"You know what?" she said. "Can we skip this part actually?"

The hand-wringing phase had never been her favorite. The endless discussion of boundaries, the promises to stay away. They had done this before and it never stuck.

"Skip it?" he said.

"It's tedious, don't you think?"

Did they really have to list all the reasons it was wrong? Was it not obvious? Was this not a common bourgeois scenario? Had they not already talked out the ripple effects on every person in their lives? Couldn't they do an abbreviated version, find a shorthand, say "it's bad but" and move on to the sex?

"I don't know that we're going to have sex," he said.

"See? You're doing it. It's boring. I liked the other night. Did you like it or not?"

"I liked it."

"Did it make you feel good?"

"It made me feel good. That's not the issue."

It had lasted maybe ten minutes. They'd sat on the bed, which was stacked with coats. He worked her underwear off with one hand while the other tried and failed to unzip her dress. She was instantly and easily wet, which he discovered by touching her with his hand. He'd paused and there was a moment where she could have stopped him, remembered her family, remembered her reservations, their mutual reservations, but she hadn't. She'd nodded and guided him in and he had closed his eyes. When he'd come, he'd made a sound, a kind of "ah," into her neck.

Then the music resumed downstairs, signaling that Christmas tree cleanup was complete. They'd pulled themselves together and Sam went out first. Cora waited, ducking into the hall bathroom to pee and refresh her lipstick. When she got back downstairs, Sam didn't look at her, and she didn't look at him. She found Eliot, who was smoking a red joint and a green joint at the same time and recounting office gossip to Marcus. She sat on his lap and he idly stroked her back.

"Do you want to do that again, or not?" Cora said to Sam.

"I haven't decided."

She drank her local gin. Just because something was produced nearby didn't make it good. She told Sam he had learned to live on the charge he got from talking about things and never doing them. A proximal charge. He got the thrill and his righteousness, too. He got to have the fun of walking up to the line, and feeling martyred for never crossing it. He had done this for years, at bars and dinner parties, in the ocean and in ponds. All the way back to the baby group and the disapproving gaze of Broccoli Mom.

"You don't think we crossed a line?" said Sam.

"This time, yeah."

"I don't do all that."

"Yes, you do. It's the main thing you do."

"Huh," he said.

He went to the bathroom and came back. "Okay fine, let's skip it."

They left the bar and walked through town. They sat on a bench overlooking the falls without speaking. A moment of tension stretched between them—someone would have to act first. With the falls frozen it was supremely quiet. Finally, he reached for her. He took his glove off and pulled her in gently by the neck. They kissed for as long as they could stand it. He put his hands inside her jacket and found her warm skin. Everything was hyperreal: his mouth, the freezing air, the waterfall, lit up blue with a floodlight as it was every night.

"We have to go inside," she said finally.

He said, "We don't."

In the other time line she was in bed with Eliot and they were rewatching a movie they'd seen many times before. He made popcorn and brought it to her in a bowl she'd bought when they first moved in together. Miles came in complaining of a nightmare and they let him snuggle between them and watch until the content became too adult. Then Cora carried him back to bed, tucked him in the way he wouldn't permit anymore, and sat with him until he fell asleep.

When Cora went home, she'd have some version of this. Eliot would be in bed reading. She could see if he wanted to turn on a movie. He would probably say yes. It was right there. It was not out of reach. If she wanted it, and could have it, why didn't she do it? But when she tried it that night—walked home, got into bed with Eliot, made the popcorn, and so on—she found it did nothing for her.

* * *

That spring, she and Sam met at the big, anonymous hotel one town away that serviced business travelers. The first time they went, they contrived to stay overnight by telling their spouses they had work events in the city. It would not make sense to come home late only to turn around and take the train back in the morning. When the affair had been imaginary, Eliot had not asked many follow-up questions. Encounters proceeded smoothly, from one to the next. In reality, he had many concerns.

"What event?" he said.

"It's an awards ceremony. They do it every year."

They were tidying up the living room, or Cora was tidying. Eliot was holding his vape, shifting from foot to foot, waiting to be dismissed so he could go outside and smoke. Cora scooped Lego pieces into a bin that was itself shaped like a Lego.

"Why haven't you gone in the past?" he said.

"They need me there this year. I'm presenting an award."

The lying made her queasy but she was good at it. The being good at it made her doubly queasy. Every time she lied to him, she imagined something supernatural happening. Like she'd open her mouth and crickets would start spilling out. Shiny and black, their legs would get caught in her teeth. They'd hop around the room, broadcasting her duplicity. But what actually happened was worse: he simply believed her.

"You are?" he said. "Why you? To whom?"

He was amused, which annoyed Cora. Why shouldn't she present an award? Was she not a person with a job? The annoyance helped with the spilling-out-crickets feeling.

"There's a girl in my department. A junior employee named Morgan. She reports to me. They're recognizing her for . . . it's not interesting. But anyway, I have to make a speech."

"Who's Morgan? You haven't mentioned Morgan before."

"Have I not?"

"I don't think so. Lily, yes. But Morgan?"

"She's from Philly? She went to UPenn? She's gluten free?"

The crickets were all over the room now, rubbing their wings together. They had filled up the Lego bin and she took a step back from it.

"Morgan," he said. "I don't think so."

"Well anyway, she exists. She . . . has a dog."

"So, you'll stay over, where?" said Eliot.

"Someplace close to the office. Midtown Ramada or somewhere. A Hilton. They're letting me expense it."

"I thought they were hardasses about that stuff."

"They usually are. I don't know why they're being cool about this one. I guess they want me there. The hotel was their idea. Maybe to convince me to do it."

"But you haven't booked yet?"

He was inexhaustible. She had planned on telling one lie, but he was making her tell forty. It was not even distrust, but a passion for logistics. Where would she stay and how much would it cost? Which train would she take in? Would she buy a paper ticket on the platform or use the app? And what time was the ceremony? And would there be food? Passed appetizers or a buffet? Which train would she take home the next day? Would she try to fit in lunch with Isabelle? If so, where would they go?

"What does Opal have that afternoon?" said Eliot.

"I think it's play tryouts."

"What does she need for that? Anything in particular? I mean besides her natural charisma and our undying support?"

On and on it went. She put the lid on the Lego bin and stowed it in the cabinet. Finally, they were through with it. The room was restored to order and Eliot had run out of questions.

"Well, all that sounds horrible."

"Do you want to come with me?"

She looked away from him as she said it, out the front windows at their street. Surely this should have tipped him off, the fact that she would not meet his eye. But no, he did not seem to notice. He looked out the window too, eager to be done with the conversation and get on with his evening.

"God no," he said. "But you have fun."

The day came and she drove to the big anonymous hotel. She beat Sam there and sat in her car listening to classical radio. He was late and she wondered if he'd lost his nerve. Possibly, he'd stand her up. Part of her even wanted him to. Then she could leave, maybe pick up takeout or a bottle of wine on the way home. She'd feel lighter, she was sure of it. It would become one of life's close scrapes, like the time she stepped in front of a cab without thinking and Eliot yanked her back. Like the time Opal got out of the apartment at one year old and, by some miracle, did not fall down the stairs.

But finally he pulled in next to her. She'd begged him to arrive first and text her the room number, or let her do the reverse. This was always how she'd imagined it. But he'd wanted to walk in with her. He thought that one of them being seen at a sex hotel was no different than both of them being seen at a sex hotel.

"It's not a sex hotel," Cora had told him.

"Right. Just a hotel we're going to for sex."

Sam was wrong that getting caught alone would be the same as getting caught together. Caught alone, you could make up a lie. You could make up an errand or pretend to be using the swimming pool. Caught together, what could you say? But each logistical exchange chipped away at the affair's mystique. She'd wanted to end the conversation, all conversations about planning, before it began to seem like a chore.

"Fine," she conceded. "It doesn't really matter."

Now he got out, took his weekender from his trunk. He fumbled for his keys, locked the car, unlocked it again to retrieve his toothpicks and a baseball cap. What was the baseball cap for? These were details she didn't need. Finally, he knocked on her window.

"Got all your shit?" she said.

He didn't laugh. She saw he was nervous, maybe anguished. She would go easy on him. She grabbed her own bag and they started across the parking lot. Though there was a man-made lake, it was lifeless. It had a multicolored sheen on the surface from chemicals. Cans and bottles were trapped in the scraggly grass. A trash can overflowed with coffee cups.

"Where are the birds?" she said.

"What birds?"

"Great blue herons . . . American kestrels . . . house sparrows?"

He looked at her blankly.

"Forget it."

They went inside and got a room. It came time to pay and he hesitated. He couldn't put down his credit card. The charge would appear on his statement. Jules would see it as early as today if she happened to open their online banking. They could be caught fifteen seconds after they checked in. The receptionist averted her eyes for this conversation, and Cora wanted to apologize to her.

"You don't have a credit card of your own?" said Cora.

"No."

So their accounts were still fully linked. Fully linked aside from Jules's secret card, which he still didn't seem to know about. Jules had used it often over the years to pay for drinks she and Cora had together. She had used it, Cora assumed, for her own affair. All those bar tabs in Manhattan. Fifty dollars here, seventy-five there. Why did she know this if Sam did not?

"She sees every dollar I spend," he explained. "It's part of my transparency with her. Former transparency."

That the transparency didn't work both ways hadn't seemed to occur to him. The automatic doors slid open and a man with a rolling suitcase queued up behind them.

"I'll get it," she said.

She handed her card over and they got in the elevator. He reached for her, held her to him, but a mother and small child got on too, wearing swimsuits and flip-flops, and they pulled apart again. The woman asked Cora if the pool and sauna were on the second floor and Cora took a step forward and studied the directory with her, determining that they were.

They reached their own floor and had trouble with the key card. The light kept turning red and Sam breathed heavily trying to get it to work. For a moment, it seemed like he'd have to return to the lobby for a new card.

"These fucking things," he said.

It opened at last, and the room was mostly as Cora had imagined it, but some of the details were off. There wasn't a bathtub, but there was a shower with a rainfall showerhead. She looked for the laminated list of TV channels and instead found a leatherette binder with a complete history of the area dating back to the Revolutionary War. The hotel didn't have room service. The only food they sold came from a kiosk in the lobby where you could get bags of chips, gum, beer, cookies, and frozen pizza.

Sam put his bag down. Cora could think of nothing to say to him and was briefly transported back to her first time with her high school boyfriend, a gentle lacrosse player named George. George's parents had gone out of town, leaving him alone in the house. Cora and George had known it was happening weeks in advance, known what they would do, and the anticipation made it heavy. When the day came, they could not shake the formality of the occasion. It made them talk in careful sentences. It made them afraid to touch each other. The house was a beautiful yellow colonial, spotlessly clean and quiet, with every food item you could imagine. They had watched *Ocean's Eleven* on his parents' big TV, putting off the sex for as long as possible. When they'd finally gone through with it, it had been out of loyalty to the premise. Cora didn't remember much else about it, except that it had done its job, which was to be over.

"Come here," said Sam.

She crossed the room and let him unbutton her dress. To anticipate something for so long and then get it. She found herself almost overcome. His warmth and heft. A strand of his hair in her mouth. The feeling of his hands on both sides of her face, then on her back. He took his shirt off, and she could see that his body had aged, though he was still muscular through his arms and chest.

She touched the tattoo, at last she touched it. Underneath, his heart hammered away. She sat on the bed and he stood in front of her and she unbuckled his belt with excruciating slowness. He wore boxer briefs and she pulled them down and pressed her face against the tangle of his pubic hair and breathed in.

He said, "Fuck."

They lay down and he was soft with her, then he was less soft, then he was not soft at all. She got on top and he had a hand on her hip and his eyes closed. She could tell he was trying not to come, trying to wait for her. She couldn't see the moment as transgressive. It was too full of uncomplicated enjoyment. When she came, she went to a place of buzzing static that was nowhere. Sam's face intercut with the backs of her eyelids. He came immediately after her, holding both of her hips, his mouth open slightly, the tip of his tongue on his lower lip.

When it was over, they lay side by side. The comforter had been kicked to the ground. The sun set over a building in the distance, which she tried not to notice was a Walmart. Now she did feel the tingling of guilt and regret. She thought of her family. They'd be eating spaghetti and listening to Opal talk about play tryouts. Eliot would suggest a round of Uno before bed. He'd send Miles up for a bath first, and Miles would protest before giving in and going upstairs.

"How was that?" said Sam.

She forced herself to stop picturing them. She told him it was good. His hair was damp with sweat and she pushed it back from his brow. They'd wanted it for a long time and that wanting had been right. Didn't this prove it?

"It does," he said and reached for her again.

Later, they ate chips from the kiosk in the lobby. They flipped through TV channels without finding anything to watch. Cora stayed up late and read the complete history of the area dating back to the Revolutionary War. Sam fell asleep and snored like the forty-year-old husband he was.

On the other side, Cora and Eliot booked an anniversary cruise on the *MS Paul Gauguin.* It took them southwest to the clear green waters of French Polynesia. Their stateroom had botanical wallpaper and a balcony. The view of endless water did not invite panic but instead fostered tranquillity. They made friends on board, an older couple. Worldly, rich. The woman wore fine gold jewelry. The man, linen suits. They drank cocktails together in the piano bar. We have kids your age, they said. They're all caught up in their lives.

What does that mean? said Cora.

It means they have their heads up their asses, said the man.

Ashore in Tahiti, Cora went topless on a white-sand beach. A palm tree craned out over the water at forty-five degrees. Eliot lay next to her in sunglasses. When they got hot, they slipped into the water. When they got restless, they wound their way up the side streets of Papeete, looking for souvenirs for the kids. For Opal, a bracelet of cultured pearls. For Miles, a carved wooden puzzle that snapped together neatly. They stopped for rum punch at a place with a straw roof and Eliot asked her if they should have another baby.

What? said Cora.

It was their last chance, he said, pretty much. Cora was about to be thirty-nine. Soon it would become too complicated, too expensive, too grueling and heartbreaking.

Remember how nice they are? Eliot said.

Cora remembered. Their pleasing heft. The soft cubes of their feet. The way they fell asleep on your shoulder with their mouths smushed to one side. Their unguarded love. The way they held out their arms to indicate they wanted to be picked up. The shared project of them. How they bound you together by making you suffer acutely. You suffered as a unit and felt yourselves erased. It was good for a person to be erased once in a while.

Remember Miles? said Eliot. He was so beautiful. Remember how he wouldn't sleep in his bassinet and you had to walk him?

They couldn't have another baby, though. They had a challenging eleven-year-old and a currently easy eight-year-old. At any moment, he could turn difficult, too.

It would be irresponsible, said Cora. We don't have enough money for three. We barely have enough money for two. We can't start over from scratch.

It would definitely be irresponsible, said Eliot. That's what makes it a good idea. Remember that was why we did it the first time?

But Cora couldn't do it. It was too exhausting. She didn't have the same energy she'd had twelve years ago. She didn't know if she had more to give.

I want a baby with you, said Eliot.

It was still an erotic thing to hear.

Back on the boat that night they met the older couple in the lounge and the woman said, Have another baby. What's the harm?

What about my body? said Cora.

Her body couldn't do a third. She was older now and there'd been changes after her second pregnancy that she didn't love. Her breasts were different. Smaller. She'd lost the weight too fast and her stomach skin had gotten loose for a minute there. What would happen next time?

Your body is going to a grave, said the woman. To a landfill. It's a single-use item. You might as well wreck it.

What about my autonomy?

The woman laughed and waved this off.

It doesn't exist, she said. You gave it away already. Forget about it. It's gone.

The woman ordered them whiskeys. They sat at the window regarding the night. The ship rocked like a giant cradle. The woman had gray-blond hair, pulled back into an elegant twist. She looked like Cora's mother.

She said, Listen to me, you'll never be free. Relinquish hope of freedom.

Do you not feel free? said Cora.

I'm rich. That gets you close.

But not all the way.

If you agree to share your life with someone, you're never free again. No one is allowed to say it, but it's true. Maybe you'll be free after he dies. That I don't know yet. Give me your email and I'll tell you in a couple of years. There are rewards, you know this. There's love. There's friendship. There are your children. Intermittently, there's sex. But the freedom goes away.

The room had cleared out. Their husbands laughed quietly with the bartender. The piano player, a handsome man in early middle age, had a sadness in his eyes that spoke of failure on the mainland. He played standards, slowed down, classed up. It was time to turn in.

Don't despair, said the woman. She motioned all around them. It's an adventure on the high seas.

Cora and Eliot made their way back to their stateroom down wood-paneled halls. She slept with him curled around her, and in the morning, they woke to watch the sunrise from the deck: A band of pink rose over the gray chop. Eliot reached out to take her hand.

Meanwhile, Cora had to work. She had to keep working. Even if you were having an affair you had to open emails. You could be living out your fantasy but you still had to chat in the elevator with Terry from accounting. You had to ask her how it had gone with her cat's cancer surgery. You had to recall the cat's name, Pepper, and say, "Hope Pepper feels better." Later, at your desk, you had to respond to the missive "I'll ping you tomorrow," from the former coworker who had become your boss.

Cora's mother came to visit. It was Eliot's racquetball night. She said, "You seem distracted. Is something going on?"

The kids painted with watercolors at the kitchen table. Cora kept getting up to check her phone in the other room. She and Sam were trying to figure out when to meet next. It turned out it was not so easy to make a standing date. Thursday was the worst day of the week—Opal had play practice and soccer back-to-back—but no other day seemed to work either. The kids had activities. They had activities on activities on activities.

"I'm fine," said Cora. "I have a lot going on at work."

She looked at her phone. *How about Friday?* wrote Sam.

It would have to be quick, she wrote. *Like an hour.*

Miles had karate that day. He was a yellow belt now, and proud of it. On the way home from karate, Cora always took him to pick up a pizza. He liked to be the one to pay and the one to carry it out of the shop and down the sidewalk. He took the responsibility seriously. The ritual was important to them.

"Can you put that thing down?" said her mother. "You're with your kids."

"It's work," said Cora.

"You guys." She meant people younger than she was. "All you do is look at your phones."

Cora made herself put it down. She made herself engage with her mother about her mother's patients and her mother's worries about Drew. She'd recently been out to La Jolla to see him. He only wanted to play tennis. All these years later, he was just a tennis bum.

"So what?" said Cora. "That's not enough? He's good at it."

"He lives in a one-bedroom apartment and doesn't have curtains. The sun comes up every morning and wakes him and instead of doing something about that, he puts a hat over his face. He has a designated hat he keeps on his bedside table for this purpose. How come he's not married? Where are his children?"

"Not everyone needs to have kids. He's fine. He's happy."

She didn't know this for sure. She hadn't talked to him in a while. Was Drew fine? He always seemed the same. He played tennis and grew hydroponic lettuce. He sold his lettuce at the farmers market. His romantic life was a mystery, which suggested either celibacy or a level of promiscuity he thought she and her mother would be unable to handle. But that was okay too; she didn't need to know. She preferred to think of him as a tennis and lettuce person, doing his thing out there, flourishing in the sun.

Cora heard her phone buzz in the other room.

"Do not get it," said her mother.

It was like the affair lived in her phone. Or her phone was an extension of the affair, an implement of it. Cora's mother wanted to know what was so important at work. Didn't her new supervisor have any boundaries? Then she got a text from work herself and put on her reading glasses to respond to it. Cora snuck back into the other room, to see that Sam had written that they would make it quick.

I'm excited, he wrote.

He sent a picture. He stood in his underwear, with the waistband pulled down. He gripped his dick matter-of-factly, like a walkie-talkie, like he was going to use it to call for help. She closed the picture quickly. Men never managed to strike the right tone in dick pics. They either made you want to laugh or made you want to cry.

Back in the kitchen her mom said to Miles, "Isn't that a gorgeous bumblebee?"

To Cora she said, "Time for a new job, maybe. If it's too demanding after-hours."

It wasn't demanding after-hours, but her mother was right that a change was overdue. Cora was ashamed to have stayed as long as she had. But she couldn't have made a move during the pandemic, could she? Not really. Not while watching the kids. And then the time had just passed, picking up speed as it went. Since Lily's promotion over her, it had become even more obvious that this job was a dead end.

"I'm trying," said Cora.

Her phone buzzed again and her mother shook her head.

In April, she had her own birthday. She and Sam both took the day off and met at the hotel. He brought her flowers and lacy black underwear. It was only their fourth or fifth time there, but they were no longer shy. She put on the lingerie, a complicated one-piece with elastic straps and garters. See-through in some places you'd expect and others you wouldn't. She looked good in it, she knew. Eliot had not bothered to buy her underwear in a long time.

Sam said, "Let me take a picture."

"You want that on your camera roll?"

He pointed out that it was no different than her sending a nude. All of it left an incriminating footprint. Jules never looked at his phone. She thought that was a violation. Besides, he had a special folder.

She climbed onto the bed and he posed her, moving her legs one way, then the other. Instructing her to let them fall open at the knee. Then he beckoned her over, unzipped his pants, and took a picture from above with his penis in her mouth while she looked up at him. He finished that way, in a final effort that gagged her. The gagging seemed to turn him on.

She realized afterward that the curtains were open the whole time.

"Oops," she said and moved to close them.

The sun shone outside. Spring was more itself when you were fucking someone new. The parking lot—even the parking lot—held an unreal beauty. The fine weather made her want to be in the world with him.

"Can we go somewhere?" she said.

"Do you have time?"

She'd cleared her schedule for the day. Eliot had volunteered to handle karate. He thought she'd treated herself to a spa day or a manicure, a day to do nothing.

"I have a couple hours," she said.

"It would have to be somewhere pretty obscure."

They ended up at an Italian restaurant, a cheesy place off the highway made to look like a Tuscan villa. It was far enough away from home that they wouldn't be seen. Jules would never go to a restaurant like that anyway; though Eliot might, Eliot didn't care. He liked places where they kept the free bread coming and stored chunky bottles of oil and vinegar in wire caddies on the ends of the tables.

They were keyed up, giddy to be anywhere together. They sat next to each other on the banquette instead of across. It was four p.m. Afterward, she'd go home and celebrate with her kids, open a box and see what they had bought her, what Eliot had arranged for them to buy her. It would be a book, or slippers, or, one year, an expensive water bottle. They would have made cards, written sincerely about what she meant to them. A cake too, supervised by Eliot. "Happy Birthday, Mom!" in Opal's cursive.

"Are we drinking?" asked Sam, and he summoned the waiter.

He came over in his long, starched apron. Cora was aware that he saw them as a couple, and this awareness made her unbearably nervous. Under the table, Sam touched her. He was working his way from her knee to the hem of her skirt.

She kept looking at the door, thinking Eliot or Jules might walk in. But no one walked in. Italian café music played, heavy on the accordion. The waiter brought them house salads with two cherry tomatoes each.

Because she had mentioned it to Anita, Cora had to join the book club. Anita had followed up with an apologetic text, *We'd love to have you as a member,* and provided the information. The first meeting Cora attended took place at Anita's house. They were discussing *The Portrait of a Lady*. The book club only read classics. The criteria for classics were that they were edifying in some way, challenging, and that the authors were dead. Cora had read the book in bed after having sex with Sam and he'd sat up on one elbow to look at the cover.

"You're reading Henry James at the sex hotel?"

Anita's house still looked like it was trying to be a farmhouse. If anything, more farm details had been added. There was a rooster made of cast iron hanging in the living room. Part of an old weathervane? Maybe selecting "farm" as a theme all those years ago had given Anita purpose. Now wherever she went she could look for farm décor. Vaguely, Cora envied this. It seemed like a more peaceful obsession than, for instance, being loved.

They sat around the living room coffee table on pillows. Jules was late. Anita had put out a spread. The wine that year was red, but the kind you chilled. Cora had dutifully brought a bottle, as had several of the other women. Liz was there, from the baby group. She had cut off her dreads, though she still wore colorful patchwork pants that were identifiably from the Tibetan store on Main Street.

"What happened to your hair?" Cora asked.

Liz told her she'd gotten rid of the dreads years ago, when she'd had to get a job.

"Outside of the arts sphere," she clarified.

It had been a tough adjustment at first, and she still missed them sometimes, but her head did feel lighter. She had normal brown hair now, shoulder length with blunt bangs. She swung it around to demonstrate.

"Bonnie likes it better this way," she said. "Remember Bonnie?"

Cora did. She remembered her as a large baby with no opinions. They began talking about *The Portrait of a Lady*. Anita moderated the discussion with one hand on her pregnant belly. She was due soon, in about four weeks.

"We are so happy to welcome a new member," said Anita. "A few of you might know her."

Then Cora had to say something about herself, so she said she was Cora, she lived on the mountain side of town, she had two kids who were eight and, wow, almost twelve, she had really enjoyed the book, and thanks for having her. The women nodded along. Frances appeared from deeper in the house. He had become lanky the way kids did in middle school, like he'd been put on a stretching rack.

"Can get I on the computer?"

Anita sighed. "Okay."

He left the room and Anita said, "He hates me."

The women said, "Nooo."

Liz said, "He's just at a difficult age."

Anita responded that he had been at a difficult age his whole life. She looked forward to a single nondifficult day. He'd always been moody, though brilliant, and things at middle school exacerbated this; in other words, he was a dork. He knew it and it drove him crazy, and the harder he strove to not be a dork the more he was branded as such.

"Now that Ichabod is on the way, things have gotten worse."

Cora had been eating a cracker and started coughing. "Sorry, Ichabod?"

"The baby," said Anita. "Family name on Brandt's side."

A man named Brandt had an ancestor named Ichabod. America really was incredible.

Jules came in saying, "Sorry. Work is a nightmare."

She wore professional clothes, a collared shirt tucked into a knee-length skirt. She held up her bottle of wine. "It's red but you have to chill it."

She sat down next to Cora, and this made Cora squirm. They returned to Isabel Archer. What a promising person she was! What a curious intellect! They were so invested in her marriage. Terrible what happened to her though . . . here conversation became vague, like maybe no one had read the whole book. Like maybe most of them had read a third of it and given up.

"I have to talk to you about something," Jules whispered to Cora.

Cora tried to interpret her tone. If Jules had found out about the affair, she probably wouldn't say "I have to talk to you about something." She might say, "I'm full of murderous rage," or simply "You bitch." She might shout those things instead of whispering. Cora followed her into the kitchen, where the cabinets had been converted to open shelving. Now you could see every bowl, cup, plate, saucer, and jar stacked by size. Some of them were not very farmhouse but Cora was willing to bet this would soon be remedied.

"What's going on?"

"Sorry," said Jules. "It's kind of stupid. It's a kid thing."

She explained that Jack had a crush on Opal and Opal was not being nice to him. A school dance was coming up and he wanted to take her and he thought she'd been encouraging. She'd sent an emissary, some child named Mia, to tell him to ask her. Then when he had, Opal had laughed at him. It was not like Jules to intervene, but he was taking it hard.

"He's been up in his room listening to depressing music," said Jules. "He painted his nails black."

This was not what Cora had been expecting. It took her a

moment to adjust to the idea that they were talking about something unrelated to Sam. The social lives of children: sorry, but who cared? Was it their business? Wasn't it better to let the kids work things out for themselves? Certainly, it didn't call for a private conversation.

"Is that all?" said Cora.

"What do you mean? He's upset."

"I get that, and I'm sorry. He's a nice kid. We all love Jack. But what do you want me to do?"

Jules sucked in a breath. She wanted Cora to talk to Opal. Did Cora not think she needed to? Opal was at risk of becoming a mean girl. She ran around with that Sarah Beth Hood and they were always laughing. Cora pointed out that the third party in this was not Sarah Beth but someone named Mia, which made Jules redouble her self-control, breathing audibly again and lowering her voice. She said that even if this Mia person had been the lackey or whatever, the stool pigeon, you could sense Sarah Beth pulling the strings.

"I don't think you mean stool pigeon," said Cora. "A stool pigeon is an informer."

"He's crushed. He is a person and he is crushed."

"If Jack knew his mom was out on the town avenging him, would that uncrush him?"

"I'm going to kill you," said Jules.

They must have heard this in the other room, because there was half a second of quiet and then Anita appeared. "What's happening? Is everything all right?"

"Yeah, it's nothing," said Cora.

"It's not nothing," said Jules. "Opal is leading Jack on."

"No, she's not. She's a kid. She doesn't know what she's doing.

And even if she were leading him on, it's not any of our business. It's not even appropriate for us to discuss this. It's between them. I guess I can talk to her, but I'm not going to yell at her or anything. How do you know Jack was telling you the truth?"

"You don't think I'd realize it if a member of my family was lying to me?"

Cora didn't know how to answer. The irony was too pronounced. Could Jules be considered a perceptive person? Cora had thought so. Certainly, she was sharp. It didn't make sense that she should miss something so large.

At a loss for what to do, Anita offered them a beverage. At the end of this they were supposed to sit back down and discuss themes of womanhood in the novels of Henry James. They were supposed to talk about marriage then and now. Perhaps what was going on was that Jules sensed tension between herself and Cora but was unable to pinpoint it precisely. She'd landed just to the left, which was too close. You got the feeling she'd guess right the next time.

"I'll find out what's up," said Cora. "Don't kill me."

They went back into the living room and sat on their pillows.

In the other time line, Cora heeded the advice of the woman on the cruise ship and got pregnant. She thought about how her body was a vehicle transporting her to eternal blankness. She thought about the act of relinquishing freedom. She decided, as always, to be amenable.

You win, she said to Eliot. Let's have a baby.

It was a fantasy world, so they conceived right away. The pink line on the home test was unequivocal. She called Eliot into the bathroom to look at it. He took the stick from her and held it up to the light. Then he kissed her on the forehead.

Well done, he said. And in record time.

After that, she was dreamy, remote, drifting around town, in and out of baby stores, up to the attic for boxes of clothes and toys she'd saved, down to the basement to see what shape the crib was in. Why was a baby at the root of so much of this? It kept coming back. There was the accidental pregnancy with Sam, and now it was happening again. She loved babies, but she didn't want another. At least she thought she didn't.

She said to Eliot, in the real world, "Do you want to have another baby?"

Eliot lay in bed reading a manuscript about seagulls or the War of 1812. "What the fuck?"

"I guess that's a no."

"We're almost done."

They weren't almost done. Miles was still in elementary school. Opal was a mean girl, or mean girl in training. When Cora had tried to talk to her about what was going on with Jack, she'd said that Jules was acting like a cop. Cora agreed but had to temper this by saying Opal should treat people carefully, especially people who made themselves vulnerable to her. Opal had rolled her eyes and said Jack hadn't made himself vulnerable, he was just some kid. Cora puzzled over this before letting it go. So really, they were in the thick of it, with many difficult years ahead of them.

"You don't want to fuck a baby into me?" she said.

This made him put down his manuscript.

"Don't talk like that with the door open."

The kids were still up. They could hear them watching YouTube, separately, in their rooms. Miles liked to watch skate tricks, though he did not skate himself. Opal watched makeup tutorials, though she did not wear makeup. Eliot told Cora he'd never liked the expression *Fuck a baby into me*. It diminished both conceiving a baby and having sex for pleasure. It also just sounded nasty.

"I don't know," she said. "It can be good in context."

"What context would that be?"

"Being disgusting for fun during sex."

He picked his manuscript back up. It was hopeless if he was not going to respond to an obvious overture. She looked at her phone to see if Sam had texted. He had. He had sent another picture of his dick. It was sweet but how many did she need? She had seen it up close a number of times by now. In this latest picture he was fully nude, standing in front of the bathroom mirror. She could see Jules's robe hanging from the back of the door and a child's Croc on the ground. He had clenched his abs and made sure he was hard, but he had not cleared the frame of Crocs.

She put her phone facedown on her nightstand.

"I'm not trying to be mean," said Eliot. "I'd have a million babies if it was free."

He resumed reading. Opal entered without knocking.

"I've decided to go with Jack to the dance. You can tell that lady if you want. I'm sure she'll be happy."

"That lady?" said Eliot.

"She means Jules."

Eliot said, "You don't know Jules's name?"

"She's a parent. They're all the same to me."

"O, should we have another baby?" Eliot asked her. "Mom thinks we should."

"Don't be pathetic," said Opal. "You guys are so old."

* * *

Rain flooded the hotel parking lot and Cora sat in her car waiting for it to die down. Propelled by the wind, a stray shopping cart from Walmart hit the bumper of a car. She was late and he would be waiting for her, sitting in the slippery upholstered chair. Checking his watch as their time together ticked away to nothing. Finally, she could wait no longer and got out and ran through the downpour, holding a reusable grocery bag over her head.

She arrived soaked, and he immediately said, "How was she?"

She went into the bathroom for a towel and started drying her hair. "Who?"

"Jules. Who else? Didn't you see her at book club?"

They had not talked about their spouses much at the hotel. The subject had seemed off-limits or bad manners, a tender spot you didn't want to touch. But now he'd brought Jules up without reservation. This took Cora aback—the rules around their families had seemed implicit and set. They would act, to the extent it was possible, as if they didn't exist.

"Oh. She was fine. Mad at me actually, over something random."

"The Jack thing," he said.

"Yeah. So you knew about it?"

"Obviously. He's been making a big deal of it. He's been sulking for weeks."

"Why didn't you tell me?"

"It's trivial. It's kid shit."

She took a step back from him. It was a callous way to put it, even if he was mostly right. It wasn't the emergency Jules had made it out to be, but nor would Cora dismiss it as "kid shit." Plus, they were intimate now. Were they not intimate? Should he not tell her about an issue that involved them both? Why would he have kept it to himself?

"Sorry," he said. "I guess I should have told you."

"Jules is pretty upset about it. She said she was going to kill me. Anita had to intercede."

He laughed and told her Jules threatened to kill him all the time. She even pretended to do it sometimes. She'd take a pillow and hold it over his face until he thrashed around. He had risen from his chair and was touching Cora's breast.

"I know about the suffocation fantasy."

"And she otherwise seemed normal?"

He unzipped his pants. He seemed to be aroused by talking about Jules.

"Yeah. We discussed *The Portrait of a Lady*. I don't think she read it."

"She never does."

They had sex, but Cora was uneasy. She was thinking of Jules, which was exactly what she didn't want to be thinking about. With thoughts of Jules came thoughts of her own family. She was only able to justify the affair to herself by not thinking of them much during the actual sex. By keeping them carefully separated in their own time line.

He pulled out suddenly. "I want to show you something."

He led her into the bathroom and pointed to the mirrors on either side of the sink. They faced each other, causing endless stacked reflections. "Have you noticed this?"

"Yeah."

It was a classic feature of inexpensive hotels. If you didn't break three hundred dollars, you faced down eternity in the bathroom.

He said, "I've always kind of liked that effect. It reminds me of that artist with the rooms that go on forever."

Cora knew the artist's name, Yayoi Kusama, and had been in an infinity room. She'd gone with Eliot to the one at the Whitney at the beginning of their relationship. They had stood in it together, just the two of them. The room had been completely enclosed, a mirrored box. Colored lights—orange, gold, and white—hung from the ceiling. It had been disorienting, oddly moving. He'd taken her hand and kissed it, and this was reflected back to them close up and far away.

Sam was touching her ass now, watching himself in the mirror. He had his hands on her hips and drove her back toward him. Occasionally, he slowed down and turned to watch the many versions of himself pull out and push in again.

Her reflections all wore the same expression. They all reached back to lightly—and there was no sexy way to put this—stroke the area behind his balls. He groped for her breasts with one hand, found her mouth instead and jammed two fingers in. Then he was finishing, pressing her hard against the sink. He had the usual vacant, openmouthed look on his face and she had to close her eyes so she would not see it replicated hundreds of times.

Sam asked her if she had come and the Coras shook their heads no. He hoisted her up onto the sink. But it was difficult to lose herself with the faucet in her back and the reflections on either side, writhing around. She was thinking about the possibility of one of the many Coras breaking rank. She was thinking about one of them getting up and leaving.

Nine

Opal and Sarah Beth Hood sat at the kitchen island, wearing eighties prom dresses from Goodwill. Opal's was black tulle, off the shoulder, and Sarah Beth's was teal. They ate gummy bears, tossing them into the air and trying to catch them in their mouths. They were in eighth grade now, pretty and popular. Sarah Beth had precocious acne. They'd already been caught smoking cigarettes in her tree house.

"Jack's dad is having an affair," said Sarah Beth.

"What?" said Eliot.

He read a magazine at the kitchen table. Cora had been cleaning out the fridge. Emptying the crisper of wilted vegetables. Throwing out old condiments. Now she froze, holding a jar of mustard over the trash. "Who told you that?"

Sarah Beth let a gummy bear bounce off her face. "My dad saw him leaving a hotel last week. That weird place out near Walmart where people, like, live?"

"It's not weird," said Cora. "It's an extended stay hotel for business travelers. Maybe it's a little anonymous, but it's clean." Eliot glanced at her, and she added, "I've seen the inside. I don't remember when."

"Why did he tell you?" Eliot asked Sarah Beth.

"He was talking to my mom, and I overheard, so then they had to tell me."

"When was this?" asked Cora.

She and Sam often exited separately now, so it could have been anytime. Sam had not mentioned running into Richard—maybe Richard had seen him from a distance. What had Richard been doing at the hotel anyway? Was there something to do there other than have sex? Cora had never seen a conference in progress.

"He's disgusting," said Opal.

"Who is?" said Cora. "Sarah Beth's dad?"

"All dads to a certain extent. But in this case, specifically Jack's dad. Isn't he like fifty years old?"

"He's forty," said Eliot.

"Whatever. It's the same," said Sarah Beth.

She touched her chin where it was broken out and Cora resisted the urge to tell her not to.

"Fifty is the same as forty?"

Sarah Beth had moved across the room so Opal could throw a gummy into her mouth. They were not good at this and it hit her in the chest and fell to the floor. "Yeah. There's no difference."

"There's a difference," said Cora.

"Which is?"

"It's a difference of ten years. You could have any number of experiences in that amount of time. It's a huge portion of your life. You could become a completely different person. You could be forty and ten years pass and a bunch of profound or bizarre or tragic things happen and remake you completely."

"I don't think that's true," said Sarah Beth. "I think you get to like, twenty, and you're done."

"What do you mean done?" said Cora.

"Done. Completed."

The girls tried the gummy bear toss again and failed again and the gummy bear rolled off under the fridge.

"Can you stop doing that?" said Eliot, and they told him no, concentrate on your doofy little magazine.

"That isn't how it works," said Cora. "You're never done. Maybe your personality stays intact from year to year, but you keep learning things. You keep changing."

Opal began eating straight from the bag. "I think I'll be done by the time I go to college."

"Same," said Sarah Beth. "If I'm not done by then, I'm gonna kill myself."

Cora said, "Don't talk that way."

Eliot said, "Hey, keep that one."

He pointed at the jar of mustard Cora was still holding. She looked down at it, a brown bottle with French writing on the label. Years ago, Eliot had received it in a gift basket for something work-related. It had accompanied salami and fancy crackers. She recalled the kids' excitement taking the items out. Miles had been a toddler.

"You can't be serious," she said.

"I'm going to use it."

"When?"

"Eventually. I'm waiting for the right sandwich."

"Does mustard not go bad?"

"I think you're fine if it's sealed. It's made of seeds and vinegar."

"Those things go bad."

Then he was googling *does mustard go bad* and reading parts of an article out loud. The article claimed it did. Mustard was food, said the article. Food went bad. Then he read a second article about the differences between American and French mustard and what the French believed about mustard going bad. The French also believed mustard went bad. Because it was food. Meanwhile, Cora had thrown the mustard away.

"Anyway, you shouldn't go around repeating that about Jack's dad," she said.

"It's probably true," said Eliot.

Cora tried to keep her voice normal. "Why do you say that?"

"Maybe it's some kind of payback."

"Payback for what?" said Opal. "Are you saying Jules cheated on him?"

"No," said Eliot quickly.

"Oh my god, she did," said Opal.

She and Sarah Beth collapsed into each other screaming with laughter. Why they found infidelity so funny Cora didn't know. Possibly because it existed in the adult realm and they were just on the outside. Outside the bubble but able to see in. Adults held fascination while also seeming pitiful and weak. That would never happen to them, they thought. They'd never be old and desperate, checking into a hotel in a sparsely landscaped business park.

"Fuck. Don't tell Jack," said Cora.

"Bad word," said Opal.

"Who'd she cheat with?" said Sarah Beth.

"We're not talking about this anymore," said Cora.

"But you do know," said Opal.

Cora said to Eliot, "Nice work. They're going to tell Jack."

"I won't tell," said Opal. "But Sarah Beth definitely will."

"I'm going to," confirmed Sarah Beth.

"This is adult stuff, girls," said Eliot. "It could mess up someone's life. Don't repeat it to any of your friends."

"Okay," they said, laughing again.

And so it got out. The part about Jules got out. It got out that Jules had had an affair, but most of the other details were wrong. Embellishments appeared. The setting was off. People thought it had taken place at the big, anonymous hotel. There was confusion about who the man was. Names circulated, but none of them made sense. No one could imagine that it might be someone they didn't know, someone from out of town. The prospect of a stranger did not occur, maybe because it was less scandalous. The part of the mind that craved narrative cohesion resisted the possibility.

The problem was that few options existed for who it might be. For this reason, Eliot's name popped up. This amused and flattered him.

"What if I stepped out?" he said to Cora.

For a second, she looked at him and wondered. Had he? But then she came to her senses and remembered that she knew who it was. They both did. It was just some guy, a lawyer who had texted Jules. A possible opportunist who had seen an opening during the pandemic with an overwrought mother of young children. Now he'd moved on to someone whose frontal cortex was not yet fully formed.

"I wouldn't be mad," said Cora.

Eliot said, "Yeah, sure."

Klaus came over for dinner and repeated the story. The pairing he'd heard was Richard and Jules, and you could see where this had originated. Richard had launched the rumor, so his name hovered nearby. He was both sleazy and game, and his involvement would have made sense. But he was innocent of all infractions, as far as Cora knew, besides flashing her that once, an act that had come to seem melancholy over the years, and harmless. What he had been doing at the hotel himself remained an open question but unrelated to the tangle of Jules and Sam.

"Who is saying Richard?" said Cora.

"Brandt."

"Oh god. The vasectomy king."

"He got it reversed," Klaus said.

"Believe me, I know."

They had book club soon, Cora realized, and everyone would want to talk about it. If Jules was there, they'd be unable to. Where would the energy of that pent-up gossip go? Into talking about the book? It had been Cora's turn to choose and she'd picked *The Master and Margarita*. Instead of talking about who was fucking whom, they were going to discuss a satirical novel by Mikhail Bulgakov.

"I didn't realize Sam and Jules were unhappy," said Klaus. "They always seemed happy."

Klaus, who had been blindsided by the departure of Freda, had thought they were happy. If Klaus thought you were happy, it almost proved the inverse. It meant there was a Jonathan on the horizon, slipping into a leather vest and biding his time.

"What made you think that?" said Cora.

"They seem to like each other."

"Do they? Jules complains about him constantly."

Cora could not recall an affectionate exchange between the two of them. Jules did nothing to hide her contempt. Over the years, Cora had been a sounding board for both of them. She could tell you their day-to-day complaints and their long-term grievances. There was Sam's lack of ambition and Jules's over-ambition. There was the elegant, useless car and Jules's temper. There was the division of household labor, and at least that one was societal.

Klaus said, "That's wives blowing off steam. I'm sure you complain to her about Eliot too."

Eliot said, "Do you complain about me?"

"No."

"What do you say when you complain about me?"

She didn't complain about him. Jules did the complaining and Cora listened. Sam did the complaining and Cora listened.

"I say you're too tall and too handsome."

She called the kids to come set the table and there was a thumping as they ran down the stairs. For some reason, the prize task was putting out forks. Nightly they raced each other for the privilege. Spoons and knives they did not care about, but forks held prestige. Opal shoved Miles out of the way, yanked open the drawer, and clutched a handful of forks in her fist above his head.

"It's my *turn*," Miles said.

Cora said, "Do you guys actually care about the forks?"

They both told her yes and that she didn't get it. Forks were important and also interesting. They barely used spoons. Only during soup season, which it was not, and wouldn't be for a while. So that concluded the conversation about Sam and Jules.

They now had to weigh in about whether soup was year-round, and how ice cream entered into the conversation.

But anyway, there was nothing to do but wait.

Jules fell out of touch. Weeks passed, and Cora texted her and got no response. This was unusual—they stayed in contact about the kids, about school, about half days, carpooling, which project was due when. For years, they'd spoken daily or almost daily. And now nothing. The silence could only indicate new levels of anger and resentment. Unless Jules had died, which would be tragic for sure but would solve a few problems.

Then it was time for book club. Everyone had brought their copies of *The Master and Margarita*. Cora had almost skipped the meeting, but by club rules, you had to attend on the day they discussed your pick. Jules arrived before her and sat on a pillow with a dangerous smile on her face. Cora had no choice but to sit next to her.

Anita began. "This book was . . . different."

"It sucked," said Jules.

"Say more," said Anita.

"I read ten pages. Even that was a slog. I'm sorry, but it's just all wrong for us."

"I thought the picks were supposed to be edifying," said Cora.

"This was too edifying," said Jules.

The other women nodded. They had not been able to get through it either. They had given up twenty pages in. It was not the right vibe. They wanted something (had Cora not gotten this?) that spoke to the experience of being a woman.

"If that was a criterion, why didn't you tell me?" said Cora.

"It's not a written rule," said Anita. "It's just something that has bound together all the choices so far."

"See, this is why we didn't want to let you in," said Jules. She turned to Anita. "I told you."

The women shifted.

Anita said, "Jules."

There was a long silence. No one would look Cora in the eye. She followed Liz's gaze and found her staring at some stalks of wheat in a vase. Then Cora saw it was not a vase, but a silver milking vessel from a dairy. So which was it supposed to be, a wheat farm or a dairy farm?

"You didn't want to let me in because you thought I'd pick something difficult?"

"It's not that it's difficult," said Jules. "We read difficult books all the time. It's that it's *wrong*."

Anita said, "We didn't not want to let you in. I don't know why she's saying this. I think we need to . . . I recently read a book about deescalating conflict and I think, well actually it was kind of about police violence, but I think we should try to use some of those strategies?"

Cora said to Jules, "Do you want to talk in the kitchen?"

Anita said, "Yeah, see, that's a good one. Moving to a new location often takes the heat out of an altercation."

Cora and Jules went into the kitchen. They were always going into the kitchen. They could not get through book club without doing it. They stood next to a weathered wooden sign on the wall that said FRUIT. Another one across the room said MEAT. These were new but did not entertain Cora as much as they should have.

"Is everything okay?" she said.

"Not really."

Jules stood with her arms crossed. Direct confrontation was rare in their lives. Conflict tended to take the form of avoidance, talking behind someone's back, slight social awkwardness, or if things got really bad, long text messages.

It was obvious that Jules blamed Cora for the spread of the rumor. But the rumor was a smoke screen for what was going on between Cora and Sam. For this reason, Cora was grateful for it, though it had set into motion a chain of events that could only end with her own affair coming to light. She could have used this moment to tell the truth, except Jules was explosively angry. Except she feared Jules generally. Except she hadn't done anything, that Jules knew of, besides tell Eliot.

"Do you know what you've caused?" said Jules.

"I'm sorry."

She knew what she had caused because it was all anyone had talked about for weeks. But actually, was Cora responsible? Richard had started the whole thing, and Sarah Beth had perpetuated it. Yes, Cora had told Eliot years ago, but she was a tenuous link, a scapegoat, maybe, for Jules's blame. Because had Jules herself not caused it? Perhaps too much attention was being paid to the third party who had simply told her husband a secret. A normal thing to do. The purpose of marriage, you might venture, now that it was no longer mostly about property exchange.

"I explicitly told you not to tell anyone," said Jules.

Cora tried to remember if this was true. She thought back on that day at the pool three years ago. Jules had sat between her and Celeste on a deck chair. They'd been drinking those watery drinks, though Jules had a lot of them. She'd told them casually. She hadn't fully made up her mind about whether she was going to do it or not, but she hadn't seemed guilt-ridden. Had she asked for secrecy? She hadn't. She had almost been bragging. She had been looking for one or both of them to sign off on her cheating and they had. Because why would they care if she cheated?

"I don't think you asked me to keep it a secret, actually."

"It's implied. Are you an idiot?"

"I only told Eliot. It's not like I leaked it to the newspaper."

"Eliot told a child."

This was an oversimplification of what had happened. Eliot hadn't deliberately told a child; he'd let it slip, which was not the same thing. And he'd only done it when Richard and Sarah Beth had already begun gossiping about Jules's marriage.

"By accident. And after keeping it a secret for a long time. Is there not a statute of limitations?"

Jules told her she had an annoying arguing style. She insisted on being wry. Being wry in a fight was worse than being nasty. At least someone being nasty was facing the situation head-on.

"Sorry for being wry!" said Cora.

"Everyone thinks I'm sleeping with Richard," said Jules.

"Is that the worst thing in the world?"

Jules asked, if she was having an affair, why would she go to that hotel out by Walmart? It was a place where people went to kill themselves. It was so gray inside and you could imagine taking a handful of pills, placing a note in an envelope, and gently drifting to the other side.

"You *were* having an affair," said Cora.

"But not there!"

It was like Jules to have an affair in a classier way than Cora. It was like her to rub it in without knowing she was rubbing it in. They fell into an exasperated silence and Cora noticed that there were no sounds coming from the other room. If they had really been in a country kitchen, they'd have heard cows lowing or the wind through the corn. The women must have been listening intently. This was prime material. They would take it with them to school pickup, school drop-off, to the various soccer fields of the town, to the dinner parties they hosted, where they'd arrange the flowers themselves, tie a bit of raffia around each cloth napkin.

Then a phone rang and the ringtone was the beginning of Cat Stevens's "Wild World," and you knew it was Liz's phone and that she'd refer to him as Yusuf Islam. She said, "Shit!" and made a series of sounds indicating she was looking for a phone, and the room went silent again.

"They're listening," hissed Jules.

"Of course," said Cora.

Jules pulled her deeper into the kitchen, into the pantry, and here the illusion of the prairie frayed because there were signs of contemporary life in the form of junk food. Anita and Brandt had a comprehensive supply of Pop-Tarts and sugar cereals. They had kettle corn on hand, three unopened bags of salt and vinegar chips, Double Stuf Oreos. They had cases of seltzer and Diet Coke, and two gallons of iced tea.

"Stop ogling their food," said Jules.

"They're really well stocked," said Cora.

Then they had to resume having an argument.

"What does Sam think?" said Cora.

"I haven't told him anything."

Sam had come to her and she had lied. Why are people saying this? Where could it have come from? She'd made a big show of being upset. She had cried. She had said they always find a way to vilify working mothers. Could Cora believe she'd used that one? He'd bought it though. He'd made a big show of believing her. *He* had cried. He had said if she was unhappy in their marriage, she could tell him anytime. He was not as judgmental as she thought he was.

"So he has no idea?"

"No, nor do I want him to. Ever. I don't deserve whatever feeling I would get from confessing. I don't want to take steps to mend our relationship. Do the things people do on TV. End up in a therapist's office with succulents everywhere and a tufted leather couch. No. All of that is bullshit. It's fake nonsense and I don't have time for it anyway. I don't have the time or the inclination or the right touchy-feely personality."

"Then, what now?"

"Now nothing," said Jules. "We wait until it dies down. I had to give him a blow job."

He did like his blow jobs. Cora considered saying this to see what would happen. In a time line far removed from their own she did say it and Jules said oh my god yes, he likes it when you look up at him, and Cora said you gotta feign abjection. Then Cora felt bad for Sam. The simplicity of his needs—he wanted to be in charge—and how Jules was mocking him. But wait, he'd also manipulated her masterfully. He could have come clean himself and instead he'd gotten a blow job.

"I wish you'd hit me," said Cora.

Jules studied her for a second and shoved her into the shelving behind her. A box of Pepperidge Farm crackers fell from a high shelf and hit her on the head. It was a multipack with several varieties, including the butterfly shape that Cora had always found special. She shoved Jules back, harder than she meant to, and more boxes rained from above. A jar with the branding of a popular Italian restaurant in the city smashed. Then they were sliding around in vodka sauce trying to regain their footing.

Anita came to the door and said, "What is happening?"

They stopped shoving each other.

"We broke a sauce," said Cora.

"Sorry," added Jules. "It just fell."

Several other items had fallen and they kneeled to pick them up. Jules put her bare knee in vodka sauce, but they couldn't laugh. Not in front of the person whose pantry they'd trashed. Cora asked Anita if she had a broom and Anita went to grab one. The shoving had worked; the aggression had evaporated. Cora suspected it would be back though. Too much was unresolved and still coming for them.

Cora and Sam found a new place to meet forty minutes outside of town. It was a motel rather than a hotel: two floors of dingy stucco in need of a power wash. You had to go outside to access the ice machine. The comforter had a paisley pattern that hid stains. When Cora arrived, Sam was already there, peering at her from behind blackout curtains. He saw that she spotted him and let the curtain fall back into place. She thought: he has lost his mind.

Inside, he said, "Everyone is talking."

"It'll pass. They'll move on to something else."

She breathed hard. She had run up a set of external stairs. He demanded she tell him what she knew about Jules.

She said, "There was a guy. I don't know his name."

"How long have you known?"

She said, "A while. Years."

She told him about how it had begun during the pandemic. She told him about her conversation with Jules on the night of his birthday party. How they had sat in the mudroom and Jules had cried. How Jules did not think she deserved forgiveness.

Meanwhile, Sam was trying to take his shirt off, fumbling with the buttons. The badness of the hotel was good somehow, as was their nearness to exposure. She got undressed and they had sex quickly. When he was about to come, he made her ask for it. She did, and meant it and said please and they came at roughly the same time. Afterward, they lay on their backs and he expressed the dire need for a cigarette and reached instead for a toothpick.

"Why didn't you tell me?"

"I didn't know how. It was hard to figure out what to do."

She had tried. But he hadn't seemed to want to hear it. Then she'd given up, figured it was best to keep it to herself. Her loyalties had been split at the time and she hadn't wanted to meddle. They looked at the ceiling, which had a popcorn texture. Flies banged against the overhead light.

"I thought we told each other the truth."

"Do we? When did we say that?"

They drank beers from the minifridge, though it was two in the afternoon. Cora sat in a chair near the bed. Scratchy, mustard yellow, the texture of burlap. Other people with uncomplicated lives were at work, running errands, considering an afternoon coffee.

"I can't believe they made a chair out of this material," said Cora.

The grossness of the motel had excited her at first but did not anymore. What was going on in the other world? She and Eliot were at an anatomy scan and declining to find out the baby's sex. A tech was printing out a 3D image for them. They were remarking that it looked like an alien, orange on a brown background. It had its eyes closed and its mouth resembled Opal's. Where had that mouth come from? Eliot's mom? Eliot himself didn't have that mouth. A mouth could skip a generation and end up on a fictional baby.

"Are you mad at me?" said Cora.

Sam lay naked on top of the comforter. It was probably made of petroleum. "I haven't decided yet."

"You didn't tell her about us."

"No."

"She gave you a blow job."

"She told you that?"

"Yeah."

"Sorry."

Cora shrugged, but it did hurt.

He wanted to know if Jules was still seeing the guy and Cora told him she wasn't. Unless she'd started seeing him again, in which case she was.

"Helpful."

"What do you want from me? I'm not a beat reporter."

Cora asked how Jules seemed, if she was acting strange, and he told her she'd been more present at the house. She'd been trying to seem less suspicious but it was making her more suspicious. She'd been working fewer hours, spending time with the kids. She'd been doing special things for them. She'd bought Jack a pair of expensive sneakers he'd been asking for. She cooked them elaborate meals that required the food processor.

"Emulsions," he said. "Pestos."

"I guess that's nice."

He sat up. "What do we do?"

He seemed to be genuinely asking. His dick was nestled between his thighs, and it was all too vulnerable. Too hat in hand. The way his gut fell forward slightly into that area. The way he seemed to be acknowledging the mess he'd made.

"I don't know," said Cora. The affair was ending now, this was obvious. It was drawing to a close. "I think it's got to be over."

"Yeah."

Part of her wanted him to disagree. When she'd imagined moments like this, he always pushed back. Rage against it, she thought. At least make a show of it out of decorum. Put on a little play about how upset you are. It wouldn't change the outcome but it might make her feel better.

"Don't just say yeah," she said.

"Sorry. What am I supposed to say?"

"Get worked up or something."

He raised his palms helplessly. She went into the bathroom and turned on the scouring yellow light. She looked at her reflection in the mirror over the sink. She was thirty-nine years old. Time had chiseled out some cheekbones for her. There was a small window next to the mirror and she slid it open. The screen had a star-shaped gash and she could see the patch of woods that grew wild behind the motel. She couldn't help but think: where you'd run during a shoot-out.

Cora prepared and made a presentation at work. She walked down to the pharmacy, down to the coffee shop. Opal performed in the school play and attended the dance with Jack. Eliot started a job at a new imprint for higher pay. Dr. Sperling died at one hundred years old, and Cora brought a wreath of white lilies to his memorial. The book club read *The Custom of the Country*, Liz's pick. There was a feeling of waiting for it to break, like you'd await the arrival of a storm or a baby.

Cora and Sam went into the city for a final hurrah. It was Cora's idea. The affair had to end—there was too much scrutiny now, too much risk. It had stopped being fun the way it had at first. But they could have a last weekend, couldn't they? They could do things properly. They could stay at a nice hotel. Make declarations that meant something. They could go out with affection.

He agreed and they arranged it.

They went to Chinatown and ate in a red and gold restaurant with fogged-up windows. It was cold out: Christmas on the way again. Christmas came every year, and just when you needed it least.

"It's almost our anniversary," Cora said. "Remember? Christmastime."

Sam didn't respond. He reached for the bottle of wine. He was drinking too much and his mood was off. She had worn a slinky black dress and he'd stoically eaten her out in their hotel room before they'd left for dinner. She'd said afterward "Thanks," and he'd nodded. He'd told Jules he was taking a weekend away from her to process what had happened, and Cora realized this was true. He was processing. He had no intention of enjoying himself.

They went to a bar for a nightcap. The light was too red, the music too loud. The two of them did not belong there. It was a place for tourists or drunk young people, the kind of bar that didn't have regulars but relied on street traffic. She ordered a water and he got a bourbon.

"The guy is successful. I guess that's hot to women."

"Guy?" said Cora.

"Jules's guy. She was with him because he's rich."

"I don't know if that's true. People are attracted to each other for all kinds of reasons."

"Do you like successful men? Obviously not."

"Hey."

Eliot was successful, though in a less flashy way than Jules's lawyer, but she didn't want to bring up yet another man with a better career than Sam's.

"You think someone loves you for who you are. But it turns out they want some kind of cheesy alpha. They want all the power dynamics they purport to despise. A guy in a suit with a bank account. It's embarrassing, really. I'm embarrassed for her."

He called the bartender over and got another bourbon.

"I found his profile." He took out his phone and showed her. "Look at this guy. He's in good shape. Bleh. He runs marathons. What an accomplishment. Running for three hours. Great work. He's got a pug named Michael. Did you know this? Dumb name for a dog. There he is. Michael the dog."

"I didn't know about the dog."

"He works at some law firm. He's a defense attorney for corporations. Maybe I should have done that too. You stay at the office until midnight every night and they give you millions of dollars. Is that so hard? Is it so hard to go to law school?"

"It's not," said Cora. "That's why a lot of people do it."

He was barely talking to her. He was talking to himself. He

chewed toothpicks one after another, working his jaw furiously. He lined them up next to his glass on the bar.

"I could go to law school. It's not too late. I bet if I did, she'd make fun of me. I bet if I said, you know what, it's been my dream this whole time to be some kind of corporate-ass lawyer sellout with dubious ethics, she'd laugh at me. She'd say, you? No way. You accomplishing something?"

Cora had to get him out of there. He was ranting about selling out. She had wanted a pleasant weekend with him, a send-off for the affair. He claimed to want that too. He had told her with a straight face that he wanted to make love to her for a long time and remember it forever. He hadn't talked like that before.

"Let's go," she said.

She signaled for the check and helped him to his feet. He weaved around, wasted.

"I love you so much," he said on the threshold of the bar.

He had pushed aside the heavy curtain meant to keep out the winter air. He leaned in to kiss her but caught the side of her mouth. They walked back to their hotel and she stayed a half step ahead of him. He did not remember the way and she had to lead. Then through the lobby, plush but dim, up to the twelfth floor, back into the room that faced downtown, toward the spire of One World Trade, which glowed blue that night, commemorating something, the fallen world of course, but what was the blue for? Had a sports team won?

"Where were you on 9/11?" she asked Sam, and even this did not make him laugh.

He thought for a beat and said, "I don't know."

He definitely did know. Who didn't know where they'd been on 9/11? The answer was that he was at school. She worked out the years in her mind. She'd been in high school and he was a few years older. He'd gone to Columbia, so that's where he'd been. He'd witnessed it firsthand.

"You were here," she said.

He said, "Oh right. Yeah."

They went to bed without having sex. He did not make love to her for a long time, or anytime. What was the point of this affair? she wondered. They slept on opposite sides of the bed. She spent most of the night cycling through guilt, dread, and annoyance. In the morning, she woke to the sound of the shower. The curtains were open and Manhattan rose and fell before them, a Lego city in the morning light. He came out looking red and scraped, sat down on the edge of the bed.

"Good morning. I have a hangover."

He put a palm on her breast.

"You had a lot to drink. It happens."

"I knew you'd understand." He studied her face. "You look pretty."

"Thank you."

"I think I should go home. I think that's what I'm going to do."

They had the room for another night. They had discussed seeing a movie or going to a museum. They had never been to a museum together, except years ago, in the other time line. Cora remembered running through the Louvre with him, and the inauthenticity of the memory, the fact that it was half grafted onto a famous scene from a Godard film, pained her. There was so much they hadn't done and would never do.

"Stay," she said, without meaning it.

"I need to go sort it out with Jules." He looked around the room. "None of this is helping. It's nice but it's not helping."

He'd ordered room service, and it arrived with a curt knock. Cora put on a bathrobe. A bellhop wheeled in a cart and whisked off the silver domes. This, in the eleventh hour, was exactly as she would picture it. The final breakfast at a small round table near a window. The ramekins of jam and salted butter. All of it loaded with nervousness and emotion held in check, as if it were over already, as if they'd never see each other again.

Sam poured coffee and Cora said thanks. He offered her raspberry compote and she said sure. He gave her first choice of omelets and she chose Greek.

"I think I'm going to tell her about us. I think it might help. Maybe she'll feel less guilty and I'll feel, I don't know. Vindicated."

He cut into his omelet.

"Right," said Cora.

"It won't help you, obviously."

"No."

"But that's okay."

He caught her eye to make sure she agreed.

"You're saying it doesn't matter if my life gets ruined?" said Cora.

"Why shouldn't yours get ruined? If mine is ruined and Jules's is ruined, why not yours too?"

She sipped her coffee and looked at him over the rim.

"I'm speaking abstractly, of course. We're talking this out. Don't you think there should be consequences for you?"

The consequences for her were already grave. She'd betrayed her husband and her children. She'd lied to Eliot repeatedly. She'd taken their shared money and used it to pay for hotel rooms. On top of all that was the toll to her sense of self. She'd

THE TEN YEAR AFFAIR

once liked who she was and now she did not. Falling in your own esteem was as bad as it got. Being unable to deceive yourself any longer about your goodness. Finding yourself severed from what you thought of as your values. Knowing yourself to be a person who mistreated the people you loved.

"I'm talking about real-world consequences," he said.

She said, "So am I."

"You're frustrating."

He said it warmly. The was a certain battered fondness between them. The TV played, she noticed, with the volume low. A woman with broad blond hair and glistening lips took a cooking lesson from a man in an apron. "You gotta stir it a lot," the guy was saying. "You gotta stir it and stir it and stir it."

"I think one of us should move," said Sam. "I was thinking this in the shower. If one of us left town that would solve it. Then we could get a fresh start, pretend this never happened."

"Sure," she said. "Put my family in a cattle car. Send us to the countryside."

"Great idea."

"We could live in a large camp with other people you find inconvenient. We could all be, say, concentrated there."

"It would work perfectly. I see no issues."

"And you wouldn't have to think about me ever again."

"That would be the aim."

"And that would make you very happy."

"Well."

He scooped up some egg with his toast. She sat waiting to see what he would say.

* * *

In the other time line, she gave birth in the brand-new obstetrics wing of a brand-new hospital. The delivery room had a view of the Hudson. Across a parking lot, a four-lane scramble of highway, an on-ramp that looped around in a circle, two bridges arched over cobalt water. It was easy, as births went. Cora had an epidural as soon as she arrived. She held still, braced against the forearms of a nurse, while two young doctors laced a catheter into her spine. The doctors wore glasses and had a perfect track record. We've never failed, they told her, to make someone feel nothing.

Then it was time to push and Eliot held her hand. My life, he called her, and dried her brow.

Her baby was cleaned up and returned to her in a tiny hat. A boy. He had pink cheeks. His silver-blue eyes brimmed with intelligence. Cora felt hope, awe, and exhaustion. On the other side of the river, a freight train churned by, car after car in muted shades of blue, teal, tan, and orange.

The next day, they took the baby home in a car seat that made him look exactly as tiny as he was. The kids met them on the front porch, speaking in hushed voices.

They had on their hands what was known as a good baby. He spent his nights in a bassinet in Cora and Eliot's room, nursed without incident, spit up minimally, grew chubby. His eyes remained open for longer stretches of time. They laid him on the bed between them on Sunday mornings, spread out the newspaper, drank their coffee and ate their toast.

Eliot returned to work and Cora stayed home on maternity leave. She was tired, but patient. She had done it twice before. The tasks came back via muscle memory, the swaddling and diapering. The careful bathing. But after a few weeks something happened. She grew bored and anxious. She had thoughts of walking out. She wasn't going to do it, but still. Who was she? What had happened to her?

A healthy person would seek out company, and so she did. On the internet, she found a local baby group. It was held in the back room of an overpriced children's clothing store. The group would not be perfect, she knew. The store would draw a certain type of parent. But the people she met did not have to be her friends forever. They could be temporary acquaintances who were going through the same thing. They could help pass the time, then disappear harmlessly from her life.

It was January the first time she went. She bundled the baby into his snowsuit. She pushed him downhill in his stroller and put on the wrist strap in case it got away from her. Past the library, the coffee shop staffed by kids with lip rings and neon Carhartt hats, through the store, which was featuring teething necklaces in primary colors. The back room smelled like broccoli. She sat at the edge of a circle of parents, set her baby down in front of her on sheepskin. A man she'd never met before handed her a toothpick.

Ten

There was no reprieve: the time lines switched back. The affair was forced again into the realm of the imaginary. In a room with blue mats on the floor, a woman demonstrated a new technique for potty training your child. Another woman said birthing a big baby makes you come. The babies grew fast. One minute they had no hair and then they did. One minute they were all soft pink gums and the next they'd cut their milk teeth. The wall clock's neon hands swooped around as the afternoons passed.

Meanwhile, in the real world, domestic life continued, the rhythms of school and work, the big and small trips to the grocery store, the seasons that were its organizing principle. Cora waited for Jules to show up at the front door. She waited for a confrontation. Maybe she'd call and Cora would pick up by accident. Or maybe she'd run into her somewhere, outside the pharmacy or dry cleaner on Main Street. Cora imagined the conversation they'd have, Jules's anger. I thought you didn't care about infidelity, Cora would say, before Jules pushed her into traffic.

But none of this happened. Cora worked from home and applied for jobs. Opal was finishing middle school; how could that be? She needed a real bra. Cora took the kids to the department store at the mall but Miles made gagging noises and insisted on staying in the car. It was a trying errand. Opal called it a grandma store, which was true—it was a place where older ladies bought hose—but the fact remained that she needed an underwire bra and this was where you got one.

The light of the department store beat down harshly and Opal snapped at her. Somehow two bras cost ninety dollars. They got back in the car and Miles complained that they'd taken forever and asked to get Taco Bell and it was easier to give in than to come up with a reason he shouldn't have it.

On the way home, they passed the big, anonymous hotel and she thought: they're in there. They had been in there, and were in there still. They were in there with the chill air and the sterile atmosphere, the birds that circled or did not circle. The worlds stacked on top of each other like playing cards.

She looked Sam up on the internet. In fact, she could not stop looking him up. She looked at the blurry picture of him with the shark. She looked at his wedding registry—why hadn't they taken it down by now? She looked at his Instagram profile, which he barely used anymore. Twelve years ago he had gone to Barcelona with Jules. Ten years ago he had tucked infant Penelope into his hoodie. Five years ago he had been shirtless at the Cape. Three years ago he'd held a hose in his backyard. A year and a half ago he'd eaten chicken wings.

"What are you looking at?" said Eliot.

"Nothing."

They were in bed, always in bed, with the windows open. Sam had not been in touch. He'd left the hotel that day and she hadn't heard from him in a few weeks. She hadn't called him either. They'd agreed, as he stood in the doorway saying goodbye, not to talk, not to text, to stay away. What she felt mostly was edgy. What was she supposed to do if she was not texting him? What was she supposed to think about if she was not meeting him?

"What are you reading?" said Eliot.

She had a book open on her chest. She genuinely could not remember what it was. She glanced at the cover and found it was *To the Lighthouse* by Virginia Woolf.

She held it up. "Book club. Anita's pick."

He asked her why they never read anything sexy like that dragon book that was so big right now. The one that groups of women loved. Why was it always so heavy?

"You know why," she said.

The women in the club had grown up a specific way and gone to specific colleges. They'd gone to Vassar or Bard or, like Jules, Columbia. Now they lived in a town that had a feel. They were not suburban in their preoccupations; they were thoughtful and sophisticated. They had to prove this to each other over and over. They had to prove it to the world too, by posting the book club picks online with the caption "Currently loving."

He said, "Couldn't you propose it?"

"You don't get it. I'm perpetually on thin ice with the book club."

She was fucking one of the ladies' husbands. Or had been. They'd had sex for the last time on that morning in Manhattan. They had the room and the lighting was flattering. A large mirror faced the bed. It seemed, as it was happening, that they were both trying to eke out meaning from it. Sam fucked her with a sort of formality, like he was trying to tell her something. Each thrust felt deliberate. Could you fuck a message into a person? Probably not. Not unless the message was "I am fucking you."

Eliot returned to his book. "All right. So read *To the Lighthouse* then. It's good."

Cora checked her phone. Sam had not texted. Checking your phone didn't make someone text. It was better if he didn't anyway. It was better if they never saw each other again as long as they lived. If he fell into a sort of metaphorical pit and never reached the bottom. She read the first sentence of her book. *"Yes, of course, if it's fine tomorrow," said Mrs. Ramsay.* She checked her phone again. He hadn't texted.

"I'm going to bed," said Eliot.

He turned off his light.

She read the sentence again. *"Yes, of course, if it's fine tomorrow," said Mrs. Ramsay.* Way down at the beginning of his Instagram, the first picture he'd ever posted was of Jules. When Cora wanted to hurt badly, to feel it in her chest, she looked at this picture. Jules was young in a striped shirt and sunglasses. She held a single daisy in front of her face. There was mischief in her expression and one inch of abdomen showing under her shirt. Who would not be in love with her?

Eliot had fallen asleep already. His ability to fall asleep quickly was uncanny. It gave the impression of a clean conscience, like a puppy or a child. But of course everyone had regrets. Things ate at him, probably. Remarks he'd made that still bothered him. Choices from the deep past he relived over and over. It was difficult, but one had to try to imagine an inner life for one's husband.

Cora forced herself to put down her phone and pick up the book. *"Yes, of course, if it's fine tomorrow,"* said Mrs. Ramsay. She turned off her own light and lay in the dark. Maybe this month she'd join the rest of the women in not reading it. Each day was a fresh opportunity to find out you were just like everyone else.

That spring, she fucked Sam in the other world, while in this world she applied for more jobs. She planned a birthday party for Opal. Opal and two friends wanted to get manicures and go to a conveyor belt sushi place in the city. Cora agreed, although the sushi place was a tourist trap. She ferried them to midtown, delivered them to their various reservations, and left them alone. She wandered around the city for a while, got a coffee, picked them up again.

Another weekend, Drew flew in from La Jolla. He had those wiry tennis arms and his face was creased from the sun. He took the kids to hit balls and then he took Cora out for a beer at the worst dive in town, the one out near the tire shop that abutted a ravine.

"Why here?" said Cora.

"I like gross places," said Drew.

Grossness had disappeared from his life. Everything in Southern California was bland and nice. It was all like a Hilton or a Tommy Bahama. The food was low carb and had avocado on top. The cars were round white SUVs like pillows on wheels. He rarely accessed raw emotion anymore. He rarely felt discomfort.

"Is something wrong with you?" he said.

"Why are you asking that?"

"Mom told me something is wrong."

He was her little brother and he had gotten old. He was like if Cora was a handsome man. He had her same ability to charm and be charmed, her same inability to put up resistance. He'd been good enough at tennis to coast on it, but not good enough to be a star. She loved Drew very much, even more now that he was slightly washed. He had his wheatgrass lifestyle, but he also preferred watery beer like their father had. She hoped he hadn't flown in at the behest of their mother.

"I'm your kids' uncle," he said.

"Oh please. You never fly in."

"Don't get mad but she said you look like shit. She said she facetimed the kids and you looked tired."

"Why is she always saying that?"

Their mother had been telling Cora she looked tired her whole life. She never said this to Drew, maybe because he never looked tired. He tended to only look golden and healthy, which was why he was their mother's favorite. But in her relations with Cora, it was a shorthand for something else. It was a shorthand for "I have an issue with a choice you have made." But also, it sometimes just meant she looked tired.

"Grandma did it to her," said Drew. "And Grandma's mom did it to Grandma. A whole lineage of women going back to Minsk or wherever, telling their daughters they look tired. You'll do it to Opal one day."

"I won't."

She'd sooner abandon her family than perpetuate that particular mistake. She'd vowed, when she'd found out Opal was a girl, to never criticize her personal appearance. But Drew hadn't come to talk about Opal. Drew had come to talk about her. He had never done this before. They saw each other once a year, at the holidays. They barely even spoke on the phone. Their text exchanges were screenshots of posts by people they'd known growing up. *Grace Cummings breast implants,* he might text her, with a picture of Cora's friend Grace in a bathing suit. *Gordon O'Toole big dumb boat,* she'd text him, with a picture of his friend Gordon's yacht.

The bartender brought more beer and set out a bowl of peanuts. Drew wore a white Fred Perry polo shirt, soccer shorts, and soccer slides. He had dressed like this every moment of his life. Opal had made him a beaded bracelet with his name on it and he wore that too, rotating and looking down at it.

"I'm trying to make sure you're all right," he said.

"I'm all right."

"Unburden yourself, Sister."

She had not told anyone about Sam, not even Isabelle. She had felt bad about it when it was going on, but now she felt much worse. She thought her punishment should be that she had to shoulder it alone. She agreed with Jules about this. She did not deserve absolution. She should look like shit. She should have to endure that assessment from her mother, for the millionth time, and from whoever else wanted to make it.

"I cheated," she said.

He smacked the bar with two palms. "I knew it."

"You're happy?" said Cora.

"No, it's just, like, cool to have my hunch confirmed."

"Why was that your hunch?"

"I think it's because we're twins."

"We're not twins."

Cora was two years older.

"No, but you know what I mean. Like figuratively. We're the same."

"You're figurative twins with your nontwin sister?"

"Do you want my advice or not?"

Was Drew's life orderly enough for her to respect his advice? She did admire how he'd never attempted to be anyone other than himself. He was a thirty-seven-year-old man in soccer slides. He put a hat over his face instead of hanging blinds. But he did, in his very fringe existence, have an almost disinterested perspective on how to conduct oneself. And he had a warmth. And he was her brother.

"I guess."

"Let yourself off the hook."

"What is that, the state motto of California?"

"Did you have fun?"

It should not have been a difficult question. There had been moments of fun, and moments of terror. Many moments of disappointment. She'd gotten to take a risk, which she hadn't thought she'd ever get to do again. She was too close to it still to know if she'd grown, but what was growth anyway? Being hurt by your own decisions and trying not to re-create them in the future? What she'd had was the full menu. She had been in love and had been disillusioned, which was one of the most bracing things that could happen to a person.

"Sort of," she said.

"You know Mom cheated on Dad, right?"

"She did?"

"No. Of course not. Not that I know of. And as you can see, I'm good at sniffing these things out. Mom is ridiculously upstanding. But anyway, you don't want to be like her, right? Isn't that your whole thing? Otherwise, you'd be delivering a baby right now and wearing, I don't know, upscale loafers."

She didn't want to be like her mom, but that wasn't why she'd had an affair. Human sexuality didn't work like that. Or actually, it did for a lot of people. Mothers were definitely in the mix. But Cora had done it for a constellation of reasons she was only beginning to understand—restlessness, a loss of self, desire to be other than what she was—and her mom so far didn't make the list.

"I feel bad for Eliot," she said.

Drew said, "He'll be all right. He cheated on you, you know."

"Did he really?"

"No. Obviously not. I think he's sexually attracted to paper."

Her brother, Drew. He'd appeared out of the ether to set her back on her feet. California had imbued him with something sage-like. Not really, but she could almost see it. It was the sandals and the tan, the impression he gave of total ease. His concern touched her. They knew each other without knowing each other, or he knew her while she wasn't allowed to know him.

"Are you seeing anyone?" she said.

He said, "Nice try," and insisted they go play darts.

They relapsed once in the back of his car. Jules's car, actually, a new hybrid model of the same Volvo. He texted her asking if they could talk. She met him in the middle of the day in the parking lot behind the movie theater. She walked down from the mountain to meet him.

He wore a knit beanie and his nose ran.

She got in the front seat. "You're sick."

"A cold," he said.

He coughed into a tissue. It was what their late pediatrician Dr. Sperling would call a productive cough. The kids brought things home. They brought things home and they brought things home. He crumpled up the tissue and threw it onto the dash.

"So?" she said.

He said, "Oh, I don't know."

She still wanted him. That hadn't abated. After all this time, she didn't even understand it. Why him? Why was she stirred by his combination of looks and personality? There was nothing remarkable about any of it. It couldn't just be that he was not Eliot. Plenty of other people were not Eliot. The town's mayor was not Eliot, nor were any of her coworkers. A man currently crossing the street a hundred yards away was not Eliot.

He took off his hat and she saw he had shaved his head. The hair loss had gotten too severe, his ponytail too thin. It was an incredible shock, and she reached up and touched his scalp without thinking. He let her, closing his eyes. She thought of a time-lapse video, a flower blooming and shriveling. That's how fast he was aging. All of them.

"Wow," she said.

The shaved head had a defamiliarizing power that excited her. He slid his hand onto her thigh and of course it was happening in the other world, too. The persistent other world, which could not be exploded, or denied, or satisfied. Which slid away when you thought you had it in your hand. He kissed her and his face was wet with snot.

She said, "Jesus Christ."

But she unzipped his pants anyway and he was hard. There was power in knowing what he liked and in being desired. He wanted her more than he wanted Jules. Was that not some kind of victory? Was that what she had been seeking? Simply to win? To beat someone primly excellent, who had, like, an administrative assistant? But God, that was lame. In the other world he finished and in this world he finished and she swallowed and they stared out the windshield.

"I told Jules," he said.

Cora had many questions like how did that go? Like where did the two of them stand now? Like what did Jules say about Cora? This last one she asked and Sam laughed.

"That's what you want to know?"

He blew his nose again, loudly. He no longer had any shame around her or any vanity, and this was probably a bad thing.

"She said you're too good for me. She said she didn't get it at all. She called you her best friend."

"No," said Cora. "She didn't say that."

Jules did not think that about her. She wouldn't accept it. Jules did not hold Cora in any kind of esteem. She treated her like a lackey. She thought her book club picks were wrong. She could *see her,* Cora had always thought. She could see her and what she saw was inadequate and less than Jules herself, and maybe she was right. But when Cora tried to come up with someone in Jules's life who might be closer to her, she couldn't. And when she tried to come up with someone in her own life who was closer to her than Jules, she couldn't. Had Jules been her best friend this whole time? It was almost too poignant to contemplate.

"She did," said Sam. "She was sad. We're going to stay together. Maybe. I'd like to try anyway."

"You might want to stop seeking outside blow jobs," said Cora.

"Probably, yeah."

"I'm sad too, you know."

"I know."

"Are you sad?"

She kind of yelled it at him. He should say he was sad. He should say he was sorry. He should start saying he was sorry and never stop. Even if it didn't make sense necessarily for him to apologize. What had he done but the same thing as her? He turned on the car to start the heat—terrible early spring.

"I'm sad," he said. "I thought you knew that."

He did not ask her anything about where she stood with Eliot or what would happen to her. He didn't ask her about herself.

"Do you want me to take you home?"

Was this their last rendezvous? She tried to read the tea leaves of the other world. Over there he had gotten her off, at least. He had gotten her off first, and then he'd gotten off, and then he'd gotten her off again. The shabbiness of real life. You had to admire its consistency.

She opened the door and got out of the car.

"That's all right," she said. "I'll walk."

Something weird happened, which was she got a call about a job interview. A woman at a literacy nonprofit wanted her to come in and chat. The job was doing mostly what she did at her current job, but for a better reason. It paid a little more than what she made now. Best of all, she would not have to ride the train to the city. The office was in the large town twenty minutes to the north of them. She could go in or work from home if she wanted.

She drove there to meet the director. The town was more depressed than Cora's own. It would be five years, ten years, never, before it gentrified. Renovated homes alternated with teardowns. There was an ongoing revitalization effort—every town in the area that was not sufficiently quaint had a program like this—but so far, blight was winning.

The office was in an old Victorian that smelled of rotting wood. The staff worked in the ballroom, under a nonoperational chandelier. They took lunch in an herb garden out back. The town had landmarked the building, so it could not be renovated, made more corporate, painted the same light gray everything was painted these days.

Cora sat with the director on the porch and drank iced tea. They spoke about literacy, the shrinking number of readers in the country. The woman was a few years older than Cora and wore a jumpsuit with a bright geometric pattern. Cora had done some research and read an op-ed she had written.

"Describe your ideal job," the woman said.

Since she'd had children, Cora had seen herself as a person who worked to obtain a salary. This wasn't noble, but it was what she could manage. She had no illusions anymore that she might achieve something that made her seem impressive. What she wanted most of all was a job with no trivial, dehumanizing bullshit. She wanted, if possible, to feel like a person.

"I would like to help someone" was how she put it in the interview.

"We do try to do that here. If we don't help anyone, we've failed, though the metrics can be hard to interpret."

The interview went well, Cora thought. She'd gotten along with the director, who seemed intelligent and reasonable. She arrived home and heard Eliot upstairs in the bathroom with a contractor.

"Come up," he shouted.

The contractor was Richard's tile guy. He'd done all the pretty green tile in Richard and Celeste's en suite. Both he and Eliot had one leg up on the lip of the tub, studying the mushroom. Recently a second mushroom had pushed through next to it. It was a two-mushroom situation now. The second one was smaller than the first, and its diminutive size somehow made it even more horrible.

"You have to retile," said the guy.

A crack existed behind the crack. A crack in the wall proper. They might want to spray something into it, he said, and then he'd seal it up.

"Something like what?" said Cora.

"Poison."

He gave them an estimate written in a sloppy tradesman's hand. It contained more zeros than Cora would have liked.

"We have to do it," said Eliot.

"Are you sure?"

"There are two mushrooms now. Where does it end? If we don't do something, it'll be three mushrooms, four mushrooms. Pretty soon we'll be living in the Mushroom House."

He said it like it was something well known from a folktale.

"What is the Mushroom House?" she said.

"No, nothing. Just a house with a lot of mushrooms growing in it."

She wanted to do it but felt she had to mount the required arguments. "It's too expensive."

"I have been pulling mushrooms out of that wall for so long," said Eliot. "I feel insane. I can't do it anymore. I can't even eat them. I got sent a book about mushrooms. The pitch was good. Mushrooms are trendy right now. Microdosing and all that. I couldn't read it. I couldn't open the file. I had to write the agent back to say that I had to pass because there's a longtime mushroom growing in my upstairs bathroom, recently two mushrooms, which has turned me off of them completely. I don't want to live my life under assault from the animal kingdom. Just passively letting it happen. Not even the animal kingdom! The fungus kingdom. I will not be defeated by mushrooms any longer."

Richard's tile guy still stood there. He nodded along as if he had heard this many times before, this rant about literary agents and longtime mushrooms.

He consulted the calendar on his phone. "You'd have to choose your tile. We'll get you some samples, and then we have to wait for the tile to come in. But we could do it in, let's see . . . four weeks."

In four weeks, they could be free of the mushrooms. It would exhaust their savings and it would not solve their other problems. It would not fix their marriage or make life with children easier. But they wouldn't have to feel the particular disgust of pulling a mushroom from the wall of their house ever again.

"I insist on doing this," said Eliot.

What could she say but okay?

There were other changes in Eliot too. He had stepped down his medicine. He had not weaned completely, but he was on a lower dose. He seemed to have more energy. His fuzziness had lessened, and his forgetfulness. Instantly, he'd lost five pounds.

He got into bed and lay there shirtless. "Do you want to have sex?"

She said, "Well, well, well."

He said, "Don't be like that."

"How the tables have turned."

"I'm going to rescind."

She studied his face and he did not appear to be stoned.

"To what do I owe the pleasure?" she said.

He said, "Shut the fuck up. I'm serious," and then he was on top of her.

It was so nice, so good, to have sex with the person you were supposed to have sex with. Why had no one ever thought of this? He was right there. In many cases, he lived in your own home. Eliot had strong arms and dark hair on his chest. When he took his glasses off, he became a less inhibited version of himself. He liked for her to leave her T-shirt on. He thought there was something dirty about this. She was wet, which pleased him. He flipped her over and nudged her legs apart with his knee. He was very hard, and as they approached the end she said, "Come for me," and he did with his eyes closed.

What happened to the time lines in these moments? When desire overlapped with obligation. Perhaps they converged. Was that what all this was about? What she wanted to do and what she had to do? What she wanted to do and what she was supposed to want to do?

"I love you," said Eliot.

He liked to say this during sex. She did not like to hear it much; it was too serious. It carried such weight, the weight of everything that had happened to them. She didn't always want to be reminded of the whole montage of events, of what she'd done for him, and what he'd done for her, the death of his parents and her father, their charmed meeting and early relationship, the birth of their children. But you know what, sure. She did love him and he was trying.

They had sex like man and wife and she had to admit she liked it. Afterward, they watched television.

She got the job in the faded Victorian. We thought you were smart, they said, in an email. We liked your ideas. Preparing to leave the digital marketing company, she took Lily out to lunch. They went to the place that made you stagger back to work like Caligula. They had oysters and Cora offered to pay. The host sat them outside at a marble table. The city churned around them like it always would.

"Take me with you," said Lily.

Cora said, "Why?"

Lily wore a shapeless dress with pastel blobs on it. She looked about five years old but was getting married soon. Perhaps she had cooled on trying so hard at work.

"Because our jobs are dumb."

They were jobs for people who did not know what else to do. Sometimes lately when one of their coworkers came to her with a question, Lily heard herself whispering under her breath "dissolve the company." What should they do for Pride Month (dissolve the company), what should they do about establishing a TikTok presence (dissolve the company). Now that she was leaving, Cora almost wanted to jump in and defend it. There were upsides, actually, to having a job that mattered little. Like you could text your illicit boyfriend pretty much uninterrupted.

THE TEN YEAR AFFAIR

"Every time someone gets out, it's like good for them," said Lily.

She'd had this thought when Ryan left, too. Now he was married to a famous restauranteur in Thailand. The public transit system there was excellent and you could live really cheaply. Which just went to show you what could happen if you no longer worked in digital marketing.

The waiter came over and explained the menu. You had to go large at this place, so they went large. Maybe Cora wanted a resolution with Lily, but the leaving would have to suffice. In time, she would unfollow Lily on social media and feel the respite of not knowing what happened to her. How beautiful to let an acquaintance slide into obscurity, as into a cool pond. How refreshing it would be for both of them.

The bill came to two hundred and fifty dollars.

"Oops," said Cora.

"How bad?" said Lily.

"No, no," said Cora. "It's on me."

Sam had paid the last time, producing a wad of cash like the high roller he wasn't. She had not even seen the bill. They went back to work and later in the week Lily threw a party for Cora in the conference room. She'd gotten a cake that said, "Good Luck" and several bottles of bad prosecco. Then that was it for the digital marketing company. She left the building and never thought of it again.

A cube appeared outside Sam's house, the kind you filled with boxes that a company hauled to your next destination. Klaus reported this while chugging water at the kitchen island. He and Eliot had just played racquetball.

"What size cube?" said Cora.

"Big one," said Klaus.

He didn't know anything specific about where they were moving, or even if they were. He'd given Jack a ride home the other day and seen it, but Jack hadn't mentioned it. He and Klaus's son had talked about video games, and then they'd talked about chip flavors they liked, and then they'd talked about how their gym teacher lived at school. Jack had not seemed like a boy on the verge of moving away from the town he'd lived in his whole life.

"Maybe they're putting things in storage," said Cora. "Cleaning out the basement."

"Do people get a cube for that?" said Eliot.

He ate a hot pickle and offered the jar to Klaus. Klaus took one.

"They're moving," said Klaus. "There's no other explanation."

Would he move and not tell her? She had seen him recently in his car. Briefly, but still. Or had they decided to move since then? She had not lived in the town without Sam living there too. What would it be like without him? Would it feel the same? Or would it be leached of excitement? Just a set of cold coordinates?

She wanted proof so she walked past their house. She could see the cube from a block away. PODS MOVING & STORAGE, it read. This should have been confirmation enough, but something made her keep walking, and then she crossed the street. She realized she was going to knock. They had played out all the clichés except this one: the wild-eyed mistress at his doorstep.

His car was there, which meant he was there. Doing his low-pressure job. Low pressure, low reward. Typing up a press release about renting baby gear at the airport. In the other world, he'd answer the door and she'd fall into his arms. She'd have large hair and he'd wear a billowing shirt. She took the porch steps two at a time. There were bikes dropped wherever and a single shin guard lying on the welcome mat. She was about to knock when the door flung open.

Jules emerged with her bag on her shoulder. "Oh!"

She was dressed for the world, in a blazer and gold jewelry. She did not look, as Cora's mother might put it, tired. She looked good, cool and sharp as ever.

Cora said, "I didn't expect it to be you."

Jules glanced back over her shoulder into the house. She noticed the shin guard and lunged for it and tossed it inside.

"Those things get so fucking disgusting," she said. "It's like they trap and preserve bad smells."

Cora could see a basket of laundry behind her in the hall. She could see an end table with its tray of sunglasses and headphones and keys. She wondered if she'd ever go inside again and the answer was probably no.

"He's not home," said Jules.

Cora restrained herself from asking where he was. Because he was definitely home. She heard sounds coming from inside of a man walking around. She heard thumping and creaking and music playing distantly that sounded like Talking Heads.

"I guess I should apologize," said Cora.

"Don't bother. I knew about it. We had an arrangement."

You always heard the word "arrangement" when a couple decided to sleep with other people. It sounded civilized. Picking things up and setting them into place. Arranging them. This was a bluff, however. If there had been an arrangement, Sam would have told Cora. They never had a conversation indicating he was permitted to fuck other women. In fact, they'd had many to the contrary. She heard more walking upstairs, the creaking of floorboards, a desk chair rolling. These crummy old houses. You could hear everything.

"You got him chained to a radiator up there?"

"You wish," said Jules.

It was time to apologize and Cora wondered if Jules would let her. Cora didn't deserve the opportunity to explain, but maybe Jules was curious.

"It didn't have anything to do with you," said Cora. "It wasn't fueled by resentment."

Maybe it had been for Sam, maybe it was personal on his end, but it wasn't on Cora's. It had been about the two of them, and it had been about sex. But what it had been about mostly was her life. Escaping it. Not that her life was stultifying or anything, but actually it was. The storybook town, the twenty-first-century marriage between friends. She had designed it, wanted it, set it into place, expected it to have meaning, and then it hadn't. If anyone could understand that, it was Jules.

"I went through his phone," said Jules.

Cora felt a wave of nausea. She had sent him a few nudes, and then there were the pictures he'd taken of her. His dick in her mouth. Not as well hidden as he'd thought. So there was no denying anything or minimizing it.

"Oh," said Cora. "Oh no."

Then she did apologize for real. She said she was sorry she had done the worst thing you could do to a friend, second to murder. She understood how awful it was and how it had made Jules feel. It was too late now and it probably didn't mean much to Jules, but she was sorry.

"Anyway, didn't you say infidelity is actually no big deal?" said Cora.

"I was talking about myself when I said that."

She was taking this too mildly. In the other world, Jules would be incandescently mad and her anger would contain an edge of sex. But this was comic, or tragicomic. She should have been letting Cora have it, like the time in Anita's pantry. Why did Cora always want to be shoved by Jules into nonperishables? She felt the need to say something cutting, to generate some feeling, even if it was rage.

"He's not that great" was what she landed on.

Jules said, "I know. Don't you know that I know?"

Then his mediocrity was out in the open, where it had been the whole time.

"Where are you moving?" said Cora.

"Oakland. I got a job offer."

"That's great."

"Two weeks and we're out. The kids are enrolled in school. We're renting a place to start, and then we'll see. It's all sort of . . . It just happened. I'm excited."

She'd said "we" and Cora wondered if this meant her and Sam or her and the kids. It was too much to ask for clarification and yet she did.

"I don't know," said Jules. "A lot is still up in the air."

"What'll happen to the car?" said Cora.

She meant the pandemic Mercedes, which had sat there all these years. Which sat there now, under the black vinyl cover Sam had finally bought for it. Even the cover had been there long enough to become sun-bleached.

"Sam is selling it back to the hippie at a loss. I am trying not to think too much about the car. I have my hands full as it is just getting us packed up."

They turned and looked at the cube. Jules was daunted by the prospect of filling it. All the years of accumulated stuff. It would be like digging out Pompeii. There were whole drawers she had actively feared for years. The shed contained a small, shitty canoe. Was she supposed to transport that to California?

"Jack's room," she said, with a shudder.

"Opal will miss him."

Was it true? Jack had been a problem for Opal, and now the problem would be solved. Likely his departure would come with mixed feelings—they'd grown up together—but one of those feelings would be relief. Opal was indomitable, though, and would move on quickly. Maybe what Cora meant was that she herself would miss Jules.

"No, she won't," said Jules.

She pulled the door shut and they both walked away.

Celeste wanted to throw Sam and Jules a going away party. They all needed to gather once more in a backyard, she told Cora. They would drink whatever the wine was that year. They would discuss the people in town. It sounded to Cora like a bad idea, like orchestrating a confrontation, and for what reason? Some nebulous sense of closure? Closure never came. There was only forgetting. There was only the slow passage of time, and rooting for the fallibility of your own brain. Rooting for the day you'd wake up and the particulars would be gone, deleted to make way for something else.

"Don't do that," Cora said.

They sat on her deck. Celeste had her long white feet up on the railing. With Jules gone, they would need a need third person. Cora worried it would be too much Celeste. Celeste and Cora all the time.

"What do you think is going to happen?" said Celeste.

She did not know about Sam and Cora, or maybe she did. She was smarter than people gave her credit for. But she definitely knew about Sam and Jules. She definitely knew that Richard was partially to blame for things falling apart. In the great unraveling, he'd pulled the first string. She definitely knew, because Cora had told her, that Sam was not necessarily moving to California with his family. Now Celeste wanted them all to eat burgers together. She wanted them to say "yum, what's in this?" about some cocktail she'd looked up on the internet.

"None of us should see each other again," said Cora.

"Ever?"

"We should sequester in our homes for the safety of the community."

But Celeste went ahead and threw the party anyway. Cora watched from her bedroom window as Richard and Celeste's yard filled with people. At some point, they had replaced the long dining table and mismatched chairs with a modern set. She saw Celeste circulating, Richard with a cocktail shaker. She did not see Sam, his newly buzzed head, but she did see Jules, in a floral dress and oversize sweater. She opened the window and could hear her laughing.

Eliot came in and stood beside her. He touched the nape of her neck, adjusted her necklace so the clasp was in back.

"It's a really nice necklace," he said, and it was. Something he had done right in his youth. When you were young, you acted by instinct and a lot of those instincts were good. People always said the opposite. But the decisions of youth were unclouded by factors such as self-knowledge or cynicism or logic. They were true like the strike of an ax. Then you had to live by them even when you were forty years old.

Music drifted in, people's voices, the shouting of children. It was dimly blue in the room, darkening outside. They saw Opal enter the gate, weave through the yard, climb the ladder to Sarah Beth's tree house. Sarah Beth's head appeared out of the tree house window and she said something and Opal said something back. Jack was up there too, his legs dangling out over the edge of the platform. They were all too big for it. Opal had to crawl through the door on hands and knees. Soon she would be gone, never to return in the same way.

"She looks tall," said Cora.

"Our girl," said Eliot.

Cora had come home from her last weekend in the city with Sam to find Eliot waiting for her in the kitchen. Both kids had been out; that could happen now. He'd been deseeding a pepper, chopping it for burritos. He asked her how her conference had gone and she paused a moment to recall her cover story. Then she told him it was as dull as you'd expect, and began to leave the room.

He'd stopped her. "This conference. It was real, right?"

They looked at each other.

"Why do you ask?"

"I don't know. Feeling."

"It was real."

"Good. Because if it wasn't real, that would bother me."

"You don't have to worry about it." She added after a long pause, "Anymore."

It was as close to a confession as she'd get. So he knew. He had known. For how long, she'd have the rest of her life to wonder. They were silent and she noticed he was listening to a podcast. A gravelly voice said, "With long molecular chains and eight times the strength of steel, High Modulus Polyethylene is the strongest known variety of rope."

"Is this a podcast about rope?" she said.

"Yeah."

It was the history of rope. Rope manufacturing, but other aspects too. The uses of rope, knot tying, rope's cultural significance. Everything you could ever want to know. This was episode eleven. He had confronted her about having an affair while listening to a podcast about rope. The world could not recognize gravitas. Every serious exchange was undermined by its particulars.

"I missed you," said Cora. "Lay down your knife."

He did and she went to him.

That had been five months ago. What had happened in the interim was an effort between them. To tread more carefully or be more passionate. To try to remember why they were there in the first place. This was what Cora had been doing anyway.

The party over their back fence had become lively now. The strands of fairy lights that Celeste had hung between trees blinked on, and this was the key to making it look charmed and enviable, especially as viewed from above. There they are, Cora thought. The people of the world. Having their private dramas, wearing their outfits, absorbing the weather.

"Do you want to go over there?" said Eliot.

She did but she said, "No."

They went downstairs and had a drink.

* * *

At the end of ten years Sam shocked them all by asking for a divorce. Cora heard it first from Jules. She was out in the yard kicking a soccer ball around with the kids when her phone rang. She looked down and saw Jules's name and felt fear.

Opal said, "Your phone is ringing."

It sat on a low table where both kids could see it.

Miles said, "Aren't you going to answer?"

Cora told him no, she'd call back later. But it rang again immediately, and Miles said, "Mom," and Opal said, "Mom," and this time Cora did answer.

"An idiot fuckhead's on the way to your house," said Jules, and hung up.

He showed up a few minutes later. They'd resumed playing soccer. It was early evening, pleasantly cool and damp. The trees shaded the yard dark green. She'd been kicking the ball too far on purpose, past the kids, into the brush, and watching them bound after it. Sam came in through the back gate.

Miles said, "What's he doing here?"

He kicked the ball at Sam. It hit him in the stomach and Sam said, "Ow."

Then Sam launched into a monologue about how she should leave Eliot. Jules was off to California and he wasn't going with her. He thought he and Cora should give it a shot. A real shot this time, free of other entanglements. He wanted a domestic life with her. He had for a long time.

He stopped talking and both kids looked at Cora.

"What the fuck?" said Opal, and Cora had to go through the theater of disapproval. Don't say fuck. It's rude. Meanwhile, Sam stood waiting for an answer. She sent the kids inside.

"I want to marry you," he said.

Cora laughed. "Marry?"

Marriage had never been the point. Marriage was the opposite of the point. She thought he'd known this. He reached out to touch her arm. His touch was hot. She felt an internal revving, but it was distant, or she thought, if she wanted to, she could will it to be distant.

"I'm serious," he said.

She considered accepting his offer to see what would happen. Various vectors appeared, like tines on a fork. He'd be a great husband and they'd be in love forever. He'd be terrible and she'd instantly regret it. She'd cheat on him with Eliot, casually and for decades. Or, by some calculation, she and Jules would end up together. They'd move to California with all four kids and Cora would let Jules work late solving their problems.

She said, "What if I told you your real life is happening elsewhere?"

He said, "It isn't though."

But it was. In the other time line, they were standing in the yard and it was the same but different. It was more vivid. The details appeared sharp and correct. She could see each tree on the mountain, each blade of grass. She wore a dress and her hair was lush and long and he certainly did not wear a free shirt from a 5K sponsored by the local weed store.

"I don't know," she said. "We tried it."

A window on the second floor opened and Opal appeared. She shouted down that the Wi-Fi had cut out. She'd already tried turning it off and on again. She needed Cora to come in and reset the router.

Cora turned away from Sam and looked up, shielding her eyes.

"I'll be right in."

A bird on the roof took flight at the sound of her voice. It rose in the direction of the mountain, a weightless silhouette against the sky. What was exalted occurred alongside the ordinary every moment, ceaselessly. But you couldn't make it stay. You couldn't claim it as your own.

Acknowledgments

The author wishes to thank: Angeline Rodriguez at WME; Carina Guiterman, Sean Manning, Anna Hauser, Martha Langford, Emily Farebrother, and the rest of team at Simon & Schuster; Sarah Jean Grimm and Kimberly Burns at Broadside; Michelle Lyn King at *Joyland Magazine*, who originally published the short story that became this novel; and my friends in the Hudson Valley and New York City for the inspiration and support.

About the Author

Erin Somers is a reporter and news editor at *Publishers Lunch*. Her first novel, *Stay Up with Hugo Best* (Scribner), was a *Vogue* Best Book of the Year in 2019. Her writing has appeared in *The New Yorker*, *The Paris Review*, *The New York Times Book Review*, *The New Republic*, *New York* magazine, *The Atlantic*, *Esquire*, *GQ*, *The Best American Short Stories*, and many other publications. She lives in Beacon, New York, with her family.